To Dave &
All the best
Simon

How to Kidnap a String Quartet

SIMON LYONS

This is a work of fiction. All names, characters, businesses, places, incidents and events are the product of the author's imagination and used in a fictitious way. Any resemblance to persons, living or dead is entirely coincidental.

Text copyright © 2017 Simon Lyons

All Rights Reserved.

Edited by Mairi Mayfield.

Cover by Malcolm English.

ISBN: 1546373810
ISBN-13: 978-1546373810

DEDICATION

To Sal & family.

With thanks to Mairi and Fenella.

CONTENTS

PART ONE

1	Goodnight Irene	Pg 1
2	The Big A	Pg 7
3	Death by Crooning	Pg 12
4	Going Viral	Pg 17
5	Mr. S	Pg 22
6	Ripperland	Pg 26
7	Return of the King	Pg 33
8	Luke, Chapter and Verse	Pg 38
9	Return of the Prince	Pg 43
10	The Last Full English	Pg 47

PART TWO

11	Wild Horses	Pg 52
12	Son of Abraham	Pg 59
13	Cell Block H	Pg 63
14	A Casualty of War	Pg 67
15	A Daughter of Abraham	Pg 71
16	A Holy Road Trip	Pg 76
17	David's City	Pg 82
18	Psycho	Pg 89
19	Hampstead Garden Suburb on Sea	Pg 94
20	R & R	Pg 100

SIMON LYONS

PART THREE

21	The 'Gooly Chit'	Pg 112
22	Ripples	Pg 118
23	Tidal Waves	Pg 124
24	Planet Tedium	Pg 130
25	Date Night	Pg 136
26	Favours	Pg 143
27	The Valley of Lies	Pg 149
28	The Signature Dish	Pg 154
29	Thunder Road	Pg 161
30	Love, Drugs and Marriage	Pg 166

PART FOUR

31	'Bristol'	Pg 172
32	Half a Person	Pg 177
33	White Girl in the Tropics	Pg 182
34	A Place Beyond Hell	Pg 188
35	The Lunatic Express	Pg 195
36	The A Team	Pg 201
37	The All Important Second Date	Pg 205
38	Steps Five (and Six)	Pg 210
39	A Song For Susan	Pg 215
40	The Fifteenth Upload	Pg 221

PART ONE

1

GOODNIGHT IRENE
(2011)

"Step four involves dousing the cellist in gasoline and threatening to turn him into a human torch!"

For the first time in the four hours since these two old friends had ordered their first drinks there was a short silence, on Stephen's part a stunned silence. He stared intently at his old roommate considering whether, in the twenty-seven years since he last saw him, the big man had remained just eccentric, rather than dangerously mad.

"To be honest," Alberto continued after a few seconds, "cousin Dino will actually do the dirty work, the dousing. I will do the threatening."

"Oh good, that's okay then," Stephen muttered, still pondering the details.

"Cousin Dino calls it the 'game changer'." Alberto laughed enthusiastically, having previously been speaking in a whisper. "What a fucking game changer hey Stevie boy."

"Yep, that would definitely be a game changer alright, but I'd have thought step two would do the job, I'm pretty confident steps three and four will not be necessary," Stephen said unconvincingly.

"I'm not so sure, you haven't met the arrogant little shits!" Alberto almost shouted. Stephen gestured for his friend to lower his voice as their fellow drinkers, on bar stools either side of them, looked round in unison.

Alberto continued in almost a whisper, "They are little shits, they totally humiliated me despite the fact I approached them with the best of intentions. Susan had talked often and with great warmth about her visits to the bandstand and when I saw and heard them myself I was greatly impressed. When they finished their last number, a superb rendition of the Beach Boys 'God Only Knows', I engaged them with courtesy and enthusiasm and they just dissed me Stevie, they fucking humiliated me."

Alberto took a large swig of his JD, Stephen could see he was pissed in both the British and American sense.

"So, there and then I introduced step one, offering them a small gratuity and their taxi fare. Not an unreasonable offer given that I clearly explained Susan's circumstances."

Stephen looked at his American friend enveloping his bar stool, Alberto had not shrunk with the passing of time, he was in fact bigger. The 'Big A', as he was affectionately known, was now an even bigger 'A'. His wild hair and beard were now grey and unkempt. His Hawaiian shirt and khaki shorts did little to conceal the mounds of flesh that glistened with sweat.

The 'Big A' would always stand out in a crowd. Stephen surveyed his neighbours, power-dressed in smart business suits and dresses. Alberto was dressed for the Californian beach, not a Midtown Manhattan hotel bar, four star at that.

"Was Susan aware of your intentions and actions?" Stephen enquired.

"Not at all Stevie, I wanted to surprise her, to put a smile on her face, God knows I owe her that. I just want, when the end comes, which is frighteningly close, that she hates me a little less. It's the least I can do for her, but those arrogant little fuc..." Stephen raised his hand as Alberto's voice raised again. "So, that was step one, my initial approach which they rejected. I walked away dejected and humiliated, but then on the subway home I thought of cousin Dino. This was his kind of situation, he wouldn't take any shit from anyone, particularly shitty little music students. Dino is old school Italian, he was the only member of the family who didn't give me a hard time when everything fell apart with Susan."

"I remember Dino," Stephen interrupted, "I remember him at the bachelor party, he was the only proper drinker there. He was in charge of the wedding present!"

"You're spot on Stevie, the wedding present, yes, best leave that in the past, halcyon days. Anyway, Dino owed me, twice in the nineties I paid his bail!"

"He was a feisty character," Stephen chipped in, "I recall him giving your colleague a slap."

Alberto let out a laugh and shook his head. "Yes I remember that, Gibson, my team leader, couldn't hold his drink, said something derogative about the Brits so Dino stepped in. Crazy days."

Stephen couldn't recall Dino's face but remembered he seemed wider than he was tall. He recalled him with affection, a loveable rogue certainly a wild one, and judging by the wedding present he organised for the 'Big A' Dino was also well connected. He smiled thinking of the present, the locked room, Alberto's delight, then the missing thirty-six hours that followed.

"I just thought of step five," Alberto said, he instantly brought Stephen back to the present. Alberto left the statement hanging as he caught the attention of the waitress, "Two more JD's Honey Pie."

The room was spinning for both of them, hurricane Irene swept relentlessly down 42nd street, which they could clearly view from their lofty perch. Stephen and Cassandra had chosen the position well. Two comfy bar stools and a stainless steel shelf that continued under a large window, which provided a grandstand view of the street below, including the main entrance to Grand Central Station, adjacent to the hotel. Most of the Irene refugee drinkers in the packed bar strained to study the storm outside.

"The eye is almost here!" Someone shouted excitedly.

"Just looks like heavy drizzle to me," Stephen chipped in, secretly disappointed that he couldn't see any cars floating below or cows flying above.

"Just hold on you English wanker," Alberto interrupted, "things are going to get crazy, trust me Irene's a bitch. Now, where was I, oh yes, step five."

Alberto was interrupted as the waitress placed their umpteenth drinks on the shelf and removed several empty glasses, winking at Alberto as she left.

"Thanks Honey Pie." Alberto attempted to wink back but it was more of a drunken squint. "Step five, it's just come to me, it's simple but brilliant and we could try it instead of step four, which I get the vibe from you Stevie that you find it a trifle over the top."

"Over the top," Stephen repeated, "that's an understatement mate. So, what the hell does step five involve?"

Alberto took a gulp of JD before continuing, "Step five would make steps two, three and four redundant, we could put them on the back burner, excuse the pun, depending on how you get on."

"What do you mean 'you'?" Stephen said, both curious and concerned.

"I was just thinking that you as a British tourist, an 'out of towner', could have a polite English word with them."

Stephen made intense eye contact with Alberto. "I'm meant to be on fucking holiday, I don't think so."

"Come on Stephen, you're stuck in New York until you sort a flight out, the airport won't open till late Monday at the earliest."

Stephen raised his voice, "Exactly, we were supposed to be on our way home this morning, I've got to get home somehow, ASAP, I'm not about to go chasing musicians around Central Park!"

The 'Big A' he knew all those years ago was one hell of a character, but the big drunk man before him was possibly insane. Stephen was beginning to regret this reunion when he noticed a scene unfolding on the street below. The congregation in the bar had watched in amazement as the police closed Grand Central Station and took up position in the main entrance which was visible from the bar window, save for the rain drops that decorated the glass as Irene slowly slipped into town.

"Look at that guy!" Stephen shouted.

The crowd could see a solitary figure bent double, walking in disorientated circles outside the station entrance.

"Jesus H Christ," Alberto exclaimed, "He's a lunatic, he'll die out there!"

"The police won't let him into the station, he probably sleeps in there," another drinker added.

"I know him, I know that poor man!"

Everyone within earshot of Stephen turned to him as the English tourist made this unlikely claim.

"You know him, what the…" Alberto said, confused.

"I mean, I've seen him hanging around the station and a couple of times on Lexington. The girls call him the 'Stooping Man', he literally stoops at ninety degrees and he is mentally as well as physically ill, he talks to himself endlessly."

"And he's stuck outside in a fucking hurricane," stated Alberto with genuine concern.

Other drinkers expressed their disgust and felt collectively ashamed. Stephen continued, "If this was back home in the UK there would be multi agency effort to help any vulnerable person in a situation like this, I can't believe that in the world's first economy we are possibly going to watch a man die, those policemen should be ashamed of themselves."

The concerned congregation considered the Englishman's words. "He hasn't even got a coat on, he's wet through, it's shocking," a business woman added.

Alberto stood up behind his stool and put his forehead to the window, almost knocking his JD over. He winced in sciatic pain as he reached for his cagoule at the base of the bar stool. "My English friend is spot on!" He shouted as he stood up fully. "This is a disgrace, someone has to do something!" With that, the big man staggered out of the bar and down to the lobby.

The crowd stretched and muttered collectively as he disappeared for a couple of minutes only to emerge on the street before them. Stephen smiled to himself as he watched his friend brave the elements through the rain-splattered window. He drunkenly marched towards the station entrance seemingly screaming and gesticulating at the police. Moments earlier this mad bugger had been formulating his five point plan to bring a string quartet to his ex wife's bedside, now he was defending America's honour.

The business women blew hot breath on the window and rubbed it with her smart jacket sleeve. "Good for him," she said, "a true hero."

"He's just bonkers," Stephen added as he wondered about his old friend's sanity. They could just about see Alberto trying to calm the stooping man, who got more animated as the big man put a hand on his shoulder and led him into the station. The two seemed to be doing a frantic rain dance when suddenly two policemen joined the dance, the scrum edged out of view into the dry sanctuary of Grand Central station.

42nd Street was totally deserted and Stephen's 'heavy drizzle' was now, he would admit, a deluge. News of death and devastation in neighbouring states was starting to dominate the plethora of screens stretched above the bar. Normally they showed different sport events, tonight there was only 'BREAKING NEWS' from in and around New York State.

Suddenly Stephen and the crowd saw the unmistakable figure of Alberto emerge back onto the pavement with his arm around an officer, his free hand was pointing towards the hotel. The two seemed to be having a friendly conversation as they both calmly walked back into the station and out of sight again.

"Looks like our hero has got your 'Stooping Man' some help," the business woman addressed Stephen approvingly.

A few minutes later a police car appeared out of the chaotic weather and pulled up outside the station entrance. An officer emerged from the passenger seat and opened the back door just as the street lit up from lightening overhead, closely followed by a fearsome thunderclap.

The crowd clapped as they saw the 'Stooping Man' helped into the back seat by officers either side of him. The officers swiftly got in the car, slammed the doors shut and drove off into the raging storm, sirens blaring.

A debate instantly started up amongst the drinkers as to where the 'Stooping Man' was heading. A cell for the night, at worse. Better options offered were a homeless hostel, social services or the New York equivalent, and possibly a psychiatric hospital.

Everyone looked forward to congratulating the big man when he braved the elements and returned to his JD. Stephen felt a touch of pride that he'd played a part in this happy ending.

Stephen's wife startled him as she slipped her arm around his waist. "Where's your friend?" Cass enquired, looking around the bar, assuming he'd gone to the toilet.

"Cass, you won't believe what's been going on." Stephen briefly explained the incident.

The business woman added, "I expect the officers or station staff are giving your friend a cup of coffee, he's one helluva guy."

"Larger than life," Stephen concurred.

His mind drifted back to his first meeting with the 'Big A', mid-August 1981 in a war zone barely two miles from the Lebanese border. The path to this strange meeting had been equally bizarre for the both of them, but it wasn't fate that brought them together. Although Alberto presumed it was, Stephen knew differently.

Reflecting on those crazy days Stephen still felt a sense of guilt, even more so given his old friend's heroics helping the 'Stooping Man'.

"Look!" Cassandra shouted, "it's him look!"

Stephen, the businesswoman and the other drinkers strained to see through the hurricane lashed window, Irene's eye was now officially over Manhattan.

"What the fuck?" Stephen swore.

"It's definitely him," the businesswoman confirmed.

"I thought you said the police had taken him away?" Cassandra was confused.

"They did!" Everyone nearby answered as one.

Despite Irene they could all make out the unmistakable figure of the 'Stooping Man' shuffling in his little circles exactly where they'd first spotted him. He was completely soaked to the bone. "What the fuck is going on?" Stephen repeated.

A sharp suited guy four stools down had a theory, "That guy we thought was your poor 'Stooping Man' could have in fact been your mad friend bent over with his hands cuffed behind his back. Your pal was being arrested!"

Stephen tried to recall the scene as clearly as possible, accounting for the poor visibility and alcohol consumption. He could only make out outlines not features, a man being handcuffed definitely would stoop if being dragged against his will. This new reality dawned on Stephen, "They've arrested Al!" He shouted and slid off his bar stool. "Shit, I'm going out there, I'm going to see what's going on."

Cassandra tried to grab him. "Don't be an idiot Steve, you haven't even got a coat!" She stopped yelling as he broke away and made for the lobby, she knew she was wasting her breath. She knew her husband too well. There was no force on earth that could stop him once he got a bee in his bonnet. She and her new friends watched as he emerged down below and ran along 42nd Street towards the 'Stooping Man', literally into the eye of a hurricane.

2

THE BIG A

Stephen and family had arrived in New York four days earlier, blissfully unaware of Irene's path. They'd done all the popular tourists sights, the Rockefeller Center, the Met, Ellis Island, Lower East Side and the Village. They were alerted to the imminent hurricane by the endless weather and news reports that interrupted the baseball footage on the TV screens, which couldn't be avoided in the numerous Irish bars they frequented.

It was only on their last evening whilst talking to their waiter in a classic Italian restaurant in 'Little Italy', that they realised they might have a problem getting home.

"You guys are from London right?"

"Yep it's our last night in the Big Apple and what a lovely restaurant to spend it in," Cassandra replied.

The waiter laughed and shook his head, "Geez thanks mam, but you ain't going anywhere till Irene passes."

Stephen, Cassandra, Luke and the girls all looked at each other perplexed.

"I'm sorry pal," Stephen responded, "we're okay, our flight is tomorrow afternoon, the hurricane doesn't get here till late tomorrow night."

The waiter put his hand on Stephen's shoulder, "I'm sorry my friend but they've just announced the airport is closing at mid-day tomorrow, so staff can get home in good time."

Stephen and family got a cab back to the hotel, it was almost midnight but he spent the next four hours on the phone trying to find a solution.

Just before 4am he was connected to Joanne at the BA call centre in Newcastle, who explained that it would be at least a week before five seats would be available. Stephen pleaded, "Look Joanne, I'm in New York with a wife and two, sorry three, kids-" it wasn't the first time he'd forgotten Luke, "-of shopping age, I'll be ruined!"

She sympathised and a few moments later offered him a flight out of Baltimore in four days time, subject to Irene's behaviour.

At breakfast the next morning Stephen gave his family a few options including the possibility of a couple of nights in Washington, if he could organise a Greyhound bus out of New York. "Wow, we could visit the Smithsonian, cool." Luke said, impressed.

Stephen, tired but pleased with his efforts, suddenly remembered his failed attempts to arrange a get together with his old mate the 'Big A'.

It was twenty-seven years since Stephen disappeared from Alberto's wedding, there had been many times he'd wondered what became of the big man. He was pretty certain the marriage wouldn't last at the time and it turned out he was right.

He received a couple of letters shortly after he returned to London but letter writing was neither man's style. The arrival of the Internet and Facebook inspired Stephen to do the odd Google search, but they were half-hearted efforts and given his sense of betrayal, along with the wedding present business, he had decided to let sleeping dogs lie.

The 'Buble' incident of course would change everything. The fourteen YouTube clips, particularly clip nine which went viral, created a subsequent chain of events that saw Stephen's past collide with the present and change his future beyond his wildest dreams.

It was Stephen's younger daughter Florence who noticed one of many comments under clip nine. Among the many insults basically describing Stephen as a pathetic woos, Florence drew his attention to one particular comment. *"OMG. This guy looks like my old buddy Stevie Ross from London England. I swear it's him but the guy I knew in the early eighties wouldn't be seen dead at a Buble concert and wouldn't be floored by a woman!"*

Florence eventually put the two in communication through Facebook. Alberto was delighted to hook up with his 'missing best man' from across the pond, but he was confused and surprised by the circumstances. Stephen was embarrassed, as he had been since clip nine went viral. He would, however, come to accept that without that moment of lunacy there would be no Luke and because of Luke they were enjoying New York.

The surprise trip was sprung on the Ross family just two weeks before departure and almost as an afterthought Stephen contacted Alberto with dates. Alberto was disappointed to inform his friend he would be at a conference and not back till Saturday night, flying into La Guardia as Stephen and family flew home from JFK.

Nature's fury suddenly opened a window of opportunity with Alberto flying back a day earlier, before Irene could do her worst to the city he loved. The two exchanged messages, a reunion in a bar in the midst of a hurricane seemed a perfect setting given their history.

Stephen and family decided on dining around the corner from the hotel, as they recommended guests were safely inside by 6pm at the latest. They plotted up in a chain Mexican restaurant they found on the west side of Grand Central. The food was so-so and they ate quickly, as the skies above Manhattan darkened.

It was as they were waiting for their bill that they noticed the 'Stooping Man' shuffle slowly past the restaurant, muttering to himself. Jessica was visibly upset, "Poor man, I wonder where he lives, what do you think came first, the physical ailment or his mental condition?"

"I guess they are linked," Luke pondered.

"I would guess they are," Cassandra added.

Florence chipped in, "We'll have to Google his condition, the stoop. I hope he has somewhere to shelter from the hurricane."

They made the two hundred meter dash back to the hotel as the rain began to get heavier. Stephen and Cassandra claimed their prime spot in the bar and the kids went up to their rooms to watch nature's wrath from the luxury of the fourteenth floor.

Cassandra could see Stephen was on edge as he surveyed the lobby beyond the bar, "Are you excited Steve?"

"I am, but it's been twenty-seven years, we're surely different people now, we may not click anymore," Stephen replied, without averting his gaze from the lobby.

"That can't take away from the good times you two shared, you've spoken so often about Al I feel I know him," Cassandra reassured him.

Stephen smiled appreciatively but wasn't sure if the 'Big A' would harbour a grudge given the circumstances of their last meeting. Had the big man learnt their first meeting, in that war zone thirty years ago, had not been by chance?

"Hold on to your hats folks, strap yourselves in, it's gonna be one hell of a night!" Herbie the bar manager hollered from his lofty perch. TV screens flickered above him, all but one was on weather stations. The last one showed a baseball game being played in glorious sunshine, LA Stephen guessed. "Tonight's special cocktail is 'Goodnight Irene', whiskey, sour ginger, a twist of lemon, soda, on the rocks. Only five dollars! When the going gets tough, the tough get drinking!" Herbie bellowed.

Stephen and Cassandra ordered a couple of 'Goodnight Irene's', clinking glasses on their arrival. "Here's to Irene," Cass toasted.

"Irene," Stephen confirmed, still staring at the lobby. The bar was filling up now and his view was obscured.

Suddenly a human tornado entered the bar and gave out a throaty roar, "Stephen Ross you English bastard, the 'Big A' is in the house!"

Stephen, Cassandra and everyone else in the bar stared at the man mountain. He was dressed in his beachwear, rain and sweat soaked through, stood in the centre of the room with his arms open wide. "Come hug the big man you English bastard!" His voice was like a primal scream.

Embarrassed, Stephen reluctantly slipped off his stool and made his way to Alberto, he disappeared into mounds of flesh as the 'Big A' embraced him.

"Twenty-seven fucking years," he bellowed, "twenty-seven years since this English bastard disappeared from my wedding!" There was laughter rather than malice as he continued without letting go of his old friend. "The best fucking man disappears into thin air. Let me warn you ladies and gentlemen, don't invite this English bastard to your wedding. He's unreliable."

The crowd's spirits were lifted by the big man's rant.

"Take me to your woman, where's that Cass, take me to your woman!"

Stephen dutifully led Alberto to the bar stools where Cassandra was cowering. She found herself joining her husband in a fleshy embrace.

They shared a couple of JDs and an hour of chit chat, mainly about their families, then Cassandra made her excuses and decided to join the kids upstairs. Stephen ordered another round. Alberto took on a serious demeanour, "Stephen Ross, it's just you and me now, no fucking bullshit, I want the truth you English bastard, the truth."

Stephen was worried. Did Alberto harbour a twenty-seven year grudge over him going AWOL after the wedding present fiasco? Or maybe he had discovered the real reason Stephen had befriended him in the first place.

Alberto cut to the chase, "What in the name of Jesus H Christ were you doing man, what the fuck was Stephen Ross, the English punk rocker who knew every word to every Clash song ever, doing at a Michael Buble concert?" Stephen instantly felt the weight of guilt and worry lift from his shoulders. "Fucking Buble man, you fucking traitor."

Their fellow drinkers either side of them were laughing as the big man harangued his old friend. "Sorry about the language ladies but this pathetic Englishman had a fist fight with The Stranglers in 1976 and spat in Paul Weller's face at an early 'Jam' concert! I'm sorry to have to tell you this but I only caught up with this mother fu- after seeing him on YouTube being beaten by a woman at a fucking Buble concert. Can you believe it, I'm still in shock!" The crowd returned to their conversations only to be interrupted by Alberto again, "Is there a Judge in the house, preferably one with a black cap? Sorry Stevie boy, Buble, that's a fucking hanging offence."

"I love 'the Buble'," a middle-aged waitress added.

"I rest my case," Alberto concluded.

Stephen imagined a familiar figure standing in the corner. "My sentiments entirely you wanker, you know how I feel about this, go on make your pathetic excuses to your fat sweaty mate you wanker." Stephen blinked and his hero, Sex Pistol Jonny Rotten, disappeared from his thoughts.

Stephen felt a wave of relief at his old friend's jibes, he didn't have to explain betrayal or spying, this was just lighthearted humiliation.

"The recession." Stephen said.

"What do you mean, recession, what the-"

"Triple dip recession, that's my excuse, I shall explain all when I've got my glass refilled."

"Bar Tender!" The big man shouted.

3

DEATH BY CROONING
(2010)

There were fourteen clips uploaded to YouTube of the fracas, clip nine got more hits than the other thirteen put together. It was clip nine that would change Stephen's life. It was this clip that would put him back in touch with the 'Big A', but more importantly, it was this clip that inspired Luke to make contact. But whilst the ripples of clip nine spread day by day, Stephen was more concerned about the possibility of a clip fifteen, he prayed there wasn't one.

Someone a couple of rows behind Stephen, Cassandra and the 'dickheads' had filmed clip nine in glorious HD:

> *At first the camera focuses on Buble, but his crooning is soon drowned out by high pitch screaming and swearing. Suddenly an altercation between a large, extremely inebriated, woman in a Blackburn Rovers football shirt and a smaller middle-aged man comes into view. The woman, in her fifties, can be seen slapping the poor man, who attempts to palm her slaps away without being too aggressive. A second much younger female, probably in her early twenties, comes into shot and literally throws a parry of punches that land right in the chap's face. The camera swings left and it becomes obvious the women belong to a hen party, there are at least eight other females in blue and white halved Blackburn shirts. Each one has 'Go Kirsty' printed on the back and they all look like they've had a long day/night.*
>
> *The camera pans back to the action and the yelps of the crowd are audible, there is a glimpse of Buble crooning in the distance. As the last punch connects, the victim turns defensively away and faces the camera. Anyone who knows or ever knew Stephen can clearly see it's him, the tick shaped scar above his right eye is visible. Both women, egged on by their friends, continue the drunken attack.*
>
> *There is a mixture of drunken rage and pure triumph etched on their faces as Stephen falls clumsily to the floor.*

HOW TO KIDNAP A STRING QUARTET

Just before the clip ends a young blonde, with 'Bride' on the back of her shirt, clambers past her mates and appears to spit towards Stephen, who has disappeared into the void between the seats.

"So my punk rocker friend from the infamous East End of London was decked by a hen." Alberto laughed loudly.

"I actually tripped backwards over the dickhead's feet." Stephen continued his defence.

"Who were the dickheads you were with?" Alberto asked, still laughing.

"I'll come to them shortly but let's go back to the triple dip recession big man, the reason why I was in the O2 arena to see the world's most popular karaoke singer in the first place." Stephen painted a depressing picture of the tough last few years, how his latest business venture, "Scam," Alberto sarcastically inserted, was brought to its knees. Both girls at Uni at the same time and attempting to help his brother pay back the Inland Revenue after a disastrous VAT inspection had led to a tale of financial woe.

Alberto nodded in sympathy, he'd struggled as well, this recession was global, but most of his problems were as a result of two expensive divorces.

Stephen admitted that he relied on Cassandra working full time, even though she loathed the job and particularly her boss Jason, aka the 'Dickhead', the best Stephen could come up with to describe the complete bore.

Some months ago they had endured a dinner party organised by Mrs. 'Dickhead', Evelyn, whose shrill voice and hyena like laugh (at anything Jason said) drove Stephen to distraction. Her only redeeming feature, or features, were her massive boobs. Cassandra insisted they were 'bought off the shelf' but they seemed to hold Stephen and the other male guests transfixed. The only light relief during a painful evening.

For some mysterious reason Jason seemed to enjoy Stephen's company and bored him senseless from hors d'oeuvres to the cheese board with tales from the world of insurance brokering. Evelyn's conversation was strictly limited to future home improvements and rubbing her guests noses in it by waxing lyrical about the villa they had purchased on the Algarve, complete with their own pool and gym. Stephen smiled when she used the word 'they' as she hadn't done a day's work in her charmed life.

His only communication with her was when she asked if anyone could recommend a good plumber to install a floating vanity unit (a sink cut into a thick shelf, Stephen later translated to Cassandra) in her en-suite. "My plumber Terry Harmer is excellent, Evelyn. I'll dig out his number for you, he's a top plumber, isn't he Cass?"

Cassandra gave him a mischievous smile and confirmed the recommendation. "Yes Terry is definitely the man for the job."

"Is he fit?" Evelyn screeched, and laughed at her own question.

"Very," Cassandra replied.

After dinner the conversation turned to music when Jason announced they had great seats at the O2 for 'Michael'.

"Michael who?" Someone questioned.

"The 'Buble', Michael Buble." The dickhead confirmed, amazed at anyone not knowing who Michael was.

"Are you a fan of the 'Buble' Stephen?" Evelyn asked.

Stephen paused before answering, *I'd rather set my own testicles on fire*, is what he wanted to say but he remembered how much they needed Cassandra in full employment. "He's a very good singer, quite a performer," he lied, feeling hot and guilty.

He imagined Jonny Rotten standing in the corner of the room holding a bottle of Bud, slowly shaking his head, "Judus," he mouthed, "fucking Judus."

"It's the recession Jonny," he tried to explain, but his imaginary hero and the thought evaporated.

On the way home they laughed about recommending their friend Terry Harmer to do the plumbing. "They don't call him 'Harmer the Charmer' for nothing," Cassandra laughed.

"Do you think Mrs. Dickhead will be safe Cass?"

"Well maybe he can confirm my theory that her tits are plastic!" A difficult night ended in raucous laughter.

Two weeks after Stephen had lost that night of his life Cassandra phoned him at his office, "I'm not sure how I'm going to tell you this but I've just had a call from Evelyn."

"Evelyn?" Stephen interrupted, surprised.

"Evelyn, Mrs. Dickhead, you know 'plastic tits'," Cassandra confirmed. "It's bad news I'm afraid, Jason's brother-in-law and wife are down with the Nora virus so they have two spare tickets for the Michael Buble concert..."

Stephen instantly knew the implications of this bad news.

"Also," she continued, "the boss has badly sprained his ankle messing about on his nephew's skateboard so..." She went on to explain that they would have to pick them up at six and battle through the Friday evening rush hour traffic to the O2 arena. Stephen felt ill. Jonny Rotten sat in the swivel chair opposite, on the other side of the Ikea desk. He sniggered as he propelled himself round and round, grinning.

"Recession Jonny, triple dip recession."

Jonny Rotten stopped revolving, gave Stephen a 'wank' gesture and was gone.

HOW TO KIDNAP A STRING QUARTET

The journey was as arduous as he thought it would be, the A12 was crawling, the rain was falling and the 'Dickhead' droned on and on about foreign drivers, punctuating his rant with more than one racist comment. Evelyn's hyena-like laugh behind him interrupted Jason's monotone whine. Stephen glanced in the rear view mirror catching a glimpse of her cleavage, he noticed Cassandra had a fixed obedient smile.

He dropped them off as near to the entrance as possible then found the closest parking space, a good twenty-minute walk away. He was soaked to the bone when he caught up with them in the O2's imposing concourse. They found a bar but he shuddered as he remembered he'd have to suffer the 'Buble' stone cold sober.

About fifteen minutes into the concert, Cassandra asked Stephen if he could swap seats with Evelyn, who was increasingly annoyed by the drunken northern women beside her. Within seconds of doing his duty Buble's latest ditty came to a climax. The crowd stood as one to applaud, his neighbour fell on him breathing neat vodka and screaming incoherently. He put his hand up defensively in an effort to calm the situation but within seconds the assault was captured on fourteen different phone and video cameras.

Security staff stepped in and removed the hen party to another area as Stephen was helped up by his shocked wife, his pride hurting more than his battered head. He glimpsed at the now empty seats, Jonny Rotten sat alone, giving him a pitiful stare.

"They were from the north Jonny, I was only helping." His imaginary hero looked sickened and disappeared into the adoring Buble crowd.

"Well now I understand Stevie Boy, these women were from Blackburn man, that explains why they were crazy." Alberto slapped his English friend on his back. "It's all those fucking holes man."

"What you on about?" Stephen asked.

"Four thousand holes in Blackburn, Lancashire," the big man sang out loudly, "you'd go crazy trying to avoid them wouldn't you?"

Stephen managed to change the subject back to the 'Big A' and his efforts to hire the string quartet Susan loved to perform at her bedside. Alberto had described her illness, which was tragically terminal, and how she still had the strength to tell him how much she hated him. He now seemed totally obsessed with the idea of a last chance peace offering, the more he talked about his efforts the more concerned Stephen grew.

Having described his initially rejected approach, the big man introduced his friend to his next moves. "So they turned down my initial approach and okay maybe the little shits were busy with their studies, waiting tables whatever, so step two was obvious. I'd return with Dino and offer them some serious corn, like a nice round thousand dollars!"

"Wow Al, that's commitment to the cause. So, what happened?" Stephen enquired.

"I went last week but Dino couldn't make it, I had a few drinks and maybe I was a bit off hand with my approach this time."

"And?" Stephen interrupted.

"I basically waved the cash in front of the female violinists nose and told her this was my final offer. She told me to fuck off Stevie, 'fuck off' were her exact words."

"You obviously didn't impress them with your diplomatic skills."

"The time for diplomacy has passed Stevie boy, I decided there and then on step three, I called Dino and told him he would have to join me for the next performance, no excuses. The little shits had turned down two reasonable and financially rewarding requests, now was the time for action." Alberto was now red in the face.

"What kind of action?" Stephen hesitantly asked.

"I shall approach them with courtesy and calmly, for a final time, explain my sincere reasons for my persistence. If, as I suspect, they turn me down I will send Dino forward and he will simply punch the second violinist on the nose. I bet that will concentrate their minds!"

4

GOING VIRAL

It was a hot sultry night in New York City, Alberto was between relationships and, more worryingly, apartments. Tonight his sofa surfing took him to his daughter's studio apartment, top floor of a brownstone in downtown Brooklyn. This particular sofa was about half the big man's size. Sleep was hard to achieve so he read and smoked a couple of joints in the hope his eyes may just give up.

Ched, his daughter's partner, kept him company sitting at the dining table on his laptop. He had ear phones plugged in and apart from the odd laugh or muttered "Jeez" he hadn't disturbed Alberto for at least a couple of hours, which suited each other just fine. Alberto didn't warm to him, maybe he was being too protective of Louisa or maybe he just found Ched aloof, too cool for school. Ched clearly found Alberto far too big and loud for the tiny living space. They just about managed to tolerate each other for the sake of the status quo, realising Louisa was loyal to both of them. "Different music, different drugs," Alberto would describe their relationship to his closest confidants.

Louisa was his only daughter, her mother Mia, his second wife, lived in Florida with a Gynaecologist whom she'd left him for. He liked to joke, "I spent every other night fiddling about with Mia's bits, 'Gyno man' has one peep and she runs off with him." The split was of course more complicated and a long time coming, but the marriage had lasted a lot longer than his disastrous four-month marriage to Susan.

It was just after 3am and his eyes were finally closing when Ched roared with laughter. "Jeez Al you gotta take a look at this man, this is right up your street."

He made his way over and sat on the arm of the sofa. "What's up?" Alberto sat up and pretended to be interested.

"It's a YouTube clip, viral clip of the day, it's from London. It's a fight at a fucking Buble concert man. This guy is totally owned by some ugly chicks, they give this spineless dude a real beating!" Obviously a dislike of crooners was common ground. Al took the laptop from him and pressed play. "Looks like a crazy British bachelorette party," Ched added.

"Hen party," Albert corrected him, "the Brits call it a hen party."

He watched the video chuckling and swearing as the two-minute clip developed. "Fucking outstanding Ched, love it. That guy deserved a good beating, the look on those soccer moms' faces."

"I loved the look on that guy's face," Ched interrupted.

"I've gotta watch this again." Alberto was wide-awake again. He watched the clip two or three times without saying another word. Each time his concentration reached a peak as the poor guy turned towards the camera. "I don't fucking believe it, can you pause this? Freeze the picture, I know this guy!"

Ched made allowances that Alberto had over done the JD and a couple of spliffs and did as he was told, pausing the clip when Alberto shouted, "Stop!"

Louisa emerged in her dressing gown, "What the hell's up with you two? Dad, you'll wake up the whole building."

Alberto's gaze never left the screen, "It's him, Jesus H Christ, it's Stevie boy, it's fucking Stevie boy, my room mate, back in eighty-two. Stevie boy, the English punk rocker!" Alberto was now screaming, sweating, and crying as he stood clutching the laptop not knowing what to do next.

Eventually Louisa and Ched calmed him down and suggested he write a message in the comments. "Your old room mate clearly isn't a punk rocker now," Ched said as he retired to the bedroom with Louisa. "A total fucking loser if you ask me."

Alberto sat down again staring still staring at the screen shaking his head, "What the hell happened to us Stevie boy?"

****

A graph of Stephen's life up to the 'Buble' incident would show a pretty steady horizontal line, apart from a hefty spike in the early eighties peaking when he met the 'Big A'. When clip nine went viral, Stephen couldn't imagine the events that would follow, this relatively uneventful graph was about to go off the scale.

Humorous sarcastic texts came first, then when clips five, nine and eleven were posted on Facebook, all hell broke loose. Various newspapers, including the New Musical Express, ran clip nine.

Lighthearted comments from friends and family were replaced by requests for interviews by tabloids and the like. Cassandra was mortified, the girls were embarrassed and Stephen humiliated. There was a family tradition of discussing problems over a Saturday brunch, the last such rare occasion was to talk about Florence's liking of legal and illegal highs.

On the positive side, Cassandra explained that the 'dickheads' were so grateful that Stephen had not only taken a beating on their behalf, but also been humiliated in every medium known to man, they had promoted her to credit control manager along with a small but handy increase in pay.

Finances continued to occupy his mind, he confessed to his family over brunch that he'd received a couple of tempting offers to sell his story. Florence guessed correctly one of them was from the Daily Mail, who were the largest news outlet to show the video on its online edition.

"I suppose your average Buble fan is a classic Daily Mail reader," she stated. Her father nodded in agreement.

Despite the temptation to earn some much needed extra money, Cassandra persuaded Stephen not to sell his soul to the devil and, with the agreement of the girls, he decided to accept the offer to appear on an irreverent comedy sports show on satellite TV. As it transpired his business also picked up after what ended up being a successful appearance, with one or two clients making fresh orders, probably out of sympathy.

Stephen's TV debut turned out to be a surprisingly enjoyable experience. The producer, not much older than his girls, warmed to him when he learnt Stephen was a fellow West Ham supporter, "Well no one can accuse us of being glory hunters," the young man joked.

There was a brief rehearsal but basically the programme went out live on a Sunday morning. Every week there was a humorous look at a popular sports related clip on social media. The attractive female co-anchor signaled his moment as he sat among the studio audience in the front row.

"We never condone football hooliganism on this programme but this week's 'Sports Gone Viral' video is an exception. Wouldn't all of us secretly love to beat the crap out of a Michael Buble fan?" The studio audience cheered their approval and this was Stephen's cue to stand up with his back to his camera, wearing a West Ham shirt with a number one and 'THE BUBLE' printed on it.

They then ran clip nine, and two minutes later, with the crowd still cheering, two huge guys wearing Blackburn shirts, blonde wigs and full make up emerged from off set and proceeded to hit Stephen with their handbags as he pretended to fall to the floor.

He lay there waiting for the adverts to roll and saw his friend standing amongst the now hysterical audience. "Fucking disgrace," Jonny Rotten mouthed, "I'd like to give you a proper fucking kicking, you are an embarrassment to your family, to yourself, and worst of all your team. You won't be able to show your ugly sissy face round East London again, wanker." Stephen was hot with embarrassment as Rotten disappeared from his thoughts.

There were post show nibbles and drinks in the studio canteen, the young producer congratulated Stephen for being a great sport and told him he could keep the West Ham shirt as a memento. He confessed to Stephen that he was surprised the Blackburn 'Hens' had turned down an invitation to appear on the programme. "My idea was to get the ladies down in their Blackburn strip and dress you up as Buble, but they weren't interested in an all expenses trip to London for a couple of days."

"Maybe they were worried I'd press charges for assault," Stephen replied abruptly. The producer seemed unconvinced.

After the show Stephen's phone went into meltdown, with people he'd never met contacting him constantly. His 'fifteen minutes' produced ripples he'd never have imagined.

A couple of weeks after his command performance he returned home from work to an uneasy atmosphere as Cassandra gave him an unusually muted welcome.

"You okay Cass?" Stephen enquired.

She had her back to him watching something revolving in the microwave as she ignored him.

"What's up Cass?" He placed his hand on her shoulder and she reluctantly turned to face him. He immediately noticed she'd been crying, her eyes were red. Stephen hadn't seen Cass like this since Florence was found unconscious in her tent at the Reading rock festival three years previously. "What's up Cass, are the girls okay?"

When she didn't reply, he poured them both a large Merlot and led her to the living room where he sat her down next to him on the brown leather sofa. He smelt gin on her breath. She'd started early.

"This young guy knocked on the door, I thought it was a salesman, but this lad just stood there."

"What did he want?" Stephen asked.

"Nothing at first, he wasn't threatening or anything, he looked nervous, he just stood there for ages."

"What did you say Cass?"

"I, I..." She hesitated for a second and tried to compose herself. "I couldn't say anything, he then stuttered and struggled for words. He really struggled to say what he wanted to say and then he shouted, 'Steve Ross, is Steve Ross here?' I told him you were at work but would be back any minute, just thinking on my feet. I asked him if I could give you a message but when he tried to speak again his stutter got worse and he just gave up and handed me this." She was holding a yellow 'post it' note and passed it to a bewildered Stephen.

He studied the barely legible writing '*Luke 07775623309*'. "What...who was he Cass? How old was he? What did he look like?" Stephen was clueless. Suddenly Cassandra burst into uncontrollable, hysterical tears. "Cass what is it, did he do something to upset you?"

She tried to compose herself, like the mystery caller she struggled to find the words. Eventually she calmed down, she released her hand from Stephen's caring clasp and looked directly at him with an intensity that startled him. "He looked like, he looked like…" She hesitated before shocking her husband. "He looked like," she took a deep breath, "like you!" Cassandra yelled, "He looked just like you Stephen!"

5

MR. S

"Of course I can never forgive you but let's put the whole Buble fiasco behind us, what's the story with Luke?" Alberto asked with an unusually serious tone.

Stephen was relieved to change the subject. "Better get another drink, it's a long story Al."

"It's gonna be a long night Stevie boy, I'm not going anywhere in a hurry."

They got another round, Stephen took a swig and delved back into the past.

****

Stephen knew it was January 1981, despite his memory problems, because he Googled 'Yorkshire Ripper' and Wikipedia quickly gave him the date of Peter Sutcliffe's capture.

He recalled taking an interest in the depressing toll of grizzly murders because of the sensational title given to the elusive serial killer and also his latest job had connections with Leeds.

He'd resisted joining his older brother in the family business due to his difficult relationship with his father. Since leaving school he'd had a succession of various jobs, or scams, as his mates described them. Despite his differences with his father he was grateful when he introduced him to a wealthy client. Over one of his mother's spectacular Sunday dinners, his father mentioned that his best customer, Maurice Saltzman, was looking for someone who could source and drive a horsebox for his daughter, who was determined to make it in the Equestrian world.

Normally Stephen would totally ignore his father's suggestions but he was desperate. His previous career, involving a home delivery service of video films, had come to an abrupt end when his supplier was arrested by the vice squad! So, he bit the bullet and phoned Mr. Saltzman's office.

Mr. Saltzman's brother-in-law Harvey interviewed him, he had a nervous twitch that unnerved Stephen. Maurice Saltzman had his fingers in many pies, the mainstay of his empire was his extensive property portfolio that spread from Brighton to Leeds and beyond. Harvey basically told him he would be starting in credit control in their ramshackle office in Finsbury Park.

Stephen's first four months were spent in the smallest office in the world, essentially an alcove with a couple of shelves and a telephone. He arrived at 9am every morning to find a list of telephone numbers and names of tenants in arrears. He had a set script for any given excuse but he quickly discovered he could create a far more menacing persona on the telephone than he ever could in person. This resulted in most tenants paying up within days, which meant a healthy commission cheque. After three months he came to an arrangement with Harvey to rent a company bedsit in Finsbury Park.

He eventually got to meet the boss himself when Harvey asked him to deliver a package to leafy Hampstead Garden suburb. Maurice Saltzman's home was unsurprisingly ostentatious. He expected the door to be answered by a butler or a housekeeper and was surprised when a small plump Mrs. Saltzman appeared with a rolling pin in her hand. "Hiya, you must be young Stephen, I'm Hilary Saltzman, do come in. You must excuse the state of me, I'm busy baking, I seem to be wearing the pastry rather than rolling it!"

He found her instantly charming and down to earth. He was led into what transpired to be a vibrant family home, with the sound of teenage children emanating from seemingly every room. She ushered him upstairs and pointed to open door at the end of a mahogany paneled corridor. "Mory, young Stephen is here!"

Stephen saw a hand beckoning him to come in. "Don't worry, he doesn't bite," she encouraged him. Stephen entered the room for a meeting which would ultimately lead him to his fateful meeting with the 'Big A', and many, many years later, Luke.

Maurice Saltzman sat behind a 'captain's table', he was busy signing cheques on a smart green baize insert. Stephen was surprised at how small he was, smaller even than Mrs. Saltzman.

He had a good head of jet-black hair and a healthfully thick tash. He was wearing a Saville Row suit, as he always did during business hours.

His left hand was still beckoning as he finished signing the last cheque of a pile. "Payday," he exclaimed, "a necessary evil." He was well spoken without being posh, his voice carried respect and authority that belied his stature. "Stephen, I've heard only good things about you," he said, shaking his hand firmly. "Every time I write out a cheque for Stephen B. Ross I hesitate, I've never paid out so much commission."

"Thanks," Stephen replied courteously.

"Harvey tells me you're an all round good lad which is a compliment coming from my brother-in-law. I'm very pleased to hear this because I only took a chance on you when your father asked me if I had a vacancy. I was concerned you might be a chip off the old block."

Stephen realised Mr. Saltzman knew his father well, "Dad is a one off Mr. Saltzman," Stephen confirmed.

"Call me Mr. S please. Yes your father isn't easy is he, he could start a fight with himself in a telephone box, but he knows all about glazing and knows I like a deal. Now you've got something for me."

Stephen handed over the package, which Maurice opened, emptying what Stephen guessed was at least ten thousand pounds in cash.

Mrs. S interrupted them, delivering a tray of tea and homemade cakes. She didn't give the cash a second glance.

Mr. S counted out a hundred pounds in tenners and pushed it towards Stephen, then passed over his wages and commission cheque. "There you are Mr. Stephen B. Ross, well done, some extra spending money for you. I'm sending you on a mission up north."

Stephen was concerned but excited by this news.

"Tell me young man, what does the B stand for?"

"Benjamin," Stephen answered.

"Benjamin," Saltzman echoed, "Stephen Benjamin Ross. You're not of the faith are you?" He enquired.

"My father's Jewish, but has never practiced his faith. I thought you might have guessed given your dealings with him." Stephen felt slightly awkward.

"And you Stephen, do you have faith?"

Stephen hesitated, "I believe in something Mr. S, to be honest my father is so negative about religion, I've actually started to study my roots. I have a cousin in Israel, I've visited him a couple of times. Harvey tells me you have a home there." He hoped he'd replied favourably.

"Interesting." Saltzman picked another hundred pounds and handed it to Stephen. "A bonus, young man, well done. Your old man may be impossible, but you I like."

Stephen thanked him and took a deep breath for courage. "Can I ask you a personal question Mr. S?"

"No young man, a business question yes, personal no."

Stephen realised he'd badly phrased the question. "I meant to ask you, my father said you needed a horse box and a driver for your daughter and I like credit control but-"

Saltzman lifted his hand to cut him short, "Speak to Harvey Monday morning he will fill you in on all you need about Leeds, the horse box is on hold for now."

Stephen felt the meeting had gone well but that he had touched a nerve with the horsebox enquiry. He met Harvey on Monday, who was his normal joyless self, and gave him a typed itinerary and a small white company mini van, which he was told was his to use for business use only until otherwise informed. The itinerary was pretty straightforward:

Saturday 9.00am. Meet Eric (the locksmith) at HQ.
Pick up hardware from address supplied by Eric (the locksmith).
Drive to hotel in Leeds. Eric (the locksmith) knows location.
Sunday 8.00am accompany Eric (the locksmith) to addresses on Eric's list.
Drop Eric (the locksmith) home.

He asked Cassandra, the pretty young receptionist Stephen fancied but hadn't found the courage to ask out, who the hell this Eric (the locksmith) was.

"Eric is the Saltzmans go-to man when clients change the locks, which is in contradiction of their tenancy agreement, as I'm sure you've read. Now and again we send him to check a whole area. Next weekend it's Leeds."

Stephen decided to take his chance and expand the conversation with Cassandra, "Why does he need me with him? I know nothing about locks."

"Eric's a nutter, he needs a babysitter and most definitely a driver as the idiot has lost his license."

'Fancy a drink one night Cass? Maybe a movie or a gig?' Stephen thought this was a great sentence but that's all it was, a thought, he couldn't summon up the actual words. He decided he'd complete the mission to Leeds and then try and ask her. He noticed Jonny Rotten sitting on her desk. "Fucking loser mate, if you don't make a move soon I'll have to fill my boots."

The following Thursday evening Stephen received a phone call from Harvey explaining that Eric (the locksmith) had food poisoning and the trip to Leeds would be put off to the following weekend. He wasn't bothered by the postponement and given the news that would break over the next few days, it would conspire to have a massive effect on Stephen's future.

6

RIPPERLAND
(1981)

Stephen decided to take advantage of the postponed Leeds mission and spent the weekend clubbing with friends. By Sunday evening he'd crashed on the sofa watching TV, covered in blankets as it was freezing both outside and in. He started watching a detective drama with Bernard Cribbins, which, despite his self-inflicted fatigue, caught his attention. The programme got darker and more gripping as it developed, but just as it was reaching its grisly climax the screen went blank. Stephen thought the rented TV had finally given up, but suddenly there was action. A deep serious voice spoke over the BBC logo, "We are sorry to interrupt our Sunday night drama but we are going straight to our news room for a news flash."

Stephen could hear his heart beating and struggled to contain his excitement, he'd never seen this happen before. His older brother often recalled the TV schedule being interrupted by the news that JFK had been assassinated. His first thought was that either the Queen or the Prime Minister were dead, he sat transfixed as the newsreader appeared without music. "Good evening, we can confirm that West Yorkshire police have released a statement detailing the arrest of a suspect in connection with the 'Yorkshire Ripper' murders. The arrest was made on Friday during a routine stop and search on Friday evening in the Leeds area. A man will appear in court tomorrow afternoon, we will keep you updated of all developments."

The next day the press divulged the name of the man arrested, Peter Sutcliffe, who was formally charged with murder that Monday afternoon.

Stephen thought no more of it until he picked up a now fully recovered Eric the locksmith the following Friday afternoon. Eric didn't speak until they approached Nottingham, he'd been busy studying his list of addresses in and around Leeds and a relevant map of the city. "I hope you've bought a good supply of condoms with you mate."

"What?" It wasn't a question Stephen expected.

"It's going to be wild up there mate, fucking mental, thank God I had food poisoning last weekend," Eric added.

"Sorry Eric, you've lost me."

"Listen mate, up to and including last weekend the women of Leeds have stayed in for the last two years because of that mad cunt Sutcliffe. If we'd gone up there last week it would have been like the fucking Moon up there, now he's been locked up every female in Yorkshire's going to be out on the town."

Stephen hadn't considered the benefits of the 'Ripper's' arrest, he'd spent most of his time thinking about how to entice out the receptionist Cassandra.

Eric continued with great excitement, "It's going to be open season up there, believe me, those Yorkshire birds will be after any geezer with a pulse, even you mate."

Stephen presumed this was banter and that Eric didn't actually know his pathetic efforts with the opposite sex. He noticed Jonny Rotten in the rear view mirror, lounging on the back seat grinning.

"Even a spineless wanker like you couldn't fuck this weekend up," he smirked, "your mate is spot on, now shape up and don't let London down."

The hotel Eric guided them to was reasonably clean and modern, most importantly it had a bar and everything was on 'Saltzman Properties'. After a wash and brush up the two met there.

"Okay mate, here's the plan," Eric was a veteran of many a road trip for the company. "Firstly rule number one, get receipts for everything. I've got a company credit card but we can't take the piss with it because the Jew boys will check every fucking transaction!"

Stephen felt uncomfortable with Eric's statement, "Jew boys?" Stephen repeated.

Eric detected his unease. "Harvey and Mr. S., nothing gets passed them, you can't take the piss."

Stephen saw Jonny Rotten on the stool next to him, "You gonna let him make racial slurs, you going to let that stand you spineless wanker."

Stephen gave Eric the 'thousand yard' stare. "Hang on pal, my old man's a 'Jew boy'. Besides I reckon that Mr. S. is okay, Harvey's a bit weird but to be fair he's only on board because he's married to Mr. S' sister."

"Your old man's Jewish?" Eric replied surprised.

"What of it?"

"Nothing mate. What about your mum, what about you mate?"

"What are you Eric?" Stephen threw the question back at the locksmith.

"I'm nothing mate, I was Christened but I got no religion mate, it's the route of all evil. The Saltzmans are alright I suppose, for Jew boys," Eric laughed.

Stephen continued his disapproving stare appreciating the thumbs up from Jonny. Eric returned to the plan, "Firstly, my friend Ahmed 'The Cab' is picking us up at seven. First stop will be his brother's in deepest Bradford for a curry, then round the corner for a massage," Eric winked, "Then it's off to 'Armageddon ' in the city centre."

"Armageddon?" Stephen repeated.

"It will be fucking Armageddon out there mate, no man will be safe, not even you. It's a top club, Armageddon, been there many times."

Eric and Ahmed exchanged banter as the cab cruised around the endless terraced houses of Bradford. Eric turned to Stephen, "Do you know how you introduce your wife in Bradford? Have you met my sister."

Stephen waited for Ahmed to laugh before joining in half heatedly. This was 1981 and political correctness hadn't been invented but Stephen found Eric totally embarrassing, even more so when they sat down to dinner with Ahmed's family.

"Don't expect me to introduce everyone mate, every time I come here there's a new arrival fresh off the boat." He made no effort to keep his voice down.

The curry was a bit too spicy for Stephen's taste but he enjoyed the experience and would agree it was a good start to their twenty-four hours up north. However, he wasn't so sure about the next port of call.

Ahmed dropped them off in a non-descript street barely half a mile from his brother's. It was freezing and beginning to snow as Eric led Stephen to a blue painted door. As he pressed the buzzer the locksmith commented, "You are about to enter paradise mate."

The door opened a fraction and Eric peered inside. "It's Eric the locksmith!" He barked and a burley Asian bouncer unlatched the chain. They followed him up the rickety stairs and pointed to a pair of maroon velvet two seat sofas separated by a glass coffee table.

They sat opposite each other, the bouncer fetched bottles of beer from a small fridge, opened them with his teeth and placed them on the table in front of them. "Cheers, here's to a Ripper free night of fun." They clinked bottles as the bouncer placed a small jewellery box on the table. Eric opened the box, which contained a couple of joints and a small bottle of blue tablets, which Stephen guessed were some kind of amphetamines. Eric picked up a joint and dug out his lighter. "What's your poison mate, fill your boots son."

It had been over a year since Stephen had taken the last of many, many 'blues', he enjoyed the odd joint but 'wizz' had been his crutch since he was seventeen. It had got to a stage where he couldn't function socially without them. They killed his shyness but then they killed his friend and supplier Kenny, whose heart attack at the age of twenty-five shocked Stephen into immediate abstinence. Though he had considered relenting and popping a couple so he'd have the confidence to ask Cassandra the receptionist out.

Eric waited for a response, Stephen hesitated. "All on expenses, the Jew boys, sorry I mean the Saltzmans," Eric confirmed without any sincerity.

Stephen noticed Jonny Rotten looking over the locksmith's shoulder. "For fucks sake don't just sit there, you're embarrassing yourself, you're up north boy, let's av it large."

Stephen looked Eric in the eye and opened the bottle, then tipped a couple of pills into his hand, placed them in his mouth and washed them down with swig of beer.

A few minutes later two blonde women dressed in white tunics entered the room. "Cindy, Angie, delighted to see you, have you missed me?" Eric stood and gave them both a kiss on the cheek.

Some inane banter passed between them as it dawned on Stephen that he was about to enjoy (or possibly not) his first professional massage. He hoped the speed would kick in but before long Cindy, the older of the two, led him to a small room and pointed to a chair to place his clothes. "You can keep pants on lad if you're shy," she said in a thick Yorkshire accent.

He lay on the massage bed and realised he was separated from Eric by a hospital like curtain. "Is your friend having the Deluxe package Eric lad?" Cindy asked.

"Why not!" Eric hollered, when a whisper would do. "It's all on the company," he confirmed.

Stephen was the colour of the crimson sofa, he hoped those pills were strong.

It took Ahmed twenty minutes to get them to their next destination, Armageddon, in Leeds city centre. Stephen monopolised the conversation for the whole journey, clearly the 'wizz' was working. Eric winked at Ahmed as they vacated the cab, Stephen was still chattering away. He wasn't surprised that the doormen knew Eric and they were ushered past the longish queue, which was almost totally female. They were taken to the 'members bar' by James, the head doorman. "It's going to be wild tonight lads," he confirmed, "most of these girls ain't been in a club for three years!" He shouted above the disco music.

"Told you mate!" Eric screamed at Stephen. Literally within seconds Eric was sitting at the bar between two highly inebriated ladies, slipping his hands around their slender waists as he introduced himself. Stephen sat on his own a few stools up and ordered a large scotch and ice, he felt good, but wanted to feel better. Unbeknown to Eric he'd slipped an extra couple of 'blues' in his pocket at the massage parlour. He found them amongst his handkerchief and loose change in his trouser pocket and popped them in his glass. The liquid and pills were knocked back in one.

Instantly the room was spinning, the music was throbbing. He noticed Eric's new friends were all over him and a group of girls, he guessed in their early thirties, standing near him laughing and giggling. He realised they were looking directly at him. One of the girls stepped forward, she was wearing silver 'spray on' jeans and an equally tight matching 'boob tube'. "Do you want to buy me a drink lad?" She asked.

He managed to avert his eyes from her body to what was a mature but pretty face. She had a 'Farrah Fawcett' hair do. "It would be an absolute pleasure, what's your poison love?" Stephen replied with an amphetamine-induced confidence.

"I'll have a gin and tonic please, large one." She turned to her friends and shouted, "I've got a Cockney here girls, that'll do me!"

The normal boy meets girl chit-chat lasted about five minutes, then Stephen mentioned almost casually, "I like your outfit, doesn't leave much to the imagination."

Jan (he'd remembered to ask her name) knocked the remains of her drink back and startled Stephen. "What you see is all I'm wearing," she winked, "listen lovely cockney boy, you seem very nice, I'm not going to waste any time, God knows we've wasted the last two years living in fear. I'm not normally like this, you're clean, you're young and from out of town, so no complications. Most importantly you're not the 'Ripper'. I'm going to powder my nose and if I haven't frightened you off, when I return we are getting a cab back to my place where I'm going to prove that there's nothing underneath."

Jonny Rotten gave him a complimentary dig in his side. "Top man, proud of yer, your pal was right, this city's gone nuts now that fucker's been locked up, now don't let London down boy."

"Where the hell are we?" Stephen asked as the cab stopped in what seemed to be a huge council estate.

"Dewsbury, come with me lover boy."

Stephen was none the wiser as she led him along a maze of dimly lit passages. As they approached her maisonette a window opened next door and a women started shouting, "You got yourself a toy boy then Jan? Send him into me when you're done!"

Jan laughed, "Piss off Suzy, go catch your own. Besides he will be totally spent by the time I've finished with him."

Stephen had learnt that Jan's husband was two weeks away from being released from prison, after serving three years for armed robbery. Hardly an aphrodisiac but the booze and pills had evaporated all inhibitions.

The 'Ripper' had given the women of Leeds a different kind of sentence for the last three years and in the next couple of hours Stephen discovered how powerful freedom can be.

He dozed off totally exhausted but was awakened by a pounding on the back door. Jan had explained that her nine-year-old son was staying with a neighbour and had a habit of coming home if he had nightmares, which he did often. He assumed the boy had ventured home.

Jan was looking out the window. "Shit," she said and wrapped a towel around her as she made her way to the kitchen door. Stephen peered out the same window and saw a mop of Jimi Hendrix-like hair, he glanced at a wedding photo on the bedside locker. "What the fuck?" He said aloud, confused. He heard raised voices downstairs and frantically got dressed, forsaking socks and pants in his panic.

Jan suddenly screamed, "Stephen help me, it's my brother-in-law, he's hurt!"

He made his way to the tiny kitchen and whispered to Jan, "Brother-in-law, I thought it was your other half."

Jan saw the panic in his eyes. "It's my husband's brother, he's a wrongen."

Blimey, Stephen thought, what a family. The brother was lying on the floor moaning, there was a trail of his blood leading to the door. They crouched down and turned him onto his front. "Jesus he's been stabbed." Stephen pointed to a bloody slit in his side just above the waist. He grabbed a tea towel and placed it over the wound and sent Jan to look for some bandages.

The Hendrix lookalike suddenly looked at Stephen and growled, "Who the fuck are you? What the fuck you doing in my brother's house?"

Stephen told him to press on the tea towel, got up and ran out the house without looking back. Stephen ran around what seemed an endless maze of alleys and cul-de-sacs, it was sleeting the whole time. With absolutely no idea where he was, he eventually came across a dual carriageway. He looked at his watch and shuddered as he realised he'd left it on the bedside locker. It wasn't expensive but he hoped Jan's fella wouldn't find it when he returned home. He guessed it was four-ish.

He walked aimlessly along the deserted road until he spotted a taxi parked in a lay-by. Stephen jogged excitedly towards the car and peered through the driver's window. He was taken aback when he saw the Asian driver sitting there, eyes closed. He tapped on the window and spotted, to his surprise, the driver was getting a blowjob from a passenger. The driver turned in shock, as did the girl, who looked no more than seventeen. "Sorry mate I didn't realise you had company," Stephen apologised quickly.

The driver wound the window down. "It's okay my friend, where do you want to go?" He asked almost casually.

"The Windmill hotel, Leeds mate."

"Get in the back then. It will be a fiver, twenty and Julie will get in the back with you."

Even after the booze and speed Stephen was repulsed by the idea, even more so as the girl smiled, showing off a rotten front tooth. "No thanks mate I'll pass, just the Windmill please."

Stephen was flooded with relief as the taxi cruised into the hotel car park and parked outside the main entrance. It had been one hell of a night and now as the first light of the new day beckoned he just wanted to have a couple of hours in his hotel bed. Calm thoughts didn't last long though. He searched his jacket and trouser pockets for his wallet and felt sick as he realised it must have fallen out in his mad rush to get dressed. He pulled his hanky out of his pocket in desperation and emptied the contents onto the seat beside him. A room key, forty-three pence, a mint, a blue tablet…and a screwed up fiver. At that moment he thanked his God.

Stephen finally got to his (and Eric's) room. He felt like his head would explode, the booze, pills, sex and mayhem of his night in post 'Ripper' Leeds had hit him all at once. Oh for a bed, oh for a couple of hours of sleep before a day doing what he was paid to do.

The first thing he saw as he entered the room was Eric snoring, wedged between the two women he'd last seen him chatting up at the bar. To his disbelief there was a man, fully clothed, and a woman, naked, asleep on his bed. He had no idea who they were but guessed the locksmith did. It was now six o'clock and Stephen slouched down against the wall opposite the strangers and closed his eyes, hoping they would be gone when he woke.

7

RETURN OF THE KING

"Jesus H Christ, man what a night, I'm guessing this has something to do with Luke?" Alberto enquired.

"I'm getting there Al, but the fun and games weren't over."

"The orgy continued?" The big man asked hopefully.

"Not quite, I'd missed all the action in the hotel room and Eric was very hazy on the details. No, things got serious."

****

Stephen had dozed off despite his uncomfortable position on the floor. He woke with a start, his eyes struggled to focus and his head throbbed like hell, he could just make out the radio clock on the bedside chest between the two beds. He was pretty sure it said eleven-thirty. *Shit*, he thought. They were supposed to be at the first address to change the locks at eight-thirty. It was then he saw what had woken him.

At the foot of Eric's bed the unknown guy who'd commandeered his bed was kneeling down looking through Eric's tool bag, which he'd told Stephen he never left in the van for security reasons. He wanted to shout but his mouth wouldn't function, nothing seemed to want respond, he wasn't even sure he wasn't dreaming.

He watched as the stranger pulled out Eric's wallet from a side pocket. They can't both lose their wallets, he pondered. The guy looked through the contents carefully and strangely ignored the cash and credit cards, placing the wallet back in the side pocket. Stephen was confused, what was he looking for, clearly not money. The guy then started looking amongst the tools and pulled out an A4 envelope, he opened it and immediately looked triumphant. Stephen realised it was the list of addresses they were supposed to visit in and around Leeds. The guy placed the document in his jacket inside pocket and then pulled out a hammer from the locksmith's bag. Stephen watched him make for the door, pausing for a brief look at the night's conquest who was spread eagled, still naked, on the bed. As he carefully opened the door Stephen's brain and vocal chords suddenly sparked into life, "Oi, what you doing! Eric wake up, the cu..."

The thief legged it down the corridor as Eric staggered to his feet. He slapped Eric's face shouting, "Eric, he's got the list, he's got your fucking list!"

Eric groaned and looked around the room trying to make sense of what Stephen was screaming, "What?" He managed, as his 'baby sitter' ran out the room bawling, "He's got the list, he's got a hammer!"

All Stephen could think of as he ran out of the hotel and passed bemused guests and staff was it was a good job he fell asleep with his clothes on, especially his shoes. It felt strange running without socks and pants, which he'd left behind in darkest Dewsbury.

As he exited the hotel he heard the sound of broken glass from across the car park. All his senses were now in full focus, which probably had something to do with the amphetamines still igniting his brain. He guessed correctly the source of the commotion and sprinted towards the company van. The stranger had smashed a window in the back right door and then forced the back door open. He was frantically searching the van for keys and locks.

Stephen stopped short and shouted, "Give me the fucking list, I just want the list!" The thief ignored him so he launched himself onto the man's back, forcing them both to lurch fully into the van, fortunately the thief had dropped the hammer when breaking the window. Stephen grabbed the list out of his hand ripping it in two, the stranger wriggled free, smashing his head on the roof as he exited the vehicle and ran off empty handed. He left a trail of blood in the fresh snow that was now falling heavily.

Stephen, in his panic, slipped as he jumped out, falling onto a metal box full of keys and locks that the thief had discarded. As he smashed into the corner of the box he felt his mouth fill with blood and teeth. He lay dazed and confused on the freezing ground, seeing stars. Suddenly, he saw Eric and a couple of green shirted hotel staff above him. "You alright Steve son?" It was the first time the locksmith had uttered his name. "Steve mate, you okay?" He repeated.

Stephen spat out a mouthful of blood and bits of tooth as his partner picked him up. He handed him the ripped schedule and smiled, "What a fucking night, what a fucking day, I need a cold shower."

They carried out their mission without fuss or enthusiasm. It was absolutely freezing without the back window, twice they made a temporary repair taping cardboard over the hole, but the biting wind kept blowing it off. It was past eight when they hit the long road home.

They were just a few miles down the M1 when Stephen saw a sign to Dewsbury, "My fucking wallet's over there somewhere!" He exclaimed, and then went on to describe the sordid story of his long night.

"Fuck me mate, I thought I was stuck with a complete knob when I first saw you, you're a fucking legend pal. Believe me, I'm going to make sure the Saltzmans hear about you son." Eric patted Stephen on the back.

"Don't tell them everything Eric," he laughed.

"Don't worry mate, what happens in Leeds stays in Leeds! Shame about your wallet getting nicked though."

"Not sure it was Eric, think it dropped out my pocket when Jimi Hendrix turned up."

Eric laughed, "Think you're a bit naive mate, I hope it didn't have your address in it."

Stephen paused to think about Eric's words, "Why's that Eric?"

"Well, I hope one of you took precautions because if the fucking husband comes home from clink, well just saying."

Stephen now felt less of a hero as he thought about the consequences of his mad night. The effects of the 'whizz' had long worn off and he felt tired and gloomy. Eric did most of the talking for the remainder of the journey, firstly he described, as best he could remember, being joined by the 'stranger' and his bird at the bar and then vaguely recalled a mass orgy back at the hotel. He reckoned his drink had been spiked. He then went on to describe how the thief was almost certainly from a local property 'firm', or possibly he was a pro burglar. Either way Stephen had saved the day and Eric was very grateful.

They got back to Eric's lock up gone midnight, after dropping the tools off, the locksmith shook his hand firmly. "Steve, it's been an absolute pleasure mate, you're a fucking legend, I'll make sure Harvey sorts out a top dentist for you. Manchester next week!"

Stephen got back in the van and looked at his broken front tooth in the mirror. Jonny Rotten sat beside him, "Nice one son, nice one."

Word spread quickly around the company, Stephen was treated like a returning warrior. Harvey sent him to a top dentist off Harley Street and explained that Mr. S was fully aware of his and Eric's bravery in foiling the gang's attack on the van. Eric had certainly embellished the story. Harvey explained his brother-in-law was preoccupied with a family matter. Rumours circulated around the company that his daughter was causing problems again, she was something of a wild child. Stephen was told he'd be going up to Manchester with Eric (the locksmith) the following weekend and would be taking a more varied role in future.

He decided to take advantage whilst his star was rising and plucked up the courage to ask Cassandra out. He'd sat in the loo for ages, having taken the surviving little blue tablet, and then just as she was leaving the office, "Fancy going for a drink Cass?" It had taken him months to utter those seven words.

"Sorry Steve, I'm very honoured to be asked out by a hero, but I've currently got a boyfriend and I don't two time."

Stephen was a veteran of humiliation but in that moment he felt this rejection would crush him, but then Cass continued, "The thing is I'm dumping him this weekend, so you might want to try again next week."

"Why you dumping him?" Stephen asked, his spirits rising.

"Bad teeth," she replied.

"Good job I got my nashers sorted out," Stephen flashed a Harley Street smile.

"Make sure you come back from Manchester with a full set then," the receptionist laughed.

He survived his trip up north and, not to appear too keen, waited until Wednesday before inviting Cassandra to a party on the Friday night, an invitation she accepted.

Life seemed perfect for him until the phone rang the following evening. He heard the beeps and click so realised it was a call box, probably The Crow asking if he was coming to the pub. A vaguely familiar accent came on the line, "Hiya is that Stevie? It's Jan, Jan from Leeds."

"Jan, hi, how are you? How's your brother-in-law?"

"He's alive, unfortunately," she laughed, "listen I've got a present for you, your wallet, it had your address and phone number in it and a shit load of cash. I thought you'd like it back."

Stephen was cautious but would in truth be delighted to reacquaint with the large bonus Mr. S had given him. "Yes, thanks but where-"

Jan cut him short, "I'm at Kings Cross Station, I don't think you live far away, I decided to have a couple of days in London."

A shell shocked Stephen arrived at the station bar and saw Jan sitting at a table wearing a short trendy red mac, an overnight bag by her feet. They were both far more sober than their previous meeting. Jan handed the wallet over, he didn't embarrass her by checking inside, just put it straight in his back pocket. She told him that her son was staying with her mum and then explained her husband's release from prison had been delayed because of an altercation between him and a warden. Stephen found this news reassuring.

She went to powder her nose, Jonny took her seat and they checked the wallet together. "Well that's a turn up, I thought you'd been shafted in more ways than one." Rotten, leaned forward and eyeballed Stephen, "Now listen up, when she comes back, you thank her for her kindness, tell her you live with your mum or something, kiss on the cheek and wish her all the very best for the rest of her natural life. Under no circumstances invite her back. That, my friend, would be the road to ruin."

When she returned he noticed she'd applied fresh lipstick, she did look good. "Guess what I'm not wearing under this coat?" She confessed.

Twenty minutes later they were in his bed.

Stephen felt awful lying to Cassandra the next morning, claiming he had to visit an uncle in hospital and could they remake the date for next week. He deservedly got a curt, "Maybe."

Stephen couldn't complain about the sex but Jan frightened the life out of him when she confessed she was looking to apply for a council flat exchange to London, anything to get away from her husband and his mad family. He should have listened to Jonny.

Things got worse over the next couple of weeks, first there were the phone calls, explaining how she'd been put on the short list for either Luton or Wimbledon. In addition to that, Cassandra had a new boyfriend. Then came the letter.

Dear Stevie,

I have to see you, I have news you need to hear, will be down two weeks on Friday to see you. Will arrive 6.30 at Kings X. Be there no fail.
All my love
Jan xxx

8

LUKE, CHAPTER AND VERSE
(2010)

Stephen waited a couple of days, he'd looked at the scrap of paper Cassandra had given him hundreds of times, reflecting on what she'd said, delving into the past and looking to the future implications but he knew he had no choice. He sat in his car and punched the number into his phone, then left a simple text. *'Hi Luke you wanted to meet me, Stephen Ross'.*

The atmosphere between them remained tense. He had shown Cassandra the message but as days passed they carried on with their 'triple dip recession' lives.

"Any news from you know who?" Cassandra asked as they headed to do the weekly shop. Stephen replied in the negative as a check out girl complimented him on his TV appearance.

Two weeks passed before Stephen woke with a start as his phone vibrated on the windowsill. He wiped the sleep from his eyes and noted it was three in the morning. There was a message on his phone. *'Luke, Chapter 15, Verse 11.'*

Stephen tried to go back to sleep but within half an hour he'd plotted up in the study and Googled the contents of the text, feeling bad that he didn't posses a Bible. It didn't take long to see the verse on the screen, *'And he said, a certain man had two sons'.*

He stared at the words for almost half hour, and then wrote the words down on the back of the notepaper with 'Luke' and the number on it. He'd given up on getting any sleep, instead he wrote and deleted at least twenty messages before daybreak. Finally, he typed out, *'We need to meet.'* and sent it.

He didn't speak of the night's shenanigans to Cassandra. He went to his office and tried to sleep, but instead stared at his phone most of the morning, interrupted occasionally by sales calls and inane texts from mates. Just after lunchtime Stephen's eyes were almost shut as he slouched back in his uncomfortable office chair, his phone buzzed, he stirred and saw the number that he'd learnt by heart in the past few days. The information was to the point. *'Tomorrow Leicester services (southbound) 11.00 am'.*

Stephen showed Cassandra the texts and asked her if she'd like to come with him. They'd not had a proper conversation since the mystery caller. She dismissed the idea without explanation and busied herself with domestic chores, Stephen was uncomfortable with the whole situation. Neither had mentioned the situation to the girls, not wanting to interrupt Uni and exams.

Stephen hardly slept that night, instead he reflected on the madness that had disrupted his ordinary life since the Buble fiasco. He wanted to discuss the situation with Jonny Rotten but even Jonny didn't want to know.

The motorway traffic was so-so, Stephen was glad he'd left plenty of time. Inevitably his mind wandered back to his pre-Cassandra days, the trips to Manchester, Birmingham and Leeds he'd enjoyed with Eric (the locksmith). Shenanigans involved wherever they went. *Whatever happened to the mad locksmith? Where was he now? Dead, probably.*

All thoughts returned back to the letter, Jan's letter, and the important news she had for him. He winced as he recalled his fear and the dreadful plan he concocted with his friend Dave, aka The Crow, to move into his bedsit for a couple of days. Dave would then explain to Jan that Stephen had joined the foreign legion and had gone to Corsica for basic training. What a dreadful lie. He winced again at the thought of the distraught northern girl realising her dreams had been shattered. Circumstances all those years ago rendered his dastardly plan redundant, but the guilt of what might have transpired at their meeting never truly left him.

Stephen pulled into the car park half an hour early, he phoned Cass to tell her he'd arrived and would keep in touch. She seemed distant and disinterested, he told her he hoped he'd recognise Luke, she replied, "Look in the mirror."

He wasted another twenty minutes looking at the texts between him and Luke, before heading to the services entrance and the conveniences beyond. Washing his face with cold water, he stared into the mirror as if to remind himself what he looked like.

He found a table in the most deserted section of the food court and tried to remain calm. Time stood still as eleven slowly became quarter past, he decided to wait five minutes more before texting the mystery man.

Six minutes passed, he tapped out a message *'I'm in the-'*

"Stephen Ross." A young man in a beanie hat sat down calmly opposite him, he took the hat off to reveal a shock of mousy hair, which he tried to fashion back into its hatless style. "I've got a letter for you, I hope it makes some sense." The lad spoke with a soft Yorkshire accent. Stephen immediately thought two things, first, how confident the lad was both in manner and speech. Second, there was not a trace of the stutter Cassandra described, just a slight camp-ness in his tone.

He took and carefully opened the envelope on which was written *'For the personal attention of Steve Ross. Strictly private and confidential'*. He concentrated on the word 'Steve' which seemed strangely informal in the context of the other words. Suddenly the young man broke Stephen's concentration, "Sorry can you show me some ID?"

They stared at each other both knowing this was an unnecessary procedure. Without averting his stare, Stephen handed him his driving license and a debit card. "Can I ask you a question Luke?" He emphasised the 'Luke'.

"Sure," Luke responded handing back the ID cards without even looking at them.

"Cass, my wife, told me you had a terrible…a bad stutter?" Stephen asked, confused.

"That wasn't me, that was Craig that called on you."

Stephen was now even more confused, he continued opening the envelope and pulled out a handwritten letter. The writing was spidery and it took some time to read it, which he did several times, his heart beating out of his chest.

Dear Steve,

> *Firstly I have two apologies to make. I lied about my age (I knew how to look ten years younger long before the tv programme), secondly I'm so so sorry I never turned up for our meeting with my news! I was about to come down, as arranged, but my mad husband turned up from prison a week early and well that was it.*

Stephen thought his head would split in two, he reflected on how many pangs of guilt he had suffered over the years due to his disappearing act and the cow never even showed up! Stephen continued reading.

> *I was coming down to tell you I was pregnant, but I had no choice but to stay in my shit world. Sadly it just got shittier and I'm writing this letter from my hospice bed.*
>
> *You will recall I was an awful chain smoker! Seems you went down hill what with being beaten senseless by a group of hens! I knew it was you the moment I saw you on YouTube.*
>
> *I recall that brief time together after they locked up that lunatic Sutcliffe as the best, freest time of my life. I thank you for that Steve.*

> *If you are reading this letter then Luke has found you, I hope you get on. I have a favour to ask you which I have no right to ask. Luke will explain. I'm tired so I will say tarrar.*
>
> *Thanks for the memories.*
> *Love Jan xx*

Stephen's head was now on the verge of exploding. He had a million questions. "Who's Craig?" He asked, relieved that he only had another nine hundred and ninety nine thousand questions to go.

"My brother, my twin brother, have you got any twins in your family?" Luke said, answering the question with a question.

"Yes, my father had a twin brother, he was killed during the D-Day landings in the war."

"Skips a generation," Luke confirmed.

"So where's Craig now?" Stephen was just too shocked to prioritise his questions, "and Jan, how's your mum?"

"She died two days after writing that letter." Luke imparted the information without emotion, then added, "I'm going to the loo, shall I get us some coffee? Then I'll explain everything."

"Sounds good Luke, maybe we should go somewhere more appropriate."

"I'm fine right here, I spend a lot of my life in these places." With that Luke disappeared.

Stephen text Cassandra to tell her he'd found Luke and would let her know when he was on his way back. He read the letter again and tried to formulate a list of pertinent questions: Craig, the favour, his job, where he lived. His mind went back to that cold snowy night in Ripper-free Leeds.

He thought she told him she was thirty, he was slightly relieved when he did the math. Seventy was still too young to die, but better than sixty. A good lie he thought.

Luke had been gone half an hour, he could see the coffee kiosk but no sign of him. Stephen was concerned. Maybe Luke had second thoughts, which might be a good thing. He thought of the impact of this meeting on Cassandra, the girls, his father, his brother, his nephews. Maybe it would be best if Luke disappeared forever, but he looked back at the letter and then stood up frantically searching for any sight of the lad.

He saw Luke emerge from the opposite direction holding two cups of 'Burger King' coffees. He felt such a flash of relief he thought he might cry.

"I met your uncle briefly, but not your father," Stephen stated ignoring the list of questions he'd organised in his splintered mind.

"Lucky you," the young man shouted almost defensively, "My sso called f f f father was an evil ca ca cunt, you met uncle Roul, he was a ca ca cunt as well."

Stephen was taken aback, the boy was stuttering. "Craig?" Stephen asked. He could see no physical difference but this lad's speech was harsher and didn't have the same confident posture as before. Stephen noticed the young man was looking round the building nervously. "You're Craig, where's Luke?"

"He, he he will be in ta ta touch ssssoon, ca ca can you, ca ca can your wife keep a sssssecret?"

Stephen put his hand the lad's shoulder to calm him, "I thinks so," he replied. "Yes, yes we can keep a secret," he confirmed.

"Ga ga good," Craig struggled, "My life depends on it."

9

RETURN OF THE PRINCE

"Wow man, heavy shit," Alberto said, "and what a coincidence."

"Twins?" Stephen asked.

"Cancer, what with Jan dying and Susan terminal, man that's heavy shit. Shame you didn't have time to say goodbye, maybe arrange a string quartet!"

"I never thought of that coincidence," Stephen said, slightly shocked by the big man's response, "and I think Jan would have preferred Rod Stewart to be honest."

"Now that's an idea," Alberto interrupted. "So, what's this big secret with the twins, the stutterer? Weird man."

"If I told you, I'd have to kill you Al," Stephen laughed, then realised he'd drunkenly given to much information. "Strictly between you and me, Craig had some problems with the police (true), doesn't want to involve Luke (true)."

Stephen concentrated on describing his further meetings with Luke, how he'd explained the situation to the girls. He described to Al how he discovered what a terrible childhood Luke endured and how his 'father' threw him out of that dismal home in Dewsbury when Luke 'came out'.

"Jesus H Christ, you should have gone on the Jerry Springer show, not that sports programme!" Alberto shouted.

Stephen had often thought that himself since that strange day at the service station. He realised that he'd told the big man enough. He reflected on what he didn't tell him, or anybody else.

****

The reality he'd learnt, mainly from Luke, was that Craig had been involved with local gang activity, which at first involved petty crimes, muggings, shop lifting, burglaries. But everything changed when the gang gravitated to drug dealing. A late payment to a supplier from Liverpool resulted in one of Craig's friends receiving a terrible beating as a warning. Revenge was soon actioned and a spiral of violence reached a terrible conclusion when both gangs obtained guns, resulting in the death of two teenagers, one a policeman's nephew.

The wrath of the law fell on the 'Dewsbury 88' and there were mass arrests. Craig hadn't directly been involved in any violence but it was a connection he made in Manchester that supplied one of the guns. He was in serious shit. Craig was offered an amnesty in return for the name of the weapon supplier, the shooter (of the policeman's nephew) and assorted historic information appertaining to various heists around the Leeds area.

Luke imparted this, and two lifetimes of information, at several meetings usually hastily arranged at service stations up and down the M1 or M6. Luke threw the fact he was gay at Stephen during their second meeting, testing him out, expecting him to immediately reject him, but Stephen surprised him with his indifference. Having passed that test, Luke furnished him with the Craig story in full, emphasising the importance of secrecy at all times.

The police had handed Craig to MI5, who got involved because the gun in question had possibly been used abroad before. They gave him a new identity and relocated him.

At the same time their 'father' was still alive and had a fearsome reputation on the estate. He had long separated from Jan and disowned Luke but he let it be known that whilst Craig knew the consequences of his betrayal, the rest of his family were off limits.

Luke explained how his older brother (the boy who'd Jan left at her mother's on that fateful night back in '81) had committed suicide on his twenty-first birthday. Jan and the lad's father never got over the shock and split soon after.

The twins made a final plan to keep in touch with pay as you go phones and when their mother became ill and they finally discovered their past, they hatched a plan to take advantage of their incredible likeness.

"As long as we are never seen together we should be okay, the meeting at Leicester was as close as we will hopefully get," Luke confirmed.

Luke explained how Jan revealed the revelation on her deathbed. "It was very emotional, Craig had come up north for the first time in four years and spent a night with mum, we swapped the next morning. Mum knew these were her last hours, she could hardly speak, I ranted on about my older brother, half brother, how it was my so called father that drove him to take his own wretched life. The bastard then disowned me, not before kicking the shit out of my partner.

"I shouted at my poor dying mother 'How could you live with such an evil bastard, I'm ashamed to be his son!' Mum croaked 'He's not…he's not your father,' she told me. She gripped my hand and said, 'How can anyone as beautiful as you be fathered by a twisted fuck like him, he's not your father.' I was shocked, she showed me the clip and the TV programme on my laptop and told me about your brief liaison, my so-called father coming out of prison the day before she was planning to take her chance of a new life in London. She gave me the letter and I conspired with Craig to find you."

Luke then described how Jan's mum had hitched up with a proper gangster in Huddersfield. When he passed away she was left his property, which was then handed over to Jan when Luke's gran passed away last year. Jan, in turn, left it to the boys but was concerned about the money trail given Craig's circumstances. Hence the 'favour' she described to Stephen in the letter.

Their third meeting was at a solicitor's office in Halifax, where a Mr. Reece explained that Jan had requested Stephen arrange the sale of the property and, together with Mr. Reece, distribute the funds by way of a monthly retainer. Luke guessed his mother, apart from taking into account Craig's situation, was also concerned about his own out of control gambling habit.

Mr. Reece read further communications from Jan including the heartfelt words, "Stephen Ross is the only decent person I have ever met, I'm willing to trust him with this transaction." It was one hell of a responsibility but Stephen, with the guidance of the solicitor, decided to be as helpful as possible.

Mr. Reese, Luke, and Stephen also discussed what to tell the girls or more precisely what not to tell the girls. In the end they decided to tell them Luke's twin brother had not accepted Luke's sexuality, had moved to Australia years ago, came back for the funeral, learnt the truth about his parentage and made one last effort to catch up with Stephen. But, had now gone back for good, leaving Luke to pick up the pieces.

Strangely, after the initial shock, Cassandra and the girls grew more accepting of the situation when they learnt that Luke was gay. Cassandra had found the Craig experience unnerving so was secretly relieved to hear the news that he'd gone to Australia.

After a couple more meetings in service stations, which Luke favoured as he worked for a courier company, Stephen invited him to meet the family. All the participants were quietly nervous in the days leading up to the meeting. Luke arrived in his van mid-afternoon, having taken advantage of his trip to London to do a couple of extra parcel drops. Stephen's family home, a modest three-bedroom semi, looked like a palace to Luke. He text Stephen *'Here'* and Stephen went straight out to meet him. Cassandra watched from the front window as the two men gave each other a manly embrace, not knowing it was their first physical contact.

It was a strange but successful get together, Stephen was proud of Jess and Flo as they warmly encouraged conversation with Luke. Film turned out to be a common denominator and music too, Luke was impressed with the girls' history of festivals and surprised to learn about Stephen's musical past.

"Dad's stuck in 1977, he's an old punk, tries to pogo now but he can't beat gravity anymore," Jess laughed.

"Yeah, he was bassist in a group called The Filth!" Flo added. "Only played one gig didn't you dad?"

"He got hit by so many missiles he gave up," Jess confirmed.

"I don't mind a bit of The Jam but I'm more of an Oasis man, my older brother got me into The Smiths, he worshiped them," Luke confessed.

"Good call," Cassandra said. She paused for a moment remembering Stephen mentioning the brother's suicide.

Luke quickly filled the silence, "But of course my all time musical God is Michael Buble!" He said, which had them all in stitches.

Stephen felt a glow as the conversation flowed naturally and warmly, the successful get together continued through dinner and Cassandra insisted Luke stay the night and enjoy some wine.

At the end of the evening she made up the sofa bed in the living room for him. She and the girls each warmly wished him goodnight with a hug and kiss. The two men were left alone, standing awkwardly in the centre of the room. Stephen put his hand on Luke's shoulder. "Well that went well," he said, with both sincerity and relief.

Luke placed his free hand on Stephen's shoulder, "Better than well, this has been the best day of my life."

They embraced without inhibition and both involuntary sobbed like babies.

10

THE LAST FULL ENGLISH

The meetings with Luke though sporadic, due to work and geography, were warm and illuminating for both of them. Stephen, with help from Mr. Reece, sold the property and came to an arrangement with the boys so their inheritance wasn't squandered. A large percentage would be put in a long-term account, hopefully a useful pension that could only be activated by Stephen (or his named dependents on his death). There would be a small monthly payment direct into their bank accounts, hopefully to help with rent and bills, not enough to gamble. Mr. Reece explained that he'd press the button as soon as probate was complete in three months or so.

Luke had communicated all this to Craig, who had disappeared back to his secret life since their brief meeting at Leicester services. Whilst Stephen enjoyed his voyage of discovery with Luke, he felt pangs of absolute guilt that he had no relationship with Craig what so ever, save for the financial arrangement.

A few months after the family get together Stephen received an email from Mr. Reece explaining that that probate had been granted and the agreed arrangements were now in place. He knew Luke had just moved to a bedsit in Sheffield having sadly split from his partner, who couldn't come to terms with Luke's new circumstances.

The madness that had followed his 'Buble' incident had subsided and life was back to some sort of normality. The girls were doing fine at uni, Cassandra was doing well at work, though she had mentioned the 'dickhead' was unusually miserable despite the company making a healthy profit. The Luke situation had turned into a real blessing and he was enjoying some cross Atlantic communication with his old friend the 'Big A', all thanks to the dickheads and the worlds most famous karaoke star!

He sat in his office, even his business had picked up, as his old hero interrupted his thoughts. "Happy as a pig in shit ain't you?" Jonny Rotten sat across from him smirking, "Got to hand it to you mate, you've surprised me, you've done well mate!" There was a knock on the door, Rotten disappeared.

"Luke," Stephen was surprised but delighted to see him standing there. He went to hug him but the visitor recoiled.

"It's na na not the fa fa fucking ga ga golden boy."

"Craig," Stephen corrected himself, "come in."

Craig sat in the chair just vacated by the punk legend. Stephen confirmed the financial arrangements were working okay for Craig and tried to make small talk, but realised that due to his struggle for words he stuck to only what needed to be said. Craig explained that due to recent events he was relocating abroad. Without emotion he explained that it was the only way his and Luke's safety couldn't be compromised, that the temptation to enjoy the happiness Luke had described to him would be too much.

"Where are you going, when are you going?" Stephen asked, knowing Craig could only answer the second question.

"Ta ta today."

"Anything I can do for you Craig?"

Craig paused before answering, "Yes, ya ya yes, la la la la love la la Luke ta ta twice over."

Stephen tried to respond but was rendered tongue-tied by Craig, who then added, "I wa wa want a fa fa fry up, a last ever proper fa fa full English."

Stephen stood up and smiled at him. He shivered as he thought of the hellish past his son had endured. "Come on son, I know just the place. You want a full English, I will treat you to one fit for a Prince, a King even!"

Stanley's café, known to all as 'Stan's', was the last old school English café in Stephen's old manor. Photos of the East End of his youth adorned the walls, pride of place was a signed photo of Stephen's West Ham hero holding the Jules Rimet trophy aloft in his glorious red England shirt. As he led Craig into the café he stopped and saluted, as he'd done a thousand times before. "Sir Bobby Moore," he said with pride, "one of the three greatest Englishman of all time."

"Who are the other ta ta two?"

"Churchill and Jonny Rotten." Stephen confirmed.

"Ja Ja Jonny fucking Rotten, I don't fa fa think so, what about Shakespeare or Dickens?" Craig added.

They went through to a small raised back room separated from the main café by an open doorway with multi coloured streamers hanging from the lintel.

"Welcome to Stan's VIP suite!" Stephen declared.

Stan, a spritely seventy-three years old stood with his niece in the open kitchen. "Morning Stan."

"Morning Steve, ow you doing son?"

"This is…" Stephen hesitated. "This is my lad, Stan."

Stan looked confused, "Oh, oh right, nice to meet you mate, 'av a seat, Wendy will come and take your order in minute."

Stephen detected a slight smile on Craig's face as they sat down.

"Ma ma my lad," Craig repeated.

"That's what I said Craig, that's what you are and that's what you will always be." Stephen realised this would be his last opportunity to say what should be said. He waited for a response from Craig but Wendy interrupted them, "What you 'aving boys?"

Craig studied the blackboard, "Ta ta two fried eggs, ba ba bacon, sssausage, beans, ma ma mushrooms, tomatoes, black pa pa pudding, hash browns, fra fra fried bread, wa wa what's ba ba bubble? Never tried it."

Stephen and Wendy laughed together. She was confused by Stephen's lads northern accent and stammer. She'd known Stephen for over fifteen years since she started working in her uncle's café and had been bored senseless by his endless stories about his wonderful girls' achievements, but never heard about a 'lad', particularly a northerner. *Maybe he'd been married before?* She thought.

"Bubble and Squeak is the food of the Gods son, take my word for it," Stephen confirmed.

"Okay," Craig nodded to Wendy.

"I'm going need a new bleeding pencil." She laughed and looked at Stephen.

"I'm having what he's having."

There was a brief silence then Craig said seriously, "I used to hate fa fa fucking cockneys, especially West Ham supporters, na na not as much as cha cha Chelsea though, I'm la la Leeds."

He went on to describe his flirtation with football violence and his disappointment with his team's demise. Stephen was slightly shocked but relieved to be enjoying an almost normal conversation with Craig.

Their mega breakfasts arrived and they surveyed the fry up before them. "Now that is a feast, that is a full English and then some," Stephen exclaimed.

"Na na nice one." Craig was impressed and the two high-fived before tucking in.

They ate in silence, a couple of builders came into the 'VIP' room and nodded at Stephen, admiring their breakfasts.

Craig finished every scrap and put his knife and fork together. "Na na nice one, if that's the la la last fa fa fucking fa fa full English I ever have, well it was a fa fa fucking ba ba brilliant one, cheers pal."

Stephen gave up on his, put his knife and fork down and high-fived his newfound son for the second time. Craig briefly had a look of contentment but it soon disappeared. He explained to Stephen that he would have lay low for quite a while, how he'd have to be out of contact with his twin brother for a year at least, maybe more.

"Have you said your goodbyes to your brother?" Stephen asked concerned.

"Sa sa sorted."

"What about a job, friends, have you a girlfriend or…?" Stephen asked frantically, as Craig stood up to leave.

Craig took Stephen's hand, clasped it firmly. "I'm na na not ga ga going alone, Luke will tell you, I ha ha have a ga ga girlfriend, sha sha she's coming with me." He was shaking Stephen's hand firmly, he released it and gripped Stephen's shoulder. "In sa sa seven ma ma months ta ta time you will be a grandad, fa fa thanks fa fa for fa for everything." He squeezed Stephen's shoulder with a last desperate burst of affection and then was gone, possibly forever.

A few weeks passed without a word from Luke, the pay as you go phone Stephen had purchased for communication with him had been frustratingly inactive. One morning out of nowhere a message appeared, *'Just returned from a lovely holiday. Got a great tan. Oh yes, I was witness to a wedding. The happy couple plus bump! send their love. x Luke (chapter 15/11)'*.

Stephen celebrated on his own with a large glass of single malt the girls had bought him on Father's Day.

A couple of months passed before he met Luke again, this time at Wycombe services on the M40. He told him all the details he could about the wedding, nothing about the bride, except she looked stunning, and of course the groom was breathtakingly handsome.

He then confessed he'd sold some jewellery that his mum had left him and had bought the Ross family a present. He handed his father an envelope, in it were five tickets to New York, leaving in two weeks time!

PART TWO

11

WILD HORSES

Cassandra, Jessica, Florence, and Luke occupied the four centre seats, Stephen was in the isle seat nearest his wife. A steward brought five glasses of champagne and Stephen proposed a toast. "To the 'Buble'."

"The 'Buble'," they all echoed.

Stephen's neighbours looked confused. "You going to New York to see Michael Buble? We love him," The lady in the centre seat chipped in.

"No, no we are on a family trip which the 'Buble' paid for, sort of."

The couple thought he might be drunk and decided to ignore him for the next seven hours, which suited Stephen, who sat back, looking sideways at his family. He felt overwhelmed with excitement, tinged with a little sadness at the thought of Craig. Where in the world he and his pregnant wife? Somewhere hot, judging by the tan Luke came back with.

His mind turned to the 'Big A' who he'd messaged about their imminent trip, but his friend replied cursing their luck due to a conference he was attending in Atlanta. *Maybe the big man doesn't want to meet me*, he thought. But it was very short notice so it was quite possible his excuse was genuine. Another drink and he was totally relaxed. The family members were engrossed in various movies, Luke and Jessica were obviously watching the same comedy as they periodically laughed in unison.

He closed his eyes but his mind was too busy for sleep, his thoughts slipped back to Jan as they had many times since the letter. He recalled his panic when he received her previous letter back in '81. He felt ashamed that he'd hatched such a stupid, devious plan with The Crow, given what he knows now. What would his reaction have been if he'd stayed put and she just never showed. Of course The Crow never had to move in and lie on his friend's behalf, Stephen didn't have to lay low at his brother's, as planned. No, a second meeting with Maurice Saltzman, Mr. S, changed everything and rendered his dastardly plans redundant.

****

(1981)

Stephen was still the talk of the company, his confidence was sky high, although now and again thoughts of Friday week brought him crashing back to earth. He recalled the locksmith's words regarding precautions, maybe Jan was coming down to tell him her gangster husband knows where he lives, perhaps she will turn up with a suitcase and a nine-year-old son expecting to move into his bedsit. He was sitting in his recess that doubled as his office when Cassandra took him by surprise. "Harvey wants you waiting in the car park in ten minutes, you're going to a meeting with Mr. She probably wants to knight you," she said, with a hint of sarcasm.

"Blimey, good job I shaved, but that was only because I'm still hoping you will give me a second chance Cass, I've got two tickets for The Jam at Hammersmith Saturday night if you fancy it?" He surprised himself, *wow I've actually asked a girl out without being drunk or stoned*.

"Okay," Cassandra shocked him with her positive response, "but only because I fancy Paul Weller, good luck with Mr. S," she added.

Stephen waited in the small car park, Jonny Rotten sat on the bonnet of Havey's Jag, "The boy has become a man, bout time, mind you, shame your bird fancies that prick Weller." The punk slipped away as Harvey appeared looking more flustered than normal. Stephen tried to engage him in conversation during the half hour ride but Harvey kept his own council. *Perhaps I'm getting another bonus*, he wondered, *would be handy for Saturday night*. Harvey dropped him off outside the front door, "Good luck boy," he said with an ominous tone and sped off.

Mrs. S was not her normal jolly self as she ushered Stephen to her husband's office, who didn't look up as he gestured to an empty chair.

There was a man he had never met before sitting in the corner of the room, Stephen noticed he was wearing sunglasses despite being indoors and the sun not having shone for months. Maurice Saltzman looked at Stephen, he noticed the boss' eyes looked heavy with tiredness. Mr. S placed a framed photo of his five children in front of Stephen and paused. Stephen looked at the photo, then at Mr. S, then at the expressionless stranger in the corner.

His boss tapped the photo with his pen, "These four boys Steve, all good bright Jewish boys, all at or going to good universities. He tapped again. "These three here will be lawyers or accountants. That is a fact Steve, non negotiable. This boy here Steve," he tapped once more, "this is Samuel, my eldest, he will take over the family business. It's a fact, non negotiable. All four boys will marry nice Jewish girls from good Jewish families. It's a fact, non negotiable. Well, to be honest, they don't have to be nice, I can compromise there, but they have to be from good solid Jewish stock," He looked at Stephen, who nodded in an attempt to look like he understood. Mr. S then put the pen down and pointed with his index finger at his only daughter, "This is my only daughter, Rachel, a real beauty eh?"

Stephen nodded again, wondering where she got her good looks from.

"I put my hands up I would have liked her to go to uni, get a good degree, but she told me she wanted to peruse a career in show jumping. Not the usual profession for a Jewish princess from Hampstead Garden Suburb, but she negotiated with those big hazel eyes and I compromised. I bought her a tip top horse, horsebox and after speaking to my window supplier, the impossible Alan Ross, I even found a reliable driver."

Mr. S got up, moved around the desk and put his hand on Stephen's shoulder. It was the first time he'd seen Mr. S stand up, he couldn't understand how two such tiny rotund parents produced such a tall slender daughter.

"Yours truly," he continued, "but unfortunately both horse and transport are redundant, though at least the driver's been put to good use." He squeezed Stephen's shoulder affectionately. "Some might say, Steve, I'm a control freak, and yes I can be overbearing but I've created a bubble for my family, a nice safe bubble. Good home in leafy HGS, a wonderful home in Herzliya, the Hampstead Garden suburb of Israel. Good schools, good universities. For all this I only ask they obey a few non-negotiable rules. The boys get this, Princess Rachel, well…" He paused to blow his nose, Stephen detected a tear in his boss' eye as he returned to his throne.

"My daughter is the family rebel Steve, I suppose there has to be one, I've made compromise after compromise but on the day I took delivery of her eighteenth birthday present, the horse, I discovered she had broken the one rule that a Saltzman cannot break! She has broken her mother's heart, she has broken the unbreakable rule!" He was now shouting and thumping the green baize leather insert on his desk. "Can you guess what unbreakable rule she's broken Steve?"

Stephen swallowed not sure what to say, he glanced at the stranger in sunglasses, whose expression hadn't changed since Stephen first entered the room. "Drugs?" Stephen reluctantly offered, hoping the guess wouldn't get him fired.

Mr. S stood up again and walked to where the stranger sat, he pointed above him at one of many black and white photos. "This Stephen is my father Jacob, he was brought up in poverty in Whitechapel, an area I know you know well. His mother, my grandmother, died in childbirth during a four-month journey from the Ukraine, after local thugs in a pogrom massacred his grandparents. My grandfather carried my newborn father and his two older sisters," he paused to point at grainy photo of his two aunts, "from Tilbury docks to Whitechapel in a snow blizzard. He never remarried but he worked fourteen hours a day as a drayman at Truman's Brewery. He made sure they were fed, just and educated.

"He died when my father was sixteen, left a small amount of money which my father spent wisely on renting a workshop where he and my aunts started a bakery. They worked all the hours God gave them and when they found their spouses they increased their staff three fold and eventually bought the warehouse, made their way out of the East End to the suburbs, and here we are." He stopped for a moment and then spoke to the stranger, "Avi, do me a favour, you're taller than me, fetch me down that Bible from the top shelf please?"

The stranger stood, he was a six-footer and very lean, he reached the book without any problem and handed it to Mr. S, both men reclaimed their chairs.

"Drugs you say Steve, good answer and yes my sources have in the past whispered a few unpleasant warnings to me. The odd 'joint' here and there maybe, but as yet not my main source of concern, though God alone knows what they would think," he pointed at the photos of his ancestors, "and of course Mrs. S knows nothing about the odd joint, she wouldn't understand. No Steve, drugs and on the odd occasion over indulging in alcohol are a concern, but that's not why you're here and nothing to do with our heartbreak." He opened the Bible at a random page, "Do you know your Bible Steve, your old Testament?"

"I know the basics," Steve replied unconvincingly.

Mr. S pointed to the photos again, "Aunts, uncles, cousins, second cousins, some relatives up there on Hilary's side, to be honest I don't even know their names. That one on the extreme left is so distant I've told Hilary it's her favourite cousin sixteen times removed. But young Steve they all have one thing in common, other then being related."

Stephen felt awkward as his boss gestured to him to answer. "They're all Jewish, I guess."

"Correct, I told you this boy was smart Avi, yes all Jews," he pointed at the Bible, "Abraham, he was the first one, Joseph, Isaac, Moses, and so on. All massive Jews and for five thousand years they have been pushed from one place to another, slaughtered from York to Palestine, from Spain to Russia, and then the Nazis tried to get rid of us, now it's the Arabs!" Maurice Saltzman was now screaming. "But we are still here and I will tell you why. Because my bloodline goes back to Abraham, I should have his photo up there, my great great great-grandfather five thousand times removed. He was the first Saltzman Steve, Avi knows, Abraham was the first Saltzman, the bloodline goes on and with respect to you, as I know your father married out, I have only one unbreakable rule, my children must marry within the faith! No compromise, no negotiation!"

Stephen was concerned his boss would have a heart attack but he had a good idea where this was going. For a brief moment he reflected on his father's story, he suddenly blurted out, "Your daughter Rachel wants to marry a non-Jew?"

The sweating Mr. S closed the Bible, took a swig of water, and turned to the stranger, "See Avi, he's our boy, he's one smart cookie. I've told Avi about your commission cheques and the action you took in Leeds, didn't I Avi?"

The stranger simply nodded.

"No, Steve, she doesn't as far as we know want to marry a non-Jew, but she has put herself in a position where she could go down that path, the pathway to hell."

"She's going out with someone?" Stephen guessed.

"Let me explain Steve, having painted a picture of my daughter the spoilt rebel without a clue, let's explain why you're here. The day of the horse business, a family member enlightened Hilary that Rachel was secretly seeing an Italian show jumper, some playboy type, dark, handsome, and attractive to an impressionable eighteen-year-old. Mrs. S wasn't her normal happy self and I sensed something was up, she reluctantly told me the truth. We confronted Rachel, who of course was very defensive, and after discussion I decided on a course of action, a kibbutz for six months. A chance for her to get what was simply a teenage crush out of her system, a chance to live outside my restrictive bubble, but surrounded by a lot of healthy Israeli boys. Not that a kibbutznik would suit my princess but that's what we arranged. I, of course, wanted her to go on one close to our home in Herzliya, but she agreed to go as long as she could choose the Kibbutz, and yes you've guessed it she headed for one less than two miles from the fucking Lebanese border."

Stephen thought this might be the first time he'd heard his boss swear.

"Anyway, all seemed well, but two weeks ago Hilary was in our home in Herztalia, where Rachel was due to come and stay the weekend, but she didn't show. After some serious worry Avi here, who looks after our business interests in Israel, drove up to the Kibbutz and discovered she disappeared with an American hippy, a Jesus freak who is part of some fucking Evangelical cult called fucking Hebrew Jesuits!"

Stephen made that three swear words, *Why am I here?* He wondered.

"Avi here has done some digging and believe me I have some very useful friends out there, but the more we discover the more concerned we are. We have reason to believe that they've left the country, possibly over the Egyptian border, so they could be anywhere. But we feel the answer lies with the cult guys who have infested Kibbutzes in Northern Israel, trying to convert impressionable teenagers.

"Apart from being out of our minds with worry, you might not know Hillary is president of the family charity that has supported Zionist charities for many years and if any of this leaks out to the community, well, it will be disastrous. So let's cut to the chase young man. How would you like an all expenses holiday, say two to three weeks in the sun?"

Stephen hesitated, he was excited but cautious at the same time.

"Avi will confirm there's a volunteers block there jam packed with attractive Scandinavian volunteers, mostly female." Avi's lip made the tiniest of efforts to give a confirming smile.

"When would I leave? I've heard there are a lot of bombs coming across the border," Stephen mumbled.

"If my daughter can hack it boy, well I'm sure you can. To be frank, we'd like you there ASAP, like yesterday, but if not, tomorrow would be good."

"What about flights, money, what do I tell my family, friends?"

"Avi will take care of all the arrangements, you tell everyone that you're going to Israel for the company, which you are, our portfolio is growing there. Going to see your cousin, spend a couple of days in Tel Aviv, then as far as everyone is concerned you've been sent up north, where we're looking to expand, and the those mean Jews the Saltzmans have put you on a kibbutz cause it's cheap."

Stephen thought this was realistic, he remembered what Eric (the locksmith) had said about the Saltzmans checking all card transactions.

"Have you got a girlfriend Steve, any immanent pressing engagements?"

He suddenly remembered Jan's visit in eight days time, this could be a lifesaver, this could solve a lot of problems, "No Mr. S nothing comes to mind, what will I be doing exactly?"

"Steve, I'm very grateful for your help, please call me Maurice, you're one of us, well almost." Stephen wasn't sure if this was a massive compliment or an insult. "Avi here will give you the fine details, but basically you turn up at the kibbutz, you have fun, socialise, be yourself, a half Jewish lad from England exploring his roots. Believe me you are just the kind of recruit this crazy cult is looking for. Do some subtle digging re. Rachel and keep Avi in the loop."

There was a pause, Stephen could feel two sets of eyes burning into him, he looked at Avi, he seemed like the kind of guy you'd want on your side. He thought about the situation with Jan, he could stand The Crow down, who'd probably mess things up by trying to sleep with her or something, he could literally just disappear from all his problems.

"One more thing Steve, if you come up with any information that directly leads to us finding my daughter there will be a substantial bonus for you," he opened a drawer and produced a wad of notes, "five grand with your name on and, more importantly, the eternal gratitude of the Saltzman family. Just think, in a few hundred years time a future head of the Saltzman family will look at a photo of me and recall how I sent a young man named Stephen Benjamin Ross to save the family bloodline."

Stephen smiled, suddenly he remembered his date with the pretty receptionist, *Shit*, he thought, *I'll have to let her down again.*

"Mr. S, Maurice, I'd better go home and pack!"

12

SON OF ABRAHAM

It was a sultry thirty degrees when Stephen landed in Tel Aviv. Avi, who hadn't said a word on the five hour flight, had given Stephen a couple of days R and R so he was going to stay with his cousin Mark and wife Rita.

They were good hosts and too busy getting on with their own lives to be curious about Stephen's plans. They weren't however 'party animals' and he was on his own when it came to Tel Aviv's vibrant nightlife. He tried a couple of beachfront bars, before heading to an English pub his cousin had mentioned. He found a bar stool and was quickly engaged by some ex-pats.

He felt relaxed after a few drinks and his thoughts drifted to the note he'd left for Cassandra, letting her down for the second time, and to Jan, who was coming down a week today. He was on a genuine mission, *why feel guilty?*

A chap from the British consulate, just a couple of years older than himself, invited him to a club they were going on to. It turned into wild night, Stephen woke Mark and Rita up in the small hours with his drunken attempts at opening the door.

He got up the next morning somewhat embarrassed and decided he'd take it very easy over the next couple of days, this was after all his job, albeit one he could get used to.

Avi picked him up a couple of days later at 9am as arranged, he hardly acknowledged Stephen as he pointed to the back of the car to place his rucksack in the boot. On this occasion he could understand why Avi was wearing sunglasses, he had his own on, it was a scorching hot day.

"It will takes approximately three and a half hours to get there, please study these on the journey."

Wow, Stephen thought, *those are the first words he's said to me*. They were also the last spoken for the entire journey. Stephen studied the photos and relevant information, Rachel's was of course familiar, the other four males were certainly an interesting bunch.

He hadn't travelled north on his previous two visits, he was struck by how green and rich the land was as they drove past established forests. He would have liked to be with a tour guide, rather than his driver, who he'd mentally nicknamed 'The Silent Assassin'.

Eventually they pulled into a lay-by, seemingly in the middle of nowhere. "You get out here and head down that track. It's eight hundred meters to the kibbutz. Find the dining room and ask for the reception, someone will take you there. This is so you arrive like every other volunteer, two buses from Haifa if anyone asks. At reception you say that Avaram is expecting you. He will be waiting for you." With that the back door sprung open. As Stephen climbed out Avi added, "If you hear the siren before you reach the kibbutz find a big tree. Lebanon is that way, north, so you make sure you're facing south."

Stephen watched Avi drive up the path leaving him in a cloud of dust. With Avi's words of advice in his mind he walked as fast as his luggage would allow.

He found the dining room without too much trouble, having inhaled the smells of the industrial chicken sheds he strolled by. He was also impressed to see a swimming pool with a couple Swedish lovelies splashing about. A friendly Danish volunteer led him to the reception, which doubled as the kibbutz HQ. A sturdy woman called Miri took his details and insisted he hand over his passport, she explained it was a new security measure. He'd told her he was to meet Avaram. She said Avaram would explain everything else but she did point out the main bomb shelter just behind an adjacent building.

Miri led Stephen on a short walk, he was impressed with the identical two story houses the kibbutzniks lived in. She stopped at a doorway and politely left him to his own devices.

Avaram opened the door and welcomed him warmly, Stephen had never experienced such a strong handshake before. He led Stephen to an open-plan dining room and kitchen. "Please sit, Avi, my namesake, I believe you know," he nodded at his chauffeur who gave the slightest of acknowledgments. Stephen suddenly twigged that 'Avi' was short for 'Avaram', which was Hebrew for Abraham, the first Saltzman. His host introduced his wife Cheryl, who spoke with a thick South African accent and busied herself putting an endless assortment of dips on the table.

"Normally we eat in the communal dining hall but we thought it best to have some privacy. Firstly Steve, Cheryl and I welcome you to our community, it's our custom that all our volunteers have a kibbutz family they can come to on Shabbat. You Steve feel free to come anytime, any problems, please just come find me."

"Thank you," Stephen politely replied, guessing his kibbutz 'parents' were only in their mid-thirties.

"These are difficult times, a very delicate situation Steve, rockets are being fired from across the border almost daily and we now have some among us that wish our children harm, in a spiritual sense, but the disappearance of young Rachel Saltzman has…as you say in English, the cat is now with the pigeons."

"Your English is excellent," Stephen complimented his host.

"Thank you, I speak three languages fluently, Ivrit, Arabic and Persian, thanks to my parents coming from Morocco and Iran. I speak French, German and English badly."

Stephen felt very inferior in comparison. "Why can't you just throw those you suspect of causing problems off the kibbutz?" Stephen asked the question he'd been contemplating.

"Fair question Steve, firstly we are a liberal democracy with freedom of speech, secondly, Avi advised us it was best to try and keep those we suspect close at hand, so we can keep fishing for information about Rachel and also try and discover who is behind this infestation in our communities."

"How can I help?" Stephen asked.

"Do some fishing."

Avi placed the photographs Stephen had studied on the journey on the dining table between the assorted plates that they picked at. Avaram placed the picture of Rachel in front of Stephen. He was surprised when Cheryl, who was standing behind him, took over proceedings, her accent grated on him.

"This young lady you know is Rachel Saltzman, just turned nineteen, spoilt rich Jewish princess. She arrived as a volunteer almost three months ago apparently wanting to sample true communal lifestyle."

Stephen looked at Avi who like him knew the real reason she came here.

"By all accounts she settled in quickly working in the kitchen, then after a couple of weeks she hooked up with this man, whom she disappeared with over two weeks ago."

Avaram placed a photo on top of Rachel's. "This is Wayne Richardson," Cheryl continued, "Thirty-three years old from Oklahoma, a Vietnam veteran, charismatic, knows his Bible, both testaments inside out. 'To cool for school', according to volunteers we spoke to."

Another photo was placed next to his, "This is Hank Bartram, from Albuquerque, thirty years old, another biblical scholar, but seems to win the youngsters over with his basketball skills, it's our national sport here, and secondly his guitar playing, very Dylan-esque apparently. Seems to be sleeping with at least three different females and may have had a one night stand with our Princess."

Avaram placed another photo down, moving a plate of hummus. "Strange boy this." Cheryl paused to look at the young man sporting a classic 1950's crew cut. "Marvin Cutts, from Kansas, twenty-three, claims to be an ex-Marine, hangs around with Hank, it's like he's his bodyguard. Rarely speaks to anyone, social phobic, did however have a rant with a girl from Canada who questioned the virgin birth. By all accounts he exploded in rage and was only calmed by Hank."

A fourth photo of a man appeared. "Ah, a fellow Brit, this is Neville Nash from Liverpool, into radical left politics, humourless but a keen worker, tried and failed miserably to gain the attention of Rachel, his politics rather than his religious views concern us."

A last photo was placed down making a line of five, Cheryl slid Rachel's photo from under Wayne's and placed it above the five males, Stephen thought the guy in the last photo looked like Frank Zappa on steroids.

"Lastly we have here Alberto Canavaro from New York, self named the 'Big A', twenty-six, loud, extrovert. Seems to be everyone's friend, doesn't seem interested in the Bible but interestingly quite openly tells everyone he's engaged to a JAP, Jewish American Princess, and he plans to convert, much to his Italian Catholic family's disappointment and of course his future in-laws."

"Sounds a familiar story," Stephen said looking at Avi.

"No one has a bad word about this gentle giant but we are interested in him because he shared a room with our boy Wayne, until he disappeared. Secondly Avi has discovered that these four guys all arrived in Israel on the same day!" Cheryl took a gulp of water before adding, "you Steve are the 'Big A's' new roommate, time to go fishing."

13

CELL BLOCK H

Avaram gave Stephen a brief tour of the kibbutz, which concluded at the volunteers' block. "Not the best accommodation in the world, we've been meaning to knock the whole block down and build proper two story houses, but the budget is tight and insurance is tricky this close to the border. We will however have to replace the asbestos roof before someone gets sued."

Stephen looked at the roof that ran across the decrepit grey block of ten 'cells', there were five blocks, a lot of roof to replace.

"Your Maurice Saltzman has offered us a generous award to find his precious princess, would go a long way to fixing these roofs. Best work as a team Steve. Avi is off to the Egyptian border to do some digging, you just see what you can find out by socialising, blending in. If I don't see you before, you're invited Friday evening, Shabbat."

Stephen knocked on the door of his new home, A6, he recognised the music coming from inside. He knocked again with more gusto.

"Enter, it's open!"

Stephen pushed and entered his new, very humble, abode. He was immediately overwhelmed by the smell of socks, he noticed there was a pair soaking in a bucket of cold water by what was to be his bed.

As he threw his rucksack down he smelt a strong whiff of weed clashing with the socks. His new roommate was lying in his bed at the opposite end of the room, the room's only window was above him, firmly shut.

"Meddle," Stephen nodded towards the 'ghetto blaster' on a small chest of drawers next to the only wardrobe.

"Good man, you know your Floyd, a Brit, welcome to the pleasure palace, will be with you in a mo' man."

Stephen noticed his roommate had graduated from Zappa beard to 'Grateful Dead' beard, he'd also cut his hair, though it was still fairly long and unwashed.

Suddenly the covers concealing the American's mighty frame lifted and a young lady's head poked out. "Hi there, I'm Sonia," she said in a delicious French accent.

"I'm sorry, I didn't realise you had company," Stephen said, taken aback.

"Don't worry man, Sonia's work is done here."

She slipped out the bed, nonchalantly picked up a pile of cigarette packets from the bedside locker and skipped past Stephen. "See you around, Englishman."

The big man stood and pulled on some tracksuit bottoms, he was wearing a t-shirt with Santana on it. "Hi man I'm Alberto, friends call me the 'Big A'."

Stephen introduced himself still feeling awkward, "Sorry about the interruption."

"Not a problem man, that wasn't what it looked liked, I'm engaged to be married to a young lady back home in the Big Apple. I only smoke weed nowadays," he said as he offered the end of his joint to Stephen, who politely declined. "We get a weekly cigarette allowance so Sonia and I do a weekly trade. It's strictly business, nothing more. Do you smoke Stevie?"

Stephen shook his head.

"Well maybe you can enjoy a trade off with Sonia as well, a double whammy, man." Alberto laughed. "Anyhow welcome to 'cell block H'. Only one thing to remember, if the siren goes head for the shelter at the end of this block no matter where you are on the kibbutz. It doubles as a disco and I'm the DJ!"

"And do you have to DJ often?" Stephen asked.

"Once a week on average due to border activity but we have an unofficial club night every Friday, as soon as the Sabbath is in, it gets pretty wild down there."

That evening Alberto took Stephen up to the communal dining room, everyone, both volunteers and natives alike, seemed to know and like the big man. They sat with a couple of Danish guys who engaged Stephen in football talk before Alberto intervened, "Hey man, soccer's a girls sport where I come from."

A couple of French girls, friends of Sonia, came over and enjoyed some lighthearted conversation. Stephen felt relaxed but hadn't yet seen any of the 'suspects', except for his roommate. He didn't have to wait long though.

On their walk back they heard the sound of a guitar and gentle singing coming from an open door. "Do you take requests?" Alberto shouted entering the source of the entertainment. "Allow me to introduce my new cell mate, Steve, from London."

Steve gave a little wave at the three figures sitting on the bed, he recognised Hank immediately.

"Hi man, I'm Hank, how you doing, these are my good friends Laila and Panina."

Stephen guessed they were kibbutzniks, in their mid teens. Stephen noticed Hank's rich southern drawl, it had an almost hypnotic quality.

"I know a song about London man, I'll play it for you, join in if you know it." He broke into the Ralph McTell classic 'Streets of London', Stephen was urged to help during the chorus. He sort of mumbled, "How can you tell me you're lonely…"

"Don't give up your day job!" The 'Big A' roared as he slapped Stephen on the back.

"I'm more 'London Calling' by The Clash to be honest, I can shout along to that," Stephen offered.

"So what's your day job here man?" Hank asked.

"Turkeys," Stephen replied.

"Wow, tough job man, good luck with that."

"He'll need it." Alberto laughed. "I hope you haven't got a strong sense of smell!"

The two Israeli girls made their excuses and left the three men chatting. Alberto produced what he called his 'magic tin' and asked if they wanted to share a joint with him.

"Given up weed and booze for lent man," Hank stated.

"Hank's a Zealot," Alberto chipped in, "do you indulge my English friend?"

"I'm more of a 'speed' man to be honest," Stephen replied sheepishly, not really sure why he declined.

"You need to see the Frenchies for pills." The big man was obviously an expert.

"What brings you to this war zone man?" Hank asked the question Stephen was hoping for.

"That's a good question Hank, I suppose I'm looking for answers, my father's Jewish, mother Christian, neither particularly religious."

"Do you celebrate any festivals as a family?" Hank asked. Stephen noted it was the first time Hank hadn't ended a sentence with the word 'man'.

"Christmas, but not so much the spiritual side, traditional stuff like presents, turkey, charades etc. But I must confess it's all about Santa Claus and Jesus doesn't get a look in I'm afraid. We do always have a 'Passover' dinner though where we follow a traditional script. Strangely my mother is keener than my father, he's very negative about his religion, particularly since the complications of his marriage to my mum."

Hank went on to explain how he was brought up in a very strict Christian God fearing household but had a keen interest in Jesus Jewish roots, explaining his fascination with the last supper, the celebration of the 'Passover'. Stephen thought it sounded like Hank was making a prepared speech. He was interrupted by a knock on the door, Alberto got up to open it.

The unmistakable figure of photo number three appeared, Marvin, with his telltale US Marine crew cut. He was wearing camouflage trousers and an army-green vest, his physique appeared rock hard. "Everything okay, Hank?" He grunted as he gave Stephen a severe stare.

"All okay man," Hank replied.

"Okay Hank, I'll see you at breakfast." He turned on his heels, slammed the door shut and was gone.

"Anyway Hank, thanks for your hospitality my man but Steve and I need to discuss our mutual faith, rock music and its saviour 'The Boss' Bruce Springsteen. See you on the morrow."

Hank winked at Stephen and drew on his joint as they made their leave.

"Well that was weird," Stephen said as they returned to their room, which still stunk of socks.

"What, Hank and his religion?" Alberto replied.

"No, that Marvin, he's creepy, couldn't stop staring at me. What's that about?"

"He's a strange one alright," the big man confirmed. "He only talks to Hank, no one else, I reckon the Marine Corps has fucked his mind up."

"Hank's an impressive guy, don't you think Al?"

"He's okay for a Jesus freak, keep him off religion and he's okay, great basketball player."

"So what happened to your previous cell mate?" Stephen said, fishing for info.

"Your predecessor, Wayne, well he's some dude, Vietnam vet. What a ladies man. Anyhow he hooked up with this frosty English bitch, a Jewish princess and disappeared with her, leaving a shitstorm behind. I got fucking questioned by the kibbutz committee and some cool Israeli cop or something, crazy shit. Don't you go crazy on me Stevie boy."

"Where they disappear too?" Steve asked, chancing his arm.

"God knows, but there's plenty of people looking, her family are loaded apparently." Alberto lowered his voice, "Between you and me, the sort-of cop guy told me there was a reward for information."

"How much?" Stephen asked.

"Five thousand of your Queen's English pounds," Alberto confirmed.

14

A CASUALTY OF WAR

Stephen's eyes were streaming, his sinuses stinging, he could hardly breathe. He stood next to the turkey farm manager Yonathan, who shouted instructions at him as fifty thousand turkeys squealed, ate and shat all around them. At first Stephen thought Yonathan was joking but soon realised he had no sense of humour.

Tomorrow morning the latest batch would be collected and transported to the slaughterhouse. Yonathan told Stephen to arrive at two in the morning, be dressed all in red, which attracts the turkeys, and stand perfectly still at one end of the shed. The birds would shuffle towards him until all fifty thousand were packed into his half of the building. A team of workers will rush in behind them with freestanding barriers, trapping them. Another team would then open the giant sliding door behind him, where the first convey of lorries would back up to the door so the poultry could be pushed in, approximately five thousand per lorry.

"Is it dangerous, do they bite?" Stephen the townie asked.

"Just don't fall over, they would peck you to death if you fell over," Yonathan replied.

Stephen wasn't exactly reassured.

He spent the next day resting before this life or death mission in the turkey house. He was hoping to run into the English suspect, Neville, but he was proving elusive. He did, however, literally bump into Marvin as he was walking into the dining room.

"Hi mate, met you briefly at Hank's last night, how you doing? I'm Steve, from London." He held out his hand but the Marine just glared at him before marching off without any attempt to communicate.

Strict to the plan at 2am Friday morning Stephen Benjamin Ross stood in a building the size of a football pitch, which housed fifty thousand turkeys, wearing a red anorak (with the hood up), red plastic trousers and red wellies. Yonathan had thoughtfully given him a pair of sunglasses to wear, explaining, "If you faint at least they won't peck your eyes out. We will see you in a couple of hours!"

After a few minutes the first beasts toddled towards him, then a throng gathered, maybe they really are attracted to red. His best mate The Crow would piss himself laughing if he walked in now.

Suddenly an old friend interrupted him. Jonny Rotten was kicking a few birds up in the air he too had on red dungarees and red Doctor Martins. Stephen found this very reassuring.

"What a pair of fucking wankers," he chortled, "are they taking the piss or what. Here we are standing like a pair of complete pillocks when we should be meeting your northern bird at Kings Cross later today!"

Stephen suddenly felt hot and faint as his friend disappeared and he considered the scenarios he had possibly escaped from. The pressure around his legs grew heavier and the floor seemed to be moving towards him.

He had no concept of time, he guessed an hour had passed as about half the turkeys had moved towards him. His wandered from his parents rowing back home to his brother, the selfish cunt, and his sister in law from hell. He thought of Cassandra, hoping she understood his hastily written excuse. He envisioned Maurice and Hilary Saltzman sitting in their opulent Hampstead Garden suburb home, worried out of their minds about their precious princess and their precious bloodline. *Where was Avi? What reward had he been offered? Did the 'Big A' know anything? What about Hank? Was Marvin a psycho? Jan, what was so important, was she…*

Bang! The corrugated roof suddenly ripped open above his head, within a split second it crashed down on top of him, sending him sprawling towards a sea of panicking turkeys. He felt a searing pain above his right eye, before he passed out.

Stephen came round a few moments later, frantic hands pushed bits of roof off him and boots kicked manic turkeys away. A siren blared across the kibbutz.

A burley man in army uniform picked him up and slung him effortlessly over his shoulder, carrying him through the sliding door and outside. The soldier ran to the nearest shelter. He clambered down the stairs as Stephen's blood dripped on his epaulettes.

The shelter was soon full of people speaking a dozen different languages. Stephen lay on a mattress dazed and confused. A familiar figure crouched down beside him, "Jesus H Christ, it's Steve, he's bleeding!" Alberto cried.

"I go get medic, look after him!" The soldier shouted.

"Way to go, Boris," the big man replied.

"You okay Steve, how many fingers?" The big man made a Churchillian salute.

Stephen smiled and made a thumbs up gesture.

"What the fuck are you wearing?" Alberto laughed.

Hank and a throng of other volunteers joined him. Amongst the chaos Stephen heard a Scouse accent, "What happened to him? What the fuck is he wearing?"

Stephen must have passed out again, a few minutes later he came round to see the kibbutz secretary, who doubled as a medic, assisting an older man in removing bits of roof out of his forehead. "This is doctor Moshe, Steve, we need to insert some stitches, you've a nasty gash above your right eye. Seems one or two turkeys didn't like you."

He could see clearly now and remembered he was wearing sunglasses at the time, what a sight he must have looked.

The soldier who rescued him appeared. "Hi, I'm Boris, you okay?" The soldier said in a heavy Russian accent.

"Yeah, thank you Boris," Stephen replied, embarrassed.

"Why you in fancy dress?" Boris asked.

Avaram arrived just as the doctor finished cleaning and stitching him up, "Stevie, wow, you okay my friend?"

"Was it a bomb?" Stephen enquired.

"Not so much a bomb, more of a projectile," Avaram confirmed. "It didn't carry any great explosive charge, you were just unlucky it hit the roof at such an angle, maybe our friends across the border have invented a missile that's attracted to the colour red!" He and the others laughed.

"Please tell me this red business wasn't a joke?" Stephen asked hopefully.

"Works every time," the kibbutz secretary chortled.

That evening Alberto came to see him in the infirmary where he was being kept under observation for twenty-four hours.

"How's the war hero?" He laughed at Stephen lying there with a big white bandage round his head. "You missed the disco, we played 'London Calling' in your honour, apparently you're the first casualty for twelve years."

Stephen remembered he was on a mission, "Was I dreaming or did I hear a Liverpool accent down in the shelter?"

"That would be Neville, a complete pain in the butt, a mad commie. Don't, whatever you do, get him onto politics or religion. You will get a worse headache than you've got now."

Stephen's roommate kept him company until there was a gentle tap on the door and Cheryl entered. The big man made his excuses and left the two of them alone. After some polite small talk Cheryl got down to business.

"We've informed Avi of your accident. He is now convinced that Wayne and Rachel are on their way to Morocco. How's the fishing?"

Stephen briefed her on the conversations he'd had with Alberto and Hank. "You were right about Marvin, what a weirdo," he concurred.

"Keep up the good work Steve, I'll leave some goodies for you here." She placed a tray of dips and cakes on a locker.

Within a minute of her leaving, Yonathan came in. "Piss off you French bastard!" Stephen barked.

"Thank the Gods I gave you the sunglasses, they saved your life, I have to say you look so handsome all in red." Yonathan was laughing so much he could hardly breathe.

"I will get you back, somewhere, sometime."

It had been a long day, he tried to sleep but his head was throbbing. *Jan*, he shuddered, *was she waiting outside his bedsit? What would she think of him? Was his injury divine retribution?*

15

A DAUGHTER OF ABRAHAM

After three eventful weeks, Stephen received three airmail letters on the same day. The first was from his mother, catching him up on family stuff, but mainly moaning about his father and brother. He was glad to be two thousand miles away. The second letter was on company headed paper.

Dear Steve,

Avi has informed me of your incident. I've asked him to find out if there is anything you need. That's twice you've taken a blow to the head whilst on active duty for our company!

Hilary and myself are now beside ourselves with worry as the information we are receiving points to our daughter traveling to third world countries. I am coming to Israel ASAP to liaise with Avi on our next moves. I'm hoping you can stay put for a while and redouble your efforts to glean any info that could be of help.

Kindest regards and heartfelt thanks for your help,
Maurice

Stephen felt their frustration and wondered what more he could do to help his employer. The bomb incident had made him something of a celebrity on the kibbutz, how could he take advantage of this status.

The third letter was handwritten, he didn't recognise the neat pen work.

Dear Steve (hero),

Having stood me up a second time I'm not sure why I'm bothering to write this letter. But your desperate note and the news of your latest head injury, well I guess I'm writing this out of pity!

I took my sister to see The Jam, thank you, you missed a great gig, we met The Crow and I'm moving in with him. Only joking. He asked me to say hi as he obviously can't write!?

You are the talk of the office, it's getting boring. Try and keep safe, maybe wear a helmet.

I do think about you, but I'm not holding my breath we will ever have that date!?

Love,
Cass

Stephen read the letter three times. He was delighted to get the letter from Cassandra but was concerned she'd run into The Crow, with whom he'd booked the tickets. Dave Smith was his oldest friend, meeting back at infant school they shared a love of football and music and enjoyed many an adventure, particularly in their teenage years.

Nobody could recall why he was nicknamed The Crow but there were no end of theories. Most assumed it was something to do with the way he would approach the opposite sex. He would swoop like a crow, "More Stone Age than New Age," Stephen would say.

The Crow was a man of action rather than words, happiest creating incendiary devices and homemade fireworks. Their close-knit gang of friends had one golden rule, 'Thou shall not covert your mates bird'. Stephen thought of this code hopefully but then remembered he wasn't technically going out with Cassandra. He felt homesick for the first time.

Despite Cassandra and Jan constantly invading his thoughts he had noticed a Canadian girl who'd recently arrived whilst she was working in the dining room. They'd overheard the 'Scouser' complain, "She's a stuck up Jewish bitch just like that cow who Wayne ran off with." It transpired however that, like Rachel, she'd resisted his Liverpool charm. Stephen was attracted to her but with everything going on, plus the lack of 'speed' about, he'd not managed to approach her.

He went to Avaram and Cheryl's house on Friday night, surprised to find the Canadian girl sitting at the dining table humouring the hosts' two young children.

"Hi Steve, this is Marci. Take a seat," Cheryl said smiling.

Stephen mumbled a hello, feeling a little flustered. However, Marci was easy company and waxed lyrical about her recent trip to London. Her parents had emigrated to Israel and were in the fur business, a subject she admitted she was embarrassed about. Stephen mentioned that his mother had a fur coat but hadn't worn it in years.

After dinner Marci joined Cheryl and the children in the garden, Avaram fetched a couple of beers.

"What you think of the additional member of the family Steve?" He said, nodding towards the Canadian girl, who was pushing one of the kids on a swing.

"Very nice," Stephen replied noticing how well put together she was.

"Careful boy, she's now your kibbutz sister. How's things, anything to report?"

"Not really, except I'm getting into some deep theological conversations with Hank, much to the dislike of that weirdo Marvin. Neville from Liverpool doesn't engage with me at all, I haven't seen him warm to anyone, spends a lot of time reading revolutionary books."

"And your big room mate?" Avaram asked.

"Very likeable, loves everybody, everybody loves him."

"Does he discuss his conversion at all, do you thinks he's genuine?"

"I don't know, he doesn't really respond to serious questions. He is either eccentric or mad, not sure which, but we are off on a road trip next weekend."

"A road trip?" Avaram queried.

"Yeah, the big man's got Boris' Jeep while he's on reserve duty, we plan to go to Jerusalem."

"That's interesting…Boris is very possessive with his Jeep. Why don't you invite our friends?" The host suggested.

"I can try." Stephen shrugged without conviction. "I was wondering, I know to my cost you have problems other than Rachel Saltzman, but have you considered using a female?"

"A female?"

"Yes, the link between Wayne and Hank, apart from the son of God, seems to be an influence over young ladies, maybe-"

"You are very perceptive Steve, I hadn't considered this angle, I don't know precisely what the figures are for this cult's conversions, but I have to tell you that whilst I might have missed a trick, you and our mutual friend Avi haven't."

"Avi?" Stephen was surprised at his mention.

"Yes, Avi has not only considered this option, he's taken action," Avaram nodded towards the attractive Canadian in the garden. "You two have got some catching up to do," he added with a mischievous smile.

The good news was Marci's roommate was away for the weekend. This would give them time and space to plot and plan but not before they ended up spending the night in bed together.

"I've never committed incest before," Stephen said as they woke early. The sun shone through the solitary window in her room.

"Well, it's all relative," Marci replied, lighting up a cigarette.

Stephen looked at his jeans discarded on the floor where Cassandra's letter was hanging out of a pocket, he felt a pang of guilt.

"So Avi sent you?" He asked.

"He's my boss, he sent me here as bait but so far the only person to have a bite is you Steve."

"Boss?" Stephen replied confused, "You're connected with the Saltzmans then?"

"You are very naive Steve. No, I work for Avi, he's my team leader."

"Team leader?" He was at a loss to what she was on about.

"Who do you think Avi is?" She blew smoke in his face.

"The Saltzmans representative here in Israel, looking after the family property interests," he coughed out.

She laughed and kissed him on the stitches above his right eye that were due out the next day.

"I don't know how much you're supposed to know, but Avi doesn't work for your Saltzmans. I know they hold a lot of influence and yes we need to find his precious daughter, but Avi is not employed by your boss Steve, he works for the government."

"The government?" Stephen repeated, feeling dizzy.

"Yes, Shin Bet, internal security," she whispered.

"But I thought they, Shin Bet, dealt with the Palestinians?" He whispered back.

"Well, yes, they certainly deal with the Palestinians, usually by torturing them, but Avi heads up a team that is concerned with security issues within the green line."

"And looking for Rachel Saltzman is a matter of national security?" Stephen queried.

"No, Miss Saltzman is an irritant, but her father and mother are big fundraisers and well connected, so we'll do our best to find her and send her home."

"And Wayne, what will you do to him?" He asked, thinking about Avi in his dark glasses looking very menacing. Come to think about it, he looked exactly like a member of Shin Bet.

"Nothing," she surprised him with her reply, "he hasn't broken any laws has he?"

"But what about the cult, the infestation?"

She paused before answering. "Wooing isn't a crime, they are consenting adults, he's gone traveling with her, not a crime, unless of course he's kidnapped her. But as whacky as his ideas are, as far as we know, she's gone willingly. Probably just sowing her wild oats, putting two fingers up to her parents and her excruciatingly boring suburban existence."

"Wow, you're probably spot on," Stephen said. "Well Rachel and I are not dissimilar, my parents are in the fur business for fucks sake. Given half a chance I'd burn their fucking factory in Haifa down. I live in fear of friends finding out how they make their money, lots of it. So I don't have friends. I just have sex now and again in the hope I'm liked for a few hours at least."

"Bloody hell Marci, that's a bit strong! Where does this leave me?"

"We both enjoyed last night, and hopefully we'll enjoy more, but you need to find out where Miss Saltzman is. I'll help if I can, but I have other priorities."

"Hebrew Jesuits?" Stephen looked for clarity, thinking that he'd never met anyone quite like this young lady.

"No, potty they might be. I know the kibbutz movement are concerned and once again Steve, any information you can give Avaram and Cheryl will be more than appreciated, no, I'm here to find out about one particular volunteer."

"Who's that?" Stephen's mind was racing.

"If I tell you, I'd have to kill you." She laughed, but he wasn't sure if she was joking.

She slipped out of bed and unlocked a combination padlock on her rucksack. She removed a magazine and pulled out an official looking piece of paper and passed it to him along with a pen.

"Sign here Steve, your full name please."

"It's in Hebrew, I can't read Hebrew," he confessed.

"It's a declaration that you are privy to classified information. Sign it and not only will I not have to kill you but I'll give you a blowjob as well."

16

A HOLY ROAD TRIP

Stephen spent the days before the road trip hanging with Hank, talking religion and occasionally women. Hank currently had two on the go, a Norwegian ice queen and a secret liaison with a young kibbutznik. Since Rachel's disappearance there was an unspoken barrier between the volunteers and the locals. Stephen had brought up the sexual tension with Alberto who, apart from his weekly trade with Sonia, seemed removed from the fun and games.

After listening to a Clash CD and sharing a joint, Stephen asked him directly. "So, Hank slept with Rachael, that must have caused a few ripples?"

"Ripples, not really, I was really surprised when Wayne came back here one night after he'd spent a week in Rachel's room. I told him I was honoured and he casually told me he'd finished his shift picking avocados and found Rachel in bed with Hank. Reckoned he could hear her screaming from the dining room."

"So was he jealous? Upset?" Stephen enquired.

"Not in the slightest, I asked him if he was okay and he casually told me that Rachel was obsessed with Hank, talked about him endlessly."

He relayed this story to Avaram and Cheryl, then to Marci, who he caught up with one rare rainy weekend. Despite signing his life away, she hadn't divulged whom she was keeping her eye on. It wouldn't be long before he found out though.

With twenty-four hours to go before the 'Big A's' road trip, there were only two takers and they were both in room 6A.

A surprise knock on the door changed the numbers instantly, the two roommates were too gobsmacked to speak at first.

"I understand you are organising a road trip to Jerusalem, if there's room maybe can I join you gentlemen?"

Stephen and Alberto looked at each other wondering who would answer first, they mumbled in unison, eventually the big man stepped forward. "Can you drive Marvin?" He asked.

"Got my international license Sir," the Marine replied, standing to attention.

"Well, yes, umm, see you tomorrow captain," Alberto saluted.

"Nine am sharp," he confirmed.

"What about your mate Hank, does he fancy a trip to the holy city?" Stephen chipped in.

The Marine seemed unsure for a moment before answering, "No, no, he's got other plans."

"Probably got a liaison with a young damsel, knowing Hank," Alberto said.

Marvin turned and left without a smile. The two roommates paused for reflection.

"Did I dream that?" Stephen wondered aloud.

"Jesus H Christ, what the fuck man, how weird is this? Well this is going to be a bundle of laughs," Alberto shook his head.

"Well, at least we can have a few beers," Stephen muttered.

"And the rest," the 'Big A' added, pulling a bag of 'grass' from under his mattress and smiling.

Marvin had only got as far as the lay-by where Avi had dropped Stephen off a few weeks earlier when they spotted a tall dark figure thumbing a lift.

"Captain stop!" Alberto shouted. "Where you heading man?" He asked the stranger.

"Anywhere out of rocket range." The hitchhiker had an American accent, but looked almost Indian.

"We're heading for Jerusalem, climb in hombre," Stephen gestured to the empty passenger seat beside Marvin.

The hitcher told them how he'd ridden a Lambretta across Europe and was hoping to write a book about his adventures. He'd even approached the Lambretta factory to sponsor his adventure. He explained his unusual background his father was an Indian Jew from Cochin, his mother, a Burmese Jew. He lived in Santa Barbra in a beachfront condo, had a successful law practice and was taking a year off to find himself. He'd been on three different kibbutzes along the northern border but was tired of the nights in bomb shelters and his scooter had died. He hoped to find some spare parts in Tel Aviv or Haifa but a trip to Jerusalem sounded good.

The Marine drove efficiently and silently while the passengers swapped tales.

"I've met some very strange dudes on the three kibbutzes, religious nutters," the lawyer noted.

"Nutters in what way hombre?" Stephen asked.

"Jesus freaks," their new friend confirmed.

"We have a few of them ourselves," Alberto said, as he and Stephen caught sight of Marvin's piercing stare in the rear view mirror.

Suddenly Marvin slammed on the breaks and swerved into the gravel beside the road.

"What the fuck!" The big man shouted, holding the back of his neck. "What the fuck you doing Marv!"

Marvin turned and ranted for three-minutes about how he wasn't going listen to the Lord's name being taken in vain.

They continued their journey in silence.

Stephen recalled the mad Marine had raved at a Canadian girl, he thought of Marci and wondered what, and possibly who, the sexy spy was up to.

They stopped for lunch in Tiberius on the shores of the Galilee, Marvin stayed in the car sulking, whilst the others enjoyed fresh fish overlooking the lake. Ronnie, the hitchhiker, entertained them with tales of his adventures on two wheels across Europe.

Stephen tried to subtlety get more info out of him, regarding the Jesus freaks.

"Seems to be an infestation of them," Ronnie claimed. Stephen recalled hearing this term before.

"Are you religious?" Alberto asked Ronnie.

"I'm pretty traditional, high holy days etc., now the scooters off the road it will give me the opportunity to get in touch with my roots. Looking forward to touching the 'wall', may also try and get to Hebron, though I hear it's pretty risky right now."

Stephen and his roommate were warming to their new friend.

"Your chauffeur's a strange one?" Ronnie nodded in the direction the car was parked.

"Yep," They replied in unison.

"I reckon he's defo a paid up member of the 'God squad'."

"Yep," they repeated.

A young woman who'd been sitting alone at the next table interrupted them. "Excuse me gentleman, sorry to interrupt but I overheard you, have you got room for another passenger? I'm trying to head south but the buses are stopping for Shabbat and I don't won't to be stuck in this place for the weekend."

Stephen recognised her accent as North London Jewish.

"Sure, where you heading sweetheart?" Ronnie was razor fast with a positive response.

"Well, Tel Aviv really but, Jerusalem will do me fine for tonight."

They returned to the Jeep where Marvin had spread a map over the bonnet. "We've found another passenger captain." Alberto introduced him to Sylvia.

Marvin didn't acknowledge the young English girl. He pointed to the route he'd designed on the map with his red marker. "Next stop is here," he pointed to a spot where the Jordan meets the Galilee, "this is the exact spot where John baptised Jesus."

"Wow." Alberto replied with surprising sincerity. "It's not on the itinerary, but hey, we can do flexibility."

They arrived at the holy spot within half an hour. "I'm going down to the river to be baptised," Marvin announced.

"Wow, okay," Alberto said.

"You're Catholic, want to join me?" Marvin looked the big man in the eye.

"Not for long captain, I'm converting remember."

"What about you?" He snapped at Stephen.

"I'll pass thanks."

"So you are happy being neither Christian or Jewish?"

"I'm happy being both." Stephen wasn't sure that was a good answer.

"You're not both, you are nothing to me and nothing to them." The Marine nodded towards Ronnie and Sylvia, who just looked embarrassed. "You will always be an outsider, this is your chance to be a whole person."

"I'll stay half a person then."

"Jesus may forgive you, but I think you're a fool." Marvin was starting to rant again.

"Hey, cool it captain, Stevie boy, is free to do whatever he wants," Alberto remonstrated.

The irate Marine glared at Stephen for a moment then stated, "Okay. One of you can take a photo of me with my camera."

"Nice piece of equipment," Ronnie said taking the camera from Marvin. Ronnie suddenly felt apprehensive with the responsibility, thinking about the photo being sent to the driver's church and a copy home to mum.

"Okay," Marvin continued, "you all go to the viewing position, I'm going to get changed."

"Way to go captain, we'll be rooting for you." Alberto slapped Marvin on his back.

"Listen," the Marine addressed them all, "listen good, this is the biggest moment of my life, any of you so much as snigger I will put my hand up your arse and rip your fucking spleen out."

The passengers stood in the viewing area just above the river, there was a party of Italian pilgrims queuing to be baptised by the resident priest. Alberto spoke to one of the party in Italian before motioning Ronnie forward into a prime position to take the perfect photo.

"No pressure Ronnie, but for all our spleens sake don't fuck this up!"

They noticed Marvin join the back of the queue in his white robe, he seemed to be in a trance and totally ignored them. They stood respectively, his threat concentrating their minds.

He was now four from the front, the priest seemed to be baptising at a brisk pace. "It must be nearly his lunch hour," Alberto whispered.

"Ssssh," the others collectively protested. The next Italian received his blessings and had his head submerged in the holy waters. They watched in disbelief as he came back for air, fully baptized, but realising his wig had come loose and was floating upstream.

The poor chap and the priest floundered about and barely managed to catch it. The watching crowd tried to conceal their laughter, but within seconds Sylvia was howling like a hyena.

Marvin, who was oblivious to this incident, stepped forward, by now his fellow travellers were in hysterics. He caught a brief glimpse of the crowd and gave a 'thousand yard' stare. Ronnie could hardly see through the lens due to the tears of laughter, his steady grip now all over the place.

The greatest moment of Marvin's life came and went. They waited for him to get changed, hoping he'd understand their merriment.

Alberto came up with an idea, they would buy Marvin a memento of his Baptism. They navigated the souvenir shop each of them choosing, then discounting, various objects, eventually deciding on a set of placemats depicting the story of Jesus. They split the cost and made their way back to the car park. The Jeep was hidden behind the Italian group's coach.

They all stopped in amazement as the Jeep suddenly emerged round the front of the coach and drove towards them. As it drew parallel with them, Marvin was shouting out the window, "Fucking heathens, you can fucking walk to Jerusalem!"

They stood motionless as he sped out the exit, leaving behind a trail of dust.

"Our bags!" Alberto shouted, as Stephen sprinted with Ronnie to where the Jeep had been parked.

"It's okay, he's dumped them, they're here," he confirmed with relief.

The four stranded passengers discussed their fate, Alberto saw the Italian tour guide getting on the coach.

"Hang on gang, I've got an idea," he said, heading to the coach front door. He engaged the guide in fluent Italian then beckoned his friends.

"They are going to Tel Aviv, there's plenty of room for us, we just have to pay a gratuity to the guide and driver."

Sylvia entertained the boys with her life story for the entire three-hour journey. Her father was a successful music producer who'd spoilt her rotten, a familiar story Stephen thought, but then ran off with a singer half his age, leaving her mother distraught. She'd taken the opportunity to escape to Israel where she'd quickly met and moved in with an Israeli in Tel Aviv.

They were eventually dropped off at the Tel Aviv beach front just in time to witness a spectacular sunset.

Sylvia said her goodbyes and Ronnie departed in search of spares for his scooter. The roommates made a surprise visit to Stephen's cousin, in the hope of somewhere free to base themselves until the buses started running after the Sabbath.

As they arrived at cousin Mark's unannounced they just caught him and Rita getting into his battered Skoda. "Mark, Rita!" Stephen called.

They stopped in their tracks and explained they were going to stay with friends in Jerusalem for the weekend, but Stephen and his friend were welcome to stay in their apartment. It was tempting, but Stephen remembered his responsibilities and forsook the temptations of TA nightlife, cadging a lift to the holy city instead.

"We've had some luck since Marvin abandoned us," Stephen observed, as his cousin drove the short journey south.

"This must be our lucky charm." Alberto uncovered the placemats they'd thoughtfully bought for the Marine.

17

DAVID'S CITY

Three hours later they arrived at the Wailing Wall, joining the throng milling around the holy stones. Within a few moments a 'Hassidic' man approached them, offering them prayers for a small donation. Before they could decline, a young man in a white shirt, black trousers and black fedora style hat ushered them away. Stephen noticed his beard was less intimidating than the 'Hassid'.

"Are you gentlemen Jewish?" He asked in a New York accent.

Alberto explained their status and they talked about Brooklyn, where the guy was from, for a few minutes.

"Let me be frank fellas, I'm what you would call 'born again'. I'm resident at a local yeshiva, which is a place of prayer. If you haven't got anywhere to go for a Sabbath meal you're welcome to come to us for a beautiful free dinner. I'm Josh, you'd be made very welcome."

"Free?" Alberto repeated.

"Completely. No strings attached," Josh confirmed.

"What about prayers, do we have to say a lot of prayers and stuff?" Stephen was skeptical.

"There are prayers, and wonderful songs, and delicious chicken and chips, plus a free bed for the night."

The two friends looked at each other.

"I'm bloody starving," Stephen whispered.

"Lead the way Josh," the big man exclaimed.

He led them down a labyrinth of alleys through the Jewish quarter of the old city. They were taken to a small apartment teaming with Josh look-a-likes and a few 'civilians' like them. Another American led the prayers and welcomed the guests. After half an hour, paper plates with the Sabbath meal were passed around. The wolfed the free dinner down not having eaten since Tiberius.

"Bit dry," Alberto observed.

"Needed some condiments," Stephen added.

After dinner Josh introduced them to a young lady in her early twenties from Boston called Rebecca and gave them an hour-long spiel about the joys of being Jewish. He was driven, just like Hank, Stephen thought. Later they were led to a room full of mattresses, which transpired to be their accommodation for the night. They slept like babies after their long day.

They woke early and strolled through the old city discussing the 'yeshiva'. They weren't sure whether the 'born again' Jews were simply generous good souls or if they had a hidden agenda. Either way, Stephen was tiring of the religious fervour being thrown at him from all directions.

They found a small café in the Christian quarter for breakfast and planned their day. They were among the first visitors to Church of the Holy Sepulchre, which houses Jesus' tomb. They spent a good hour in the imposing building, leaving just before the throngs of tourists made things uncomfortable. After, they mooched about the endless shops and stalls selling Christian artifacts until they reached the Muslim quarter. As they made their way through a maze of butchers and various food sellers, they noticed an increased number of soldiers on patrol.

Alberto paused by a vegetable stall, Stephen assumed the heat was getting to the big man, but Alberto reached into his back pocket and took out a small map of the old city. There was an 'X' marking a spot in the Muslim quarter, he looked to see if there were any street names in view but as these weren't exactly streets he had no idea where he was.

"What you looking for Al?"

Alberto looked around him nervously, he waited for a couple of tourists to pass, "A restaurant," he whispered. "Wayne, my old room mate, told me he changed his dollars there on the black market and also scored some grass. I'm running low so thought I might give it a try."

Now Stephen looked around nervously.

They found a local, who sent them down two long alleys, then sought the help of a man selling 'Afghan' coats, who told them the rest of the route.

"That's it," Alberto said, pointing to a sign in Arabic and English.

"I'll hang around here," Stephen said. He didn't want to get involved in his roommates dodgy dealing.

"Okay, if you see any police or military coming this way, let me know."

Alberto checked his rucksack, making sure he knew where his dollars were. He walked briskly twenty meters or so to the restaurant, Stephen went into a souvenir shop to waste time whilst Alberto did his business. The shop owner pounced on him, trying to sell him an expensive chess set, "Each piece is a hand carved biblical figure my friend, you impress your family in America my friend."

"I'm English, I'm not a rich American," Stephen replied and moved to the postcard section, he thought Cassandra deserved a reply to her letter. He swirled the stand around looking for a card that best showed off Jerusalem.

"Steve," Alberto hissed from the shop doorway.

Stephen beckoned him in, "That was quick Al, not open yet?" He asked as the big man joined him at the back of the shop. Stephen immediately noticed he was as white as a sheet and in a terrible sweat.

"Blimey Al, you look like you've seen a ghost."

Alberto looked back at the door nervously. "You won't fucking believe it Steve," there was panic in his voice, "fucking Wayne, my old roommate, is in there!"

"Wayne?" Stephen said.

"Yes, the guy who disappeared with the Jewish girl from London and that's not all, he's sitting with our fucking Marine, fucking Marvin!"

Stephen was momentarily dumbstruck. "Is she there?" He asked.

"Didn't see her."

"Did they see you Al?"

"No, I'm sure they didn't."

They both looked at the door. Stephen grabbed a couple of postcards and put a few shekels on the counter, ushering Alberto to the door. They looked up the street towards the restaurant, a few tourists milled about and a couple of traders pushed carts down the narrow passage.

"What the fuck." Alberto was unable to think straight.

"Okay Al, stay around here, Wayne doesn't know me. Give me Marvin's gift and your dollars. I'll go in there, tell him it's a coincidence and see what happens."

"I don't know Steve, Wayne's involved in some heavy shit, I'm sure of it. I know there's a reward but I'm not comfortable with any of this."

Steve was taken aback by the state the New Yorker was in. "Okay big man, keep out of sight but see if there's a telephone anywhere. If we get split up I'll meet you at that hotel near the Jaffa gate that Ronnie recommended, Hotel Amman."

Alberto nodded looking anxiously towards the restaurant then watched the Englishman stroll casually up to the front door. He hesitated, appearing distracted by something opposite. Stephen stepped away from the restaurant and mimed making a phone call, pointing to the building across.

Stephen noticed a youth hostel opposite and guessed correctly they had a pay phone. He entered the hallway, the phone was adjacent to the hole in the wall which was the reception. A small Arab man with a mighty tash shouted from the top of the stairway, "I be five minute!"

Stephen gave a thumbs up and dug out some shekels, he wedged his bag between his feet and dialed the number with his index finger, holding Avi's business card in his other hand. His heart was thumping as he got the dialing tone. *Oh for some speed,* he thought.

A female answered, "Shalom."

"Hi, is Avi there please?"

"He's in a meeting, who wants him?"

"It's urgent, please tell him it's Stephen Ross."

"I'm afraid he can't be disturbed, I'll tell him you called, can you give me a number please?"

"No, it's urgent, I'm in a call box, tell him I'm with Rachel Saltzman's boyfriend!" Stephen was trying not to shout.

The lady paused, before asking, "Rachael Saltzman?"

"Yes, her boyfriend is in a restaurant opposite me." He guessed from her tone she knew the situation.

"Give me your number in case you're cut off, where are you, Morocco?"

"No Jerusalem!"

"Jerusalem! Give me the number." She sounded both surprised and concerned. He gave her the number, seconds later the line went dead.

"Shit!" He shouted. He looked through the glass door, he could just about see the unmissable silhouette of the Marine across the passage.

"You want room friend?" The moustached man shouted from the landing.

"Maybe, I'm waiting for a call from a friend, we were cut off."

"Okay, just shout when you are ready, it's ten dollars, including breakfast."

The phone gave a shrill, causing Stephen to jump. He clasped the handset as if in a sprint relay. "Avi?"

"What's up?" Avi was his normal, detached self.

"I'm in Jerusalem, the old city, opposite the Star restaurant. I'm in a hostel, I don't know the name, in the Muslim quarter. Wayne is here, Rachel Saltzman's boyfriend. He's in the Star restaurant."

"Slow down Stephen, are you sure it's him?"

"Yes, my roommate, Wayne's old roommate, is with me, he spotted him. He's with the mad Marine Marvin."

"No sign of Rachel?" Avi enquired.

"No, what do I do now, can't you send someone here now to arrest him?" Stephen pleaded.

"Arrest him for what? He hasn't committed any crime as far as we know." Avi rebuffed him.

"But, Rachel, he-"

"Rachel is nineteen now, she is a consenting adult, they have run away together. Not a crime in this country or yours. Yes, we want to know where she is, but nobody needs to be arrested."

"So what the fuck do I do now?" Stephen asked in desperation, frustrated by Avi's coolness.

"Go and ask him where Rachel is?" Avi suggested. "One thing Stephen, Avaram called me an hour ago, there was apparently an attempted burglary last night in the reception office."

"What was stolen?" Stephen asked.

Nothing as far as we know, we think they were looking for passports, but our friends Hank and Neville have disappeared from the kibbutz."

The hostel manager came down the stairs. "What's the name of this place sir?" Stephen asked.

"The Scanda Hostel," he confirmed.

Stephen related the information to Avi as he handed fifteen dollars to the Arab.

"Don't forget Maurice Saltzman's generous reward Stephen," Avi concluded.

"I said the room was only ten dollars my friend," the Arab held out a five dollar note.

"I want one facing the street," Stephen gestured to the passage.

The manager handed him a key to room four, explaining it had the best view in the building.

Stephen took a breath and strode across the passage, turning to where he'd left Alberto. He saw the big man wave from a small junction beyond the gift shop. Stephen gave him a thumbs up and entered the restaurant.

There was a Norwegian couple sitting near the door eating a collection of strange looking meats. There was an open plan kitchen with two unsavoury looking characters busy over a red-hot grill. He spotted Wayne and Marvin deep in conversation at a discrete table against the far wall. They hadn't seen him come in, he felt surprisingly calm as he approached them.

"Marvin!" He shouted in mock surprise. "You made it to the holy city then? I've got something for you."

Wayne turned in surprise as Stephen came up beside them.

Marvin stood up and aggressively grabbed his t-shirt sleeve, "What the fuck you doing here, I'll break you in two you little shit." Marvin's eyes were wild, he was almost frothing at the mouth.

"Cool down Marv," Wayne remonstrated.

"Yes, calm down Marvin," Stephen said.

"This is the Englishman who took your place sharing with Alberto, one of the idiots I left in Tiberius."

Stephen tried to explain why they were laughing and showed him the memento they'd bought him.

"Shove it up you arse," the Marine suggested.

"It's okay Marvin, cool down man." Wayne put a calming hand on his torso, ushering him to sit down.

The owner emerged from the kitchen, asking if all was okay.

"What exactly you doing here, how's the 'Big A'?"

Stephen sat down at the next table and ordered a beer, "He's good. I'm making my first visit to Jerusalem, I'm in that hostel over the road, coincidentally it was the 'Big A' who told me about this place being good for changing dollars."

Marvin averted his manic stare from Stephen and looked at the pony tailed Wayne, hanging on his every word.

"Yes, I remember marking his map, told him this was the place to take care of all his needs."

"Exactly," Stephen confirmed. He then surprised himself with his directness, "You're infamous at the kibbutz Wayne, apparently there was a shitstorm after you ran off with your English girlfriend. Poor Alberto was almost tortured, everyone thinks you're in Morocco."

"Young Rachel isn't my girlfriend, I think she's gone to Morocco, but I haven't seen her since the day after we left the kibbutz. I've been hanging round here, I've no idea what that crazy chick is up to."

Stephen was considering how to get more information about this revelation without seeming too interested.

"Rachel was never my girlfriend, she's obsessed with someone else. I understand you know him." Wayne said.

"Do I?" Stephen asked, wondering where this was heading.

"Hank, she's obsessed with Hank, she basically paid me to be a decoy, she told me she was going to Morocco and he would follow."

"Enough," Marvin snapped, "none of this is his business."

"But Hank's my friend, I've learnt so much from him, I don't think he'd leave us." Stephen impressed himself with his quick thinking.

"Hank's not your friend," the Marine snapped, "not until you accept Jesus Christ into your heart."

"Everyone wants to be Hank's friend," Wayne said.

"Hank has a magnetic personality, God knows he has sucked us all in and none more than Rachel, she told me she would give up everything for him."

"What do you mean by everything?" Stephen asked.

"Her comfortable materialistic lifestyle, her family, her religion, it's as if Hank's hypnotised her."

Stephen's head was spinning with this new, conflicting, story of events. He certainly couldn't disagree with Wayne's description of Hank, people, particularly females, were drawn to him. He finished his beer and just about remembered to change the big man's dollars. He suddenly recalled Avi telling him about Hank and the missing passports, he needed to get back to him and discuss these new details. He returned to the Americans, who seemed to be having a heated disagreement.

"Where's the Jeep Marvin, I take it we are still heading back north tomorrow?"

"Fuck you," the Marine snapped.

"With respect, the 'Big A' came to an agreement with Boris to borrow it, so I think we need to go back together."

"Where is the 'Big A' anyway?" Wayne interjected.

"Left him back at the Jordan river, he was pissed off, decided to head back to the kibbutz," Stephen lied.

"Where you staying Marvin? I'll come and find you tomorrow tenish."

Marvin didn't answer and looked mighty upset when Wayne answered for him, "We're at the hotel Amman, near the Jaffa gate."

Shit, Stephen thought. He said his goodbyes and hurried off to find Alberto. The big man was nowhere nearby, so Stephen sprinted through the hustle bustle of the souk. It took him a good ten minutes to get to the hotel, he reckoned he had about the same amount of time before Wayne and Marvin turned up. He hovered around the front steps, it was thirty-four degrees, the street near the Jaffa gate was wider but choked with traffic, the noise and the heat were suffocating.

He heard panting as the big man emerged from a passage across the street, swigging a bottle of water. Alberto sat down on a step barely able to breathe.

"Al, listen we haven't any time, Wayne and that fucking psycho Marvin are on their way here!"

Panic spread across the 'Big A's sweaty face.

"It's okay Al, I told them you'd gone back north. Get a taxi to the bus station, lay low for a couple of hours till the buses start running again."

"What you going to do Steve?" He croaked.

"Try and get the Jeep back. I'll see you back at the ranch come what may, now leg it."

18

PSYCHO

Stephen sat in a small café across the square thinking about his next move. He felt a pang of guilt about sending Alberto on his way. It made sense though, he clearly wouldn't be comfortable running into his old roommate.

He was surprised to see his mate Jonny sitting beside him. "Nice one fella, got rid of the competition, good move, the five grand is all yours for the taking. Not sure about Morocco though, could be a ruse. Watch out for that mad Marine mate, he's well dodgy!"

Rotten slipped away as Stephen noticed the pony tailed figure of Wayne emerge out of the souk and disappear into the hotel Amman.

He waited for a good hour but there was no sign of Marvin, which troubled him. He decided to head back to the hostel, he had spent fifteen dollars on it after all.

As he reached the scene of the earlier drama he felt a foreboding sense of danger, *was the mad Marine waiting for him?* He bolted the last few metres and was relieved to find the hostel alive with activity. A large group of Danes had arrived and were busy checking in. He waited for the crowd to thin before phoning Avi, this time he answered immediately,

"What's happening?" Avi asked casually.

"I've been earning my five grand," Stephen quipped.

"Excellent, so where's our girl?" Avi replied.

Stephen hesitated, embarrassed that he'd been so flippant. "Listen Avi, I'm seriously concerned, Wayne's in the hotel Amman, but Marvin never returned with him. Wayne reckons Rachel is in Morocco, but it's not him who she's run off with, he's a decoy, it's Hank."

"Slow down. I'm coming to collect you, you can tell me everything on the way back."

"That's good because I'm concerned about Marvin, he's a psycho. Where shall I meet you?"

"Go to your room and stay there, I've already arranged some back up for you. Don't open the door to anyone unless they know your middle name."

"What?" Stephen was now seriously concerned.

"Listen Steve, we've had some disturbing information about Marvin. He wasn't a Marine, he failed his medical on psychological grounds. He's apparently jumped bail."

"What's he charged with?" Stephen interrupted.

Avi hesitated, then decided the truth was the best option. "Manslaughter," he reluctantly informed the Englishman, "I'm on my way, go to your room and lock the door. Remember what I told you, Benjamin."

Stephen flew up the stairs and locked the door behind him. There was no bolt or chain to reinforce it. He scoured the room for anything that could be used as an improvised weapon. The room wasn't much bigger than the bed, there wasn't one piece of furniture to suit his needs. His only means of defence was to look out the window at the narrow passage below.

The lights in the restaurant illuminated his whole line of vision, he could hear laughter coming from the diners sitting on outside tables. He felt exposed looking out the open window, but the room was stifling. He kept an eye out for anyone who could possibly be Avi's back up. He thought he saw Marci 'the sexy spy' walk by, but that was wishful thinking.

He heard his hero, who was sitting on his bed, but he didn't dare take his eyes off the action below. "It's just me and you matey, fuck the yank, he's no match for a couple of Londoners."

He turned around, but the room was empty. He looked back at the passage and blinked disbelievingly, Marvin was standing in the street looking up, hold all in one hand. Stephen dived onto the bed hoping the deranged non-Marine hadn't noticed him, but then he heard him shouting, "I've seen you Ross, come to the window I've got something for you!"

Something? What the fuck has the lunatic got for me? He thought, hardly able to breathe.

"For fuck sake you English cunt, don't make me come up there!"

Had he purchased a gun from the Arab restaurant owner? He recalled Marvin's rant about how he'd rip their spleens out. Reluctantly he peered over the window ledge, trying to give the psychopath the smallest target possible.

"I've got the Jeep key for you, it's parked in a public car park at the Hebrew University!" He shouted.

Stephen thought he might cry with relief.

"I'm heading south by bus, you can take the Jeep. Here!" Marvin threw the key up at the window but it fell short. He tried again, this time it hit one of the window bars and nearly fell down a drain grill.

"Shit, I'll bring it up, wait there."

Stephen's relief turned to outright panic but he realised that Marvin had genuinely tried to throw the key through the window.

The American knocked on the door.

"You're not coming in Marvin, leave it outside." Stephen saw the door handle rattle. "Pass it under the door Marvin, you ain't coming in." The feeling of relief returned as he saw the Jeep key slide a good six inches into his room. "Good man Marvin, where you heading?"

"I'm on a mission, I'm on my way to complete it," Marvin replied cryptically, trying the handle again. "Listen Ross, I know you're looking for that Jewish chick, it's too much of a fucking coincidence you showing up at the kibbutz and now here, I've got you sussed. Let me tell you Ross, your Jewish bitch will be with Hank by now. He's going to marry her and show her the glory of Christ and there's not a God damn thing you can do about it."

Stephen was about to betray his roommate again but desperate times, desperate measures. "Alberto told me about the reward, fucking hell Marv five thousand pounds is a tidy sum. Tell me where she is, where Hank is heading, and we can go fifty fifty."

"Fuck you Ross, I'm the gate keeper, no one's going to stop Hank, I'll make sure of it." Marvin tried the door again, Stephen picked up the key and put his weight against the door. He heard a dull thud and then a groan followed by a few seconds of quiet.

"Benjamin, open the door."

Stephen was dizzy with confusion.

"Steve. Benjamin Ross. It's Boris, quick open the door."

He turned the key and opened the door a fraction. Boris, the soldier who'd carried him down to the bomb shelter was holding his M16 gun like a baseball bat. Marvin lay semi conscious on the floor.

"Help me," he requested as he tried to drag the prostate figure into Stephen's room.

It took all their combined strength to get Marvin into the room, which was now very crowded.

"Where's my fucking Jeep?" Boris asked, Stephen twiddled the key in his fingers.

Boris ripped up some sheets and tied Marvin's hands behind his back. They had just managed to roll him onto the bed when there was a knock on the door. "Benjamin, it's Avi."

He opened the door, Avi had his sunglasses on despite it being ten at night. He looked at Marvin moaning on the bed. Stephen started to describe what happened but Avi cut him short, "Do you think he knows where Rachel Saltzman is?"

"Possibly," Stephen replied.

"How possibly?"

"Very."

"Okay, go get me a bucket of cold water from the toilet please." Stephen hadn't heard Avi do politeness before.

There was a metal pale in the loo, he returned to the room and handed it to Avi. Boris turned Marvin over so he was face up. Avi poured the water over his bloody face and Marvin came round, coughing and spitting out blood. Boris took aim with his weapon whilst Avi sat on the bed next to the prisoner. "Where's Rachel Saltzman?" He asked calmly.

"Fuck you."

"Where's Hank?"

"Fuck you," Marvin repeated.

"If you're squeamish Steve, you might want to leave the room," Avi coldly offered the civilian.

"I'm okay Avi, you carry on."

Avi tore a pillowcase and gagged Marvin. "When you are ready to talk just nod twice Mr. Cutts," he stated as he took a lethal looking lock knife from his jacket pocket.

"Look out the window Steve, what do you see?"

Stephen had to crawl over Marvin's legs to get to the window. He couldn't believe his eyes, the passage was completely deserted, except for at least eight soldiers in full combat gear all in attack positions, he described what he saw to Avi.

"There is another platoon surrounding the hotel Amman." He was dragging the knife around his prisoner's eye sockets. "The wonderful thing about being an officer is that I get to torture bad people, I really quite enjoy it. Of course I've only tortured Palestinians before, never an American, but as you are wanted in Kansas for manslaughter, at least you appear to be a bad one so I don't feel so terrible. Please Stephen, this is going to be quite shocking, I must insist you leave the room." He unzipped Marvin's 'fly' and slid out his penis, "You're definitely not Jewish are you Mr. Cutts?"

Marvin's head rolled frantically from side to side as he felt the cold steel move around his foreskin.

Stephen felt sick, he took Avi's advice and left the room.

"You and your fucking friends have lost us some Jews so it seems right that I convert you to the chosen race."

Avi drew a little blood, Marvin nodded his head, his eyes bulging like they were about to burst.

"You want to tell us where Rachel Saltzman is then Mr. Cutts?"

Marvin nodded furiously, Avi loosened the gag. "Morocco," he gasped.

"Morocco," Avi repeated, "where in Morocco exactly?" He put more pressure on the knife.

"Casablanca."

"And Hank is on his way there I presume?"

Marvin nodded, with a twisted smile.

"Thank you for your cooperation Mr. Cutts, my boys outside will escort you to your embassy, good luck."

Avi put his knife back in his pocket after wiping it clean on the ripped bedclothes.

"Okay Boris let's go and see what Wayne Richardson has to say."

19

HAMPSTEAD GARDEN SUBURB ON SEA

It was a mixed night, Marvin was on his way to be handed over to the Americans custody but the raid on the hotel Amman had come to nothing as Wayne had slipped the net. Boris was reacquainted with his Jeep so Avi drove Stephen to his apartment in Tel Aviv, where he slept on an airbed in the living room.

He woke in the morning to the loud happy voices of small children. "Good morning." An attractive dark haired woman stood over him with a tray containing freshly squeezed orange juice and filter coffee. "Hi I'm Irit, Avi's wife, would you like some eggs?" Stephen was staving and she could tell from his enthusiastic response he could handle a big breakfast.

After freshening up he joined Avi's family at the breakfast table. Avi was playing the clown with his two small children and he wasn't wearing sunglasses. Stephen thought about the doting father opposite him threatening to circumcise Marvin just a few hours before, he wondered if he'd dreamt it all.

Irit talked about her sister living in Brighton and how she loved London parks. Avi was almost pleasant throughout the conversation.

After Stephen wafted his four-egg omelette down, Avi put his shades back on and gestured to the door.

"Where we heading?" Stephen asked as they ventured north out of Tel Aviv.

"Not far, just up the road." Avi was back to his usual surly self.

They drove in silence for twenty minutes following the coastal road as far as well healed Herzliya. He drove down several side roads, the houses got bigger and grander and they finally came to a stop outside a Swiss chalet style property that overlooked the sea. Avi flashed his lights at a car parked just up the road, the car responded with its hazards.

"Friends," Avi confirmed, "there's been a development."

"A development?" Stephen echoed.

"A breakthrough," Avi added nonchalantly.

Stephen contemplated the words Avi had used, 'development' and 'breakthrough', these were significant words and Avi used his words very sparingly.

"A significant breakthrough?" Stephen asked.

"Very," Avi confirmed.

"Whose house is this?" Stephen enquired.

"How many people do you know who live in a house in Herzliya Pituah Stephen?"

"Only Maurice Saltzman," Stephen replied.

Avi nodded towards the house beside them. "He arrived last night, he's waiting for you Steve."

"For me?" Stephen was confused.

"He will only see you, don't ask me why but whilst all hell was breaking loose in Jerusalem last night your boss arrived in Israel with a letter."

"A letter, what letter?"

"A letter from his daughter."

"Fucking hell, what did it say?" Stephen couldn't believe it.

"I've no idea, Mr. S will only discuss it with you." Avi removed his shades so Stephen could see he was serious. "He called me early this morning and after I briefed him on recent developments, he told me he'd received a letter from Rachel but he would only discuss the contents with Stephen Ross."

Stephen swallowed hard, mesmerised by the sudden turn of events.

"Go knock on the door Steve, I'll wait here."

Stephen reluctantly climbed out the car.

"One more thing Steve," Avi shouted as put his sunglasses back on, "I told your boss how well you've done!"

Stephen rang the bell, shortly after a Filipino housekeeper answered the door. "Hi I'm Steve, I've come to meet Mr. Saltzman."

"Yes, he wait for you out back by pool."

He made his way through the palatial building to the manicured garden at the bottom of an amply size swimming pool, complete with changing rooms and bar.

He spotted his boss sitting at a green metallic garden table with a garish yellow canopy offering shade.

He stood and shook his employees hand, apart from the novelty of seeing him in a casual shirt and 'Bermuda' shorts, Stephen was shocked to see how Mr. S had aged. He could see the worry lines above his sunglasses, he'd lost a shit load of weight.

"Good to see you Steve, help yourself to whatever you want."

Stephen poured iced water into a plastic cup, he was alarmed to see his boss had what looked like a brandy at barely eleven am.

"Nice gaff eh Steve?" He said, nodding towards the house. "Hillary calls it Hampstead Garden on Sea." Saltzman tried to smile but was a shell of the confident millionaire Stephen had met a few months previously in North London. "Apart from this and our wonderful home in London my company has a portfolio of over hundred properties." Stephen noticed his boss twirling an airmail letter in his hand. "I'm in fact a billionaire on paper, not bad eh, the Saltzmans have come a long way since my grandfather dragged his children through the snow from Tilbury Docks." He paused, briefly removed his glasses and wiped a tear. Stephen noticed heavy bags under his eyes. "But my point is Steve, I wish I could swap lives with you, it's all meaningless, my money can't cure the pain Hillary and I are going through."

Stephen wondered if he should say something about the last twenty-four hours but he felt they might not be relevant now.

"I received a letter Steve." He placed the letter flat on the table and took a swig of his brandy. "It's from Rachel." He paused, an ambulance siren wailed in the distance.

"Is she okay?" Stephen asked.

His boss opened the letter, stared at it and then started to read.

"My darling daddy," his voice cracked, Stephen wondered why Avi wasn't invited to hear this vital information.

"There are two pages here Steve, I've read it over a thousand times, Hillary doesn't know it exists and never will, I will read you the last line, 'You are my shining light Daddy, all my love, Rachel.'"

Stephen watched in amazement as Mr. S produced a lighter, placed the letter on a plate containing a half eaten bagel, and set it alight. Stephen watched it burn, aware his boss was watching his reaction.

"Only three people know this letter exists Steve, my princess, me and you and I want you to swear you've never seen it."

"Of course Maurice, I don't know what was in it anyway," he replied looking at the smouldering ashes.

"The letter didn't exist okay?" Saltzman said with a frightening intensity.

"Okay, do you know where she is?" Stephen chanced his arm.

"Doesn't matter anymore Steve, que sera sera, possibly Morocco where the letter's from, maybe India where she mentioned she was heading, it doesn't matter anymore." He poured some water over the ashes.

Stephen was struggling to understand his boss' sudden apathy, he recalled the history lesson in the wood panelled office back in HGS. "What do I do now Mr. Saltzman, Maurice?"

"Take a couple of weeks off I guess, God knows you deserve it young man. We could do with you back in the office, plenty of debts to pay."

Stephen noticed Saltzman was beginning to slur his words. He raised his hand and waved towards the house, within a few seconds the little Filipino housekeeper came scurrying across the lawn.

"Please fetch Avi, thank you Maria."

Stephen wondered what Avi the torturer would make of all this. There was an uncomfortable silence before Stephen asked, "How's Harvey doing?" He'd noticed how depressed and morose his boss' brother-in-law had become. Most in the company felt sorry for him having to be humiliated on a daily basis by his wife, the boss' sister, who by all accounts was a complete bitch. The female staff all found him a bit creepy.

"He's dead," Saltzman replied without emotion.

"What?" Stephen mumbled.

"He's dead to me, I'd rather you not mention his name again."

Avi joined them, he noticed Stephen looking ashen and the host's changed appearance since they'd last met. They shook hands functionally.

"I'd like to thank you for everything Avi but I've just been explaining to young Steve here that my family matters are concluded, Maria will be down with coffee and croissants for you, enjoy them. Let yourselves out when you're done, I'm going to have a lay down." They watched him trudge up to the patio doors a little unsteadily. For the first time Stephen noticed Avi looked lost.

"What the fuck Stevie?"

"He basically told me he'd accepted his daughter was free to do as she chooses and that's it." Stephen shrugged making sure not to mention the letter, he hadn't read it anyway.

"Did he say where she is?"

"Maybe Morocco or India, but he doesn't care."

Avi sighed and shook his head in disbelief trying to understand the situation.

"She's probably in a church somewhere marrying Hank," Stephen offered.

But then Avi added, to his total confusion, "Wherever she is I can tell you for certain she's not with Hank."

"What?"

"Hank has spent the last two days on Kibbutz Ein Hapoel near Haifa. In fact he spent the night with a Swedish volunteer, definitely not with Rachel Saltzman."

"But he stole his passport, Marvin said he was on his way to her?" Stephen protested.

"Not sure you can steal your own passport, a window was broken during the forced entry but I can tell you for a fact he never took his passport."

"How can you be so sure?"

Stephen looked in amazement as Avi placed Hank's passport on the table next to the plate containing the ashes of the airmail letter.

"What the fuck," he exclaimed.

"When I went up to the kibbutz following Rachel's disappearance Avaram and I met with all the volunteers and collected their passports to be kept in the office safe. We explained it was a security measure so we'd know when people were leaving, of course mostly legitimately. Anyway, Hank's never made the office, they ended up in my pocket. Here, I've got a couple of others."

Stephen read the names on the two more passports Avi threw on the table.

"Neville Nash and Alberto Canavaro, wow Avi you're a slippery so and so."

"I'll take that as a compliment."

"Don't think you need to worry about Alberto though, he was scared shitless about running into Wayne," Stephen said.

"Well he doesn't have to worry about Wayne now," Avi stated.

"Why?"

"He's in custody at Ben Gurion Airport. He was arrested last night and is still in a cell awaiting my visit."

"Wow, but you said he hadn't committed any crime, surely he was legally just leaving the country, was he going home?"

"He was charged with theft. He slipped out the hotel Amman in a hurry, maybe understandably, but he forgot to pay, so…"

"And where was he going?"

"Egypt," Avi paused before adding, "and then on to Casablanca."

"Morocco," Stephen whispered.

Avi gave a knowing nod.

"Shit, do you think Wayne was using Hank as a decoy?"

"Or maybe the other way around," Avi responded.

"Shame you handed Marvin over to the American embassy."

"I didn't."

"What?"

"Our friend Boris gave him one hell of a bang on the head, my boys were worried about his condition so he's in hospital. After I've chatted to Wayne I'll go and revisit Marvin's private parts."

"You've got a busy day Avi."

"It's the job Steve, it's what I do."

"One last thing Avi, Maurice Saltzman told me Harvey was dead, his exact words were, 'He's dead to me', what was that about?"

Avi shrugged. "Crazy fucking Jew," he muttered ironically. "Enjoy your time off Steve, it's been a pleasure."

20

R & R

Tel Aviv beach, thirty degrees, cold beer, burger and fries, no watch and most importantly, no mad Jews or Christians. Stephen reclined on his deck chair and reflected on the craziness of the last few days. He wondered if Marvin still had his testicles. What Avi might do with Wayne's ponytail. He thought about whether the five grand reward was null and void. What would he do with his two weeks? What was Cassandra up to? Would they ever have that date?

He closed his eyes for a few minutes but his peace was disturbed not soon after. "How's the road trip London boy?"

He looked up and saw Sylvia, the hitchhiker, standing above him in a revealing swimsuit. "Sylvia, how you doing? Pull up a chair."

The two chatted for a couple of hours, though to be fair Stephen hardly got a word in. She repeated the story about her music producer father. He had success with a song that won the Eurovision Song Contest but fame had turned his head and he'd left her and her mum in poverty. She'd followed an Israeli male model here but she wasn't sure how keen he was on her. She then confessed she had spent the weekend with Ronnie, the other hitcher. Stephen wasn't surprised, he knew he was a charmer. He wondered if he'd found his Lambretta part.

"Where's your male model now?" Stephen enquired.

"Flies in from Amsterdam this evening, he's been filming an advert."

Stephen felt quite drunk, he realised he'd overdone the sun and beers. "Shame Sylvia, I'd have liked to have had a night on the town with you."

She lent over and kissed him playfully on the lips, "Some other time London boy, see you around."

Stephen enjoyed the incredible sunset and took a taxi to the bus station. Since Sylvia had floated off he decided to head north. Three hours later he was settled into the back seat of his connecting bus as it left Haifa. It was only a third full, mainly with soldiers heading to the Lebanon border.

It had only moved a few yards when a latecomer banged on the front doors. The lights were red so the driver let him on, Stephen blinked as he recognised the lucky passenger headed for a seat half way along the bus. He considered hiding but something told him to make contact. "Hank," he whispered forcefully.

Hank looked round in fright, Stephen clambered down the bus and sat next to him. "Steve, what's happening man, thought you were on a road trip in Boris' mean machine?"

"I was but I slipped off to my cousin's in Tel Aviv for a couple of days, left your friend Marvin in charge of the Jeep."

"Well I hope Marv took good care of it, that mad Russian doesn't take prisoners." Hank laughed, Stephen found that statement quite ironic.

"What you been up to then Hank?"

"Well it's been a long weekend man, seems the kibbutz have mislaid my passport, so I went to the Consulate and tried to sort things out."

"Any luck?"

"Got to go back next weekend which is a real bummer man, but I went to see a friend on a kibbutz near Haifa, nicer place, had a sweet couple of nights there."

"Funnily enough I ran into Marvin and an old friend of yours in the old city," Stephen chipped in, "the guy who was supposed to have run off with the English girl."

"Wayne," Hank confirmed, but didn't seem over surprised.

"Yeah, nice guy, asked after you and the 'Big A'."

"I thought he was in Morocco with her," Hank pondered.

"That's what I said to him," Stephen said honestly, before continuing with a lie, "he reckons the spoilt Jewish princess has gone back home to mummy and daddy."

Hank looked confused and a trifle agitated on hearing this news. "He thinks she's in London?"

"That's what he said," Stephen repeated.

"Wayne's a liar man, no way that Rachel's gone home man." Hank seemed stressed.

"Ask your man Marvin, he was there with us." Stephen was enjoying himself now. He wasn't sure where all this bullshit was coming from.

Hank sat deep in thought for a couple of minutes before confiding in Stephen. "Steve, I need a favour man."

"Sure Hank, what is it mate?"

"Well the thing is man, I left the kibbutz the other day with no intention of returning, but today was post day and I'm expecting a very important letter, do you think you can get it for me? I'll hang around Rosh Pina tonight, maybe you could meet me tomorrow morning at the bus station. I'll treat you to falafel."

"That's an offer I can't refuse," Stephen quipped.

"The thing is Steve, I left under a cloud, that idiot Neville told me he'd been refused his passport from the kibbutz office and decided he'd break in and get it. I stupidly asked him to get mine but he claims neither of ours were in there."

"Wow, complicated," Stephen agreed.

"Yeah man, I reckon this heavy Israeli dude took them, he questioned us after Rachel disappeared, real slippery guy."

Avi would be delighted with this description, Stephen thought.

"One more favour Steve, can you bring Marvin with you? I'd like to say goodbye to him."

"Sure Hank, he's a strange one though."

"Sure is man but he loves Jesus and that's good enough for me."

It was almost midnight when Stephen arrived at his room, he was surprised to see the light still on, he could hear the big man's laugh reverberating around A6. He tried to open the door but, most unusually, he found it locked from the inside.

"Al, open the fucking door mate!"

"Fe fi fo fum, I smell the blood of an Englishman!" Alberto bellowed as he made to open the door.

The room was empty of guests, Al appeared pleased to see his roommate. "Where the fuck you been?" He rasped. "I've had to entertain your visitor, he arrived this morning."

"What visitor?" Stephen asked mystified.

Alberto gestured towards Stephen's bed. There was someone hiding under the quilt, Stephen noticed a small suitcase beside his bed. He ripped off the quilt and was stunned to see The Crow with a great big stupid grin on his face. "Dave!" Stephen shouted with joy.

"The crow has landed," Alberto laughed.

"Where these Scandinavian birds?" Stephen's oldest mate asked.

"What the fuck Dave, what the fuck you doing here?"

"I was made redundant last Thursday, booked my flight, packed my case, here I am. Now where's the free love Stevie boy?"

"Do you smoke Mr. Crow?" Alberto asked.

"Like a chimney," Stephen replied for his mate.

"Got any cigarettes with you?" The big man asked.

The Crow opened his duty-free carrier bag and tossed a multi pack of Rothmans onto his bed. Alberto and Stephen looked at each other. "Sonia," they both said.

"Follow me Mr. Crow." Alberto led the guest to the volunteers' house, E9, and knocked on the door. It was past one in the morning, Sonia answered the door completely naked.

"Hi Sonia, this is Stephen's friend from London," Al handed her the duty-free, she took The Crow's hand and pulled him to her bed.

"Thank you Al, I'll bring him back in a couple of days."

Stephen threw The Crow's stuff off his bed and saw a couple of letters his friend had obviously hand delivered. His parents wrote two sides of tittle-tattle, which left him underwhelmed. He recognised the writing on the other envelope and ripped it open clumsily.

Dear Steve (hero again),

This is getting tedious. News has filtered through that you continue to use your superpowers in the company's cause. I'm very jealous of The Crow, who by now will be causing havoc. As if they haven't got enough problems in that part of the world. I might just be tempted to make a visit myself before anything else happens to you. Rumour has it you are coming back to the office shortly. Things are really bizarre here. Harvey has apparently left, or been sacked?

Let me know your plans as I have an army of rich good-looking guys pursuing me.

Love Cass

"So what the hell happened with Wayne and Marvin?" Alberto asked.

Stephen wanted to sleep but gave a summary of events that bore little relevance to reality or the story he told Hank, whose name he didn't mention. He needed to rest, his scar was sore and his brain was frazzled.

Sleep was spasmodic though, he spent most of the night mulling over recent events. He was relieved that his boss was calling off the search but mystified and curious as to why. The letter, Harvey…nothing added up. The reward would have been handy. *Enjoy the break.* That ain't going to happen with The Crow about. No rest anyway, but plenty of recreation.

He was woken first by Alberto clumsily getting ready for his early shift in the kitchens, then by a visit from Avaram asking him to pop by the office.

Cheryl let him in and then put a 'Back in 20 mins' sign on the door. Avi had fully briefed her by phone and fax as to Stephen's adventures on the road trip. She showed Stephen a fax that had just arrived from Maurice Saltzman.

Dear Avaram and Cheryl,

Further to my previous communication I would like confirm my daughter is safe and well.

I am leaving Israel this evening and would like to thank you for your help and concern. I'm sorry my daughter caused you so much trouble. I shall be making a donation to your wonderful kibbutz shortly.

Yours faithfully,
Maurice Saltzman

Stephen shrugged. "Strange."

"Very," Cheryl replied. "The weekly post arrived early this morning, take a look at this." She handed him an airmail letter with a Moroccan stamp. It was addressed (typed) to Alberto Canavaro.

He read the brief contents aloud, "Dear Al, hope all good with you. Could you do me a massive favour and get the enclosed envelope to Wayne. You know where he hangs out. Thank you so much, love you big man, Rachel."

Stephen handed the envelope to Cheryl, there was nothing written on it, just a small cross in a heart drawn in the corner where a stamp would normally be.

She opened it carefully and read aloud, "My dearest Wayne. Please please come and save me from my fucked up family ASAP. I've contacted my father and I'm now free to take whatever path I choose, even if it leads to you and Jesus. I'll be where I told you to meet me. Don't take forever, but I would wait forever. All my love and devotion, Rachel."

"Shit, Hank's the decoy after all," Stephen muttered.

"What?" Cheryl queried.

"Have you got any post for Hank?" He asked her, explaining about their meeting on the bus. She searched through the pile of volunteers' letters, mainly bearing Scandinavian postmarks. Eventually she came across a solitary letter for Hank. She handed it to Stephen, who ripped it open and began reading.

Hank,

On my way to sort problem!? But run into unexpected trouble, which I will sort now.

By the time you read this, the road will be clear.

Jesus is with us.

Marvin.

"What the fuck." Cheryl's harsh South African accent made her swearing more vicious.

"Shit!" Stephen thought his head would explode. "What about my meeting with Hank, he's waiting at Rosh Pina!"

"I'm going to phone Avi, I don't like any of this. Go and get Avaram we need a plan of action."

Stephen ran to the metal factory where Avaram worked but halfway there the sirens blasted, followed by an Israeli fighter jet screaming low overhead heading towards the border. The ground shook from the boom created as it went through the sound barrier. Stephen turned and ran to the volunteers' shelter. "Shit, shit, shit!" He yelled as he ran. As he reached the shelter another thought added to the confusion, he hadn't seen Marci or the strange Scouser Neville. *Where the hell were they?*

The volunteers streamed down the stairs with more urgency than normal, a couple of thuds had been heard in the far distance. Alberto headed straight for the turntable as Sonia and her fellow French friends led an exited Crow down to the dungeon. He made his way over to Stephen, who was still deep in thought.

"Bloody hell Steve, I've only been here twenty-four hours and I've been raped and bombed, this is some place."

Alberto took the microphone and announced, "Welcome to the pleasure pit boys and girls, fasten your seat belts, apparently Israeli planes have hit the Iraqi nuclear plants, there's going to be a shitstorm of revenge so could be a long day. This goes out to our first casualty, Steve Ross, and his guest, the legendary Crow." The first riffs of The Clash's 'London Calling' blasted out from the speakers located at each corner of the shelter.

Day turned into night and still they waited for the all clear, Stephen wondered if Hank was still waiting for him. He patted his jean back pocket to make sure the letter was still there.

The big man was in full flow when Avaram interrupted his 'Motown medley' to address the throng. "I'm sorry to inform you but there's been a large amount of rockets fired across the border and consequently a lot of retaliation. The Airforce headquarters has informed us that a jet seems to have accidentally dropped a 'sidewinder' missile somewhere in the valley. The good news is it's not armed, but naturally until it's found we are all confined to our shelters."

There was a mixture of groans and cheers. "Fucking hell, I came here for the famous Israeli weather and I've not seen the bloody sky yet!" The Crow shouted.

"One more thing everybody!" Avaram shouted into the microphone. "There's been a direct hit on the bus station in Rosh Pinna, there are reports of many casualties." There was a hush in the room before Avaram added, "It's vital you all have patience and sit this out, I will keep you informed."

Stephen sat against the wall, his forehead was stinging, The Crow was back on the dance floor boasting to any Swedish looking female about his remaining stash of cigarettes.

Alberto managed a straight twelve-hour shift of DJ-ing before collapsing in a sweaty heap on the floor. He had a second wind at five in the morning with some mellow sounds. Stephen woke up to the strains of Pink Floyd's 'Comfortably Numb'. He saw The Crow snoring, entwined with a Norwegian beauty. Jonny Rotten was standing nearby shaking his head. "Fucking Floyd, bunch of public school tossers, they are fucking history, who listens to guitar solos nowadays?"

Stephen nodded towards the DJ.

"Wanker," Rotten snarled before he ran up the shelter stairs.

In total they spent a kibbutz record of thirty-eight hours in the shelter. It was well into the following evening when they emerged, at least it was dark so they didn't have to worry about their eyes. As they went en-masse to the dining room the relief amongst the volunteers and the kibbutzniks was audible. Kids reunited with their parents and swapped stories, teenagers couldn't stop themselves shouting. Stephen saw the imposing figure of Boris destroying the buffet and they exchanged knowing glances. Avaram came over, "Have a good nights rest, come to our place seven am," he whispered.

His friend seemed to be enjoying his trip and Stephen was thankful his guest was spending the night in the Scandinavian block. He passed out on his bed in the clothes he'd worn down the shelter for two days.

Stephen had planned to shave, shower and change clothes in the morning but he overslept and had to run straight to Avaram's. Cheryl opened the door to him. "You're late," she said coldly. "Boris is in the car park, he's waiting for you," she stated and shut the door.

He paused for a few seconds and then ran through the kibbutz to the car park. He jumped in the open passenger door of the Jeep. Boris started the engine without speaking and they headed down the main road. "Where we going Boris?" Stephen asked.

"Haifa."

Stephen wondered why he seemed to be surrounded by people who spoke in mere syllables. Boris, Avi and The Crow were all verbally challenged, though the 'Big A' made up for all of them.

They arrived in a small town near Haifa, Boris turned into a ramshackle industrial estate and drove past all manner of factories and warehouses before they reached a dead end and stopped. Stephen could see a smouldering shell of a building surrounded by a barbed wire fence. Boris reached for a canvas bag on the back seat and took out a clumsy looking Polaroid camera, "Avaram's" he said, gesturing to the camera, "what a piece of shit."

"Bomb damage?" Stephen guessed, "I didn't think they could reach this far south."

"Not a bomb, wait here." The Russian didn't elaborate.

Stephen watched him take a few photos as he walked along the length of what he assumed had been a factory. He returned to the Jeep shaking the prints in an effort to make them develop quickly.

They then drove in silence to Haifa, where they turned into the city's hospital. Boris parked the vehicle and led a mystified Stephen down several corridors. He stopped by a room with Hebrew writing, which seemed to look important, and knocked on the door.

"I wait down there, take these," Boris said, handing him the Polaroid photos of the wrecked building. Stephen had just found a chair in the corridor when a familiar face opened the door.

"Avi," Stephen said, surprised.

"Come in Steve, I haven't got long, come with me."

He led him through another door that had a combination lock, Stephen knew immediately it was a mortuary. There were three bodies inside on steel trolleys, white sheets covered each of them. On the middle one was a small canvas bag that Stephen thought looked familiar.

"Okay," Avi said, "it's been an interesting few days."

Stephen nodded in agreement.

"So, Hank arranged to meet you in Rosh Pina with a letter." Avi put his hand out, Stephen pulled the Marvin's letter from his pocket and handed it to him. Avi read it quickly and placed it by the backpack. "So whilst Marvin recovered from his bump on the head, a Danish tourist staying at the Scanda hostel found this under a cabinet in the hallway near where our friend fell." Avi handed the bag to Stephen who shuddered as he pulled out a small handgun.

"Jesus Christ, it's Marvin's, he was going to-"

"Kill you," Avi interrupted, "and then sort Wayne according to the letter."

"Please tell me he's in custody," Stephen pleaded.

"Sorry, firstly you may have noticed we're at war, my bosses wanted this nonsense over, so I let him go with the intention of following him. But the attack on Iraq messed up my plans."

"But he wants to fucking kill me!" Stephen shouted in panic.

"Yes, exactly Steve, and he must have made contact with Hank because they were waiting to finish the job, but God works in mysterious ways." Avi pulled the sheets off two of the bodies, Stephen recognised them instantly.

Hank was on the first trolley, his face was badly burnt on one side but his Elvis quiff was unmistakable. Marvin was on the middle trolley, his mad stare no different to the last time they met, he went to pull the sheet off his torso but Avi stopped him.

"You don't want to look, trust me it's not pretty."

Stephen was shaking unable to speak from the shock.

"A direct hit on the bus station, they died instantly. You must have friends in the PLO, they've done us one hell of a favour."

Stephen looked at the third trolley, "Please don't tell me that's Wayne."

"Alas no." Avi sounded disappointed as he revealed the third victim was an Arab labourer from Nazareth. "Just a poor guy on his way to work in the wrong place at the wrong time, I'm not going to lift the sheet, his head was blown half off, it's not a pretty sight."

"So where's Wayne?" Stephen was regaining his composure.

"He's been deported back to the States," Avi confirmed.

"But Rachel Saltzman, you've seen this letter." Stephen handed over the letter from Rachel to Wayne. "My roommate is meant to get it to him."

Avi got out his lighter and ignited the letter. *What's good enough for Maurice*, Stephen thought.

"Finally, you have some photos for me," Avi remembered. He placed them on top of the poor Arab. "One last piece in the jigsaw Steve. This was a factory, can you guess what kind?"

Stephen shook his head clueless.

"It was used for the manufacture of fur coats."

It took a few seconds for Stephen to compute this information. "Marci's parents?" He said, still none the wiser.

"Neville from Liverpool," Avi replied.

"Neville?"

"Neville the communist, we thought he had a political affiliation with the Palestinians, he spent time in the West Bank, had a cousin interned in Belfast a few years ago for belonging to the IRA. We were more concerned about him than our friends here, but we fucked up."

"Fucked up?"

"We were set up, he was none of these things, we've been played."

"Played, who by?"

"Your Canadian nympho friend."

"Marci." Stephen guessed.

"Yep, the Englishman is not a member of the PLO, he's in the ALO, The Animal Liberation Organisation. Marci and Neville used the cover of the rocket shower to set fire to the fur factory and disappear."

"Marci colluded with the Scouser to burn her parents factory down."

"Seems that way, plus they helped themselves to a substantial amount of cash out of the factory safe!"

"What now?" Stephen asked.

"I'm going to take the rest of the day off," Avi quipped.

"What about me?"

"Well Steve if I were you I'd head back to London, I'm sure Mr. Saltzman will have plenty of work for you. Besides, after the Iraq business and today's fatalities it's going to be very lively, probably a war." Stephen knew Avi was not a man to exaggerate. "Two God fearing Americans were killed today, Washington will not give us a free hand, do yourself a favour go and pack."

PART THREE

21

THE 'GOOLY CHIT'
(2011)

The kids were on their third movie and Cassandra was away with the fairies, Stephen's mind moved from recollecting the dramas of '81 to mulling over his difficult relationship with his father. "The Impossible Alan Ross," Maurice Saltzman had described him as all those years ago. He liked to think he was the complete opposite of him in every possible way, he couldn't think of a single thing they had in common. He blamed his shyness and lack of confidence as a young man on his father being an overbearing control freak. Maybe in that aspect he could sympathise with Rachel Saltzman. He could never recall a time he loved his father or even respected him, he just feared him. His father's endless rants against the Jewish side of the family, whom had never accepted Stephen's mother, were full of bitterness and the grudge held for life.

As a young teen he gave up asking him for permission to go anywhere as it would be met with resounding no or ridiculous time constraints. Because of this he consciously disengaged from his father and learnt the dark arts of deceit. This came in handy when he found himself caught up in those shenanigans many years ago.

He'd tired quickly of his father repeating stories from the Second World War, except the one about the 'gooly chit'. There was one particular time this story was told after he found himself on the receiving end of his father's terrible temper.

****

Stephen had explained calmly that the goods had been delivered, signed and paid for so it wasn't important, but Alan Ross was in a strop for days over the missing delivery note, a worthless piece of bureaucracy, he just wouldn't let it go. After a few days Stephen told him to stuff the job and went to work on a scam with The Crow.

A few weeks later they ran into his father and older brother in Stanley's café, they reluctantly joined them and made small talk until Stan came to take their order.

"Hi Stevie, hear you've joined the family firm."

"I've sacked him!" Alan Ross roared.

"I resigned," Stephen countered.

"The thing is Stanley, the younger generation have no understanding of the importance of paperwork."

Stephen rolled his eyes.

"Paperwork is the cornerstone of any successful business Mr. Ross," The Crow interrupted, to the amazement of Stephen and his brother.

"Exactly young man, let me tell you something, when I was in the north west frontier in the Second World War," Stephen yawned as his father continued, "which is now Pakistan, there were a lot of dangerous tribes out there. They had a liking for capturing our lads tying them to a post, cutting their goolies off and stuffing them in their mouths. A British General came up with the brilliant idea of issuing every soldier with a piece of paper that, in twenty different dialects, said if they returned the captured soldier to the nearest British garrison, rather then cutting off their goolies, they would be rewarded with the King's gold sovereign. This document was affectionately known as a 'gooly chit' and you will appreciate why no 'Tommy' would go out without it. And that is why I'm so fucking fastidious with my paperwork!"

****

The pilot gave an update on their progress, they were approximately three hours from New York and weather conditions there were good. He mentioned a hurricane brewing off the coast of Florida as an afterthought. Stephen got up to let the Buble fan next to him squeeze past so she could go to the toilet. As soon as she was on her way Jonny took her seat. "I'm not used to fucking pleb class," he snarled, "been reminiscing have you? At least we had some fun back then, well, until you betrayed me for those wankers."

Rotten left him with his thoughts of those 'fun' days. His mind wandered back to the events that occurred after his conversation with Avi at the morgue.

****

As Boris drove him back from Haifa they talked about the looming war. Boris had been invited to be an officer in the bomb disposal unit. The mad Russian was quite excited by the idea. "After that, if I'm still alive, I leave this fucked up country for America."

Stephen let him know he was planning to slip away quietly and thanked him for saving his skin on more than one occasion. They arrived back as the sun set, he asked Boris to give his apologies to Avaram and Cheryl.

"What about the 'Big A'?" Boris asked.

"I'm gonna miss the big man," Stephen answered honestly.

"You think he's involved in the craziness Stevie?"

Stephen hesitated before answering carefully, "He's either the nicest fucking loon on the planet or he's the ring leader. Either way he's crazy."

Stephen found The Crow in-between Sonia and her roommate. "Get your pants on Dave, we're heading to the bright lights of Tel Aviv."

They collected their baggage quickly and headed out the kibbutz. "Fuck me Stevie, I've been in this country for five days and I ain't seen the sun yet."

They waited at the bus stop for a few minutes before a truck emerged from the kibbutz dirt road. Stephen held out an apathetic thumb and to his surprise the battered old vehicle stopped.

"Jump in Steve!" Yonatan the turkey manager shouted. "I will drop you off on the highway!"

On the way they reminisced about the night the roof fell in and Yonatan admitted that he didn't have a clue whether turkeys were attracted to red clothing. Stephen still swore that he would get revenge one day.

Once on the highway they knew it would be easier to hitch a lift to Haifa. Stephen thought about his morning at the hospital and the smouldering shell of Marci's parents' factory, he could still see the wild-eyed stare on Marvin's dead face. His morbid thoughts were interrupted by the shrill of a motorbike horn. The bike slowed and drew level with them.

"How the fuck are we both going to fit on there?" The Crow exclaimed.

Stephen recognised the machine, a Lambretta, before the driver took his helmet off. "Stevie, where you heading man?"

"TA. Good to see the beast back on the road Ronnie, I hear you had a good time mate."

Ronnie was curious to know how he knew about his trip.

"I ran into Sylvia on the beach on my way back up north, good luck to you."

"I'm on the way there now, meeting her on the usual stretch of beach, might catch you there buddy." With that the scooter revved off into the darkness.

They spent the night at Stephen's cousins, The Crow managed to behave himself, sleeping on his own for the first and last time on his holiday.

In the morning Stephen booked his flight home, the same flight as his friend, leaving in a couple of days time. They went to Stephen's favourite beach in the afternoon as The Crow was on a mission to go home with at least a bit of colour.

They were sat watching another glorious sunset when The Crow nudged Stephen. "There's your Lambretta mate over there."

Ronnie was strolling past, hand in hand with Sylvia. Stephen caught their attention and signaled them over. They engaged in some small talk before adjourning to a beach bar for cocktails. They spent the night barhopping and then gate crashed one of the dozens of beach parties that spontaneously sprang up during the Middle East's scorching heat waves.

Stephen sat supping on a bottle of local beer, content that he was out of rocket range and there were no mad Jews or Jesus freaks on his case. The Rachel episode was behind him. He briefly wondered about her whereabouts and where the hell Wayne was, but it wasn't his problem anymore.

He managed to persuade his pal to start the stroll back to their lodgings. It was three in the morning by the time they headed up the less salubrious end of Dizengoff Street. The Crow saw a bouncer outside a black door, he could hear the faint sound of disco music.

"This looks like our kind of place," he said.

There was a small neon sign flickering overhead. "Bar Exotic," Stephen read aloud, "classy."

Within five minutes Stephen sussed out the kind of establishment they were in and called it a night. He left The Crow making conversation with a heavily made up brunette. His mind went back a few months to Eric the locksmith and that mad night in Leeds.

He didn't see The Crow again until they met at the airport two days later. The queue for security was chaotic to say the least and Stephen was keeping an eye out for the elusive Crow. He looked at the sun-drenched taxi rank outside and felt a pang of regret that he was leaving this crazy place. He was, however, looking forward to getting back to his normal boring life, which seemed to have spiraled out of control since Peter Sutcliffe had been arrested. Of course he hadn't considered his father's own 'ripples'.

Suddenly, The Crow emerged out of the crowd. "Fuck me it's the Scarlett Pimpernel." Stephen noticed his exhausted looking friend had no luggage. "Where's your case?"

"Long story Stevie, that young lady you left me with only lived in an apartment above the bar! I spent most of the last two days there and when I said goodbye she asked for two hundred dollars!" The Crow sounded surprised.

"So at no stage did you suss out that the over painted, under clothed tart who lived over a dodgy bar was a prostitute?" Stephen laughed.

"I thought she was a nice Jewish girl," The Crow shrugged, "anyway, I had no cash left so that door man came and took my case!"

"Her pimp," Stephen confirmed, wondering just how naive his mate was.

They shuffled slowly towards the front of the queue, a female security officer barely out of her teens came and questioned them as to where they were flying and where they had been. "Where is your bag?" She asked The Crow.

"It was stolen in a bar," he replied. Stephen glared at his idiot friend.

"In a bar?"

"Yes it was stolen by a prostitute and her pimp," he confirmed all too honestly.

"Idiot," Stephen muttered to himself.

"Okay. Have a good flight," she casually told him. She then turned her attention to Stephen, "That scar looks new, how did that happen?"

Stephen tried to explain as simply as possible. She asked him to wait and then returned with a supervisor. "Could you come with us sir," he politely but firmly instructed.

They led him to a side room and put his bag on a metal table. "Shall I open it?" he offered.

"No sir, an officer will be here shortly," the supervisor confirmed.

Stephen was at a loss how The Crow had been sent on his way despite his dodgy answers but he was about to be interrogated, possibly strip-searched.

A stern, important looking soldier entered the room. He looked at Stephen's passport and gestured for the young lady and supervisor to leave the room. Stephen was suddenly very concerned. "Have you met this man during your stay here Mr. Ross?" He placed two photos of Avi on the suitcase, in one he was wearing sunglasses, the other not. Stephen swallowed and considered his answer. "Think very carefully before you answer Mr. Ross," the soldier advised.

Stephen studied the stars on his epaulets. "No I'm sorry," he replied hopefully.

"So," the soldier continued slowly and clearly, "you have never seen or met this man, yes or no?"

"No," Stephen confirmed.

"You have never spent time with this man in Haifa hospital have you?"

Stephen was sure this was a threat rather than a question, he could almost feel his inquisitors stare penetrating his gaze. "Yes or no?"

"No," Stephen replied with all the sincerity he could muster.

"Thank you for your time Mr. Ross, I'm arranging an upgrade to first class as a gesture of our appreciation for your cooperation, if I could just get you to sign this please." He placed an official document on top of the case, Stephen recognised it was similar to the one Marci had got him to sign. He briefly thought of the reward he got last time. A blowjob and an upgrade, not bad compensation for keeping secrets for several lifetimes.

"Do you read Hebrew Mr. Ross?"

Stephen shook his head.

"It's basically a medical form, as long as you stick to the answers you have given me you will continue enjoy full use of both testicles."

Stephen remembered his father's story. *I now have my own 'gooly chit'.* The soldier slowly picked up the photos of Avi and winked. "Have a good a flight Mr. Ross."

22

RIPPLES

Another of his father's traits that annoyed the hell out of him was his oft-repeated sayings he managed to introduce into every conversation. However there was one that resonated as he returned home first class, whilst The Crow was stuck in pleb class with a huge family of Hassidic Jews. 'The bigger the stone you drop in the water, the bigger the ripples'.

On the tube from Heathrow The Crow casually mentioned that Cassandra had left her job after the Harvey business. The Crow had phoned her and asked her out but she refused his offer of a night at the Camden Palace. Stephen was relieved that she had resisted The Crow's charms but was not at all comfortable with the news of her leaving the company. He would phone her as soon as he could to get the gossip.

As he entered his bedsit he felt a wave of uncertainty. He sifted through the pile of mail wondering if there was a message from Jan but to his relief there was nothing. The sky was grey and the air chilly compared to the Middle East, but no one was likely to come and bomb him, or for that matter shoot him. The room felt very empty without the 'Big A', Stephen, not for the first time, felt a pang of guilt for not saying goodbye to the big man.

After a week catching up with friends and family, Stephen arrived early at Saltzman HQ and found his 'recess' more or less unchanged. There was a long list of rents outstanding, at least two weeks work he reckoned. He noticed there was a new name on Harvey's office door, Colin Davis. *Never heard of him,* he thought. He didn't have to wait long to meet the new managing director though as the man's Mercedes roared into the car park.

"You're keen," he snapped at Stephen, who was admiring his car through the window.

Stephen noticed he was wearing a Saville Row suit. He introduced himself and was pleased to hear the new man knew all about him.

"You're a legend in these parts."

It was the last compliment he would get from Davis, who had been brought into the company to streamline everything from the accounts to the staff, who all seemed to fear him. Well nearly all, Stephen would soon discover there was one new member who answered to nobody, not even to Maurice Saltzman.

He hit the list of rent arrears with a new confidence, possibly born out of his recent adventures. He noticed that whoever the new receptionist was, she didn't bring him a cup of coffee at 10am like Cassandra used to. After hopefully positive outcomes to seven out of twelve calls he took a break.

Rotten was back, full of negativity. "You're back where you belong mate, planet tedium. Party's over mate, get on with your pathetic list, you're a fucking parasite."

Stephen turned to face his hero. "What do you mean 'parasite'?" He surprised himself with his bravery.

"There's a fucking depression out there, Saltzman tenants are hurting and the last thing they need is fucking 'scar face' on their case."

Stephen looked Rotten in his crazy eyes. "Fuck off Rotten you're history, you're a joke, you've done fuck all since the Pistols, you're nothing without Steve Jones, just fuck off and leave me alone. You're a has been."

Stephen's overdue rant was interrupted by his telephone, which he noticed had been upgraded in his absence.

"Hiya, call for you." The new receptionist's voice sounded younger but more refined than Cassandra's.

"Thank you, who is it?" Stephen enquired.

"I think he said his name was Eric Locksley."

Stephen laughed as he realised that she'd misheard 'locksmith'. "Eric, what's up?"

"Can I have your autograph mate?" The locksmith chortled.

They made arrangements to meet up for a night out before Stephen suggested, "Hopefully we'll be out on the road shortly."

"No chance mate, the new man Davis has dispensed with my services."

"Fucking hell Eric, I'm the last man standing."

"Yeah, watch your back mate, Davis is ruthless. I've got your girlfriend's new work number by the way."

"Girlfriend?" Stephen asked.

"Cass, she's got a decent job in Holborn, you better call her sharpish, there's a lot of competition there."

He gave Stephen the phone number and added, "What do you reckon about Cass's replacement, bit of a turn up eh?"

Davis entered the office without knocking, Stephen hung up abruptly.

The new manager went through a few of the new systems he'd implemented, Stephen took an instant disliking to him but would admit he was far more on the ball than Harvey. *Poor old Harvey, what the hell had he done to get sacked?*

It was just after midday, Stephen picked up the phone and buzzed the receptionist.

"Yes," she replied curtly.

Stephen decided to make an instant impression. "Two sugars please love and don't be to slow about it," he demanded.

There was a few seconds silence before the new girl replied. "Maybe you'd like something a little stronger for your leaving drink?"

There was a confidence in her voice that unsettled Stephen. "That's a no then," he countered.

"It's more than a no, it's a final warning, now get on with your fucking job."

She meant business. Stephen decided to restore his faith in receptionists and dialled the number Eric had given him. Cass' slightly cockney, "Allo," was reassuring.

"Cass, it's me, Stevie, I'm back."

"In one piece?" Cassandra enquired.

"Just about. Hey what's going on, why is there a hard nosed bitch breaking my balls here?"

"Quite a turn up Stevie but I can't talk now, can you call me back later."

"I can do better than that, how about that long awaited date? How about you give me all the goss over a Chinese on Friday night?"

"Sounds good, but I've told you before I don't two time and Friday night I'm out with Toby."

"Toby, who the…who is Toby and when you going to dump him?"

"He's my manager and has fallen in love with me and he has a racy sports car, so it's going to take quite an incentive to dump him."

"So we're talking Chinatown, not the 'Mandarin' Romford," Stephen concluded. *Toby*, he thought, *bit posh.*

He needed some air and a coffee desperately so he decided to take his lunch hour. As he walked through the reception, the new receptionist was bending over a bin sharpening a pencil. Her suit looked classy and expensive, the skirt was short, revealing legs that went on forever. He tried to slip out unnoticed but she turned quickly and caught his eye. She had her hair tied back in a bun, a pleasant face, no make up, she reminded him of a plainer version of Rachel Saltzman. "So you must be the guy who spends his day on line five in the alcove?" She could kill with one lash of her tongue.

"I think technically it's a recess rather than an alcove." Stephen wasn't sure where these lines came from. "I'm Steve," he muttered, his confidence draining as he looked into her un-missable deep green eyes.

"Hi, I'm Rachel, nice to meet you Steve."

Stephen didn't get his coffee, he sat against the wall by the car park trying to compute what had just happened. "What the fuck," he said aloud. A thousand thoughts went through his mind, many questions, no answers. *Did she know who he was?* He didn't think so. *Did she know he'd been to the kibbutz?* He wasn't sure, but he couldn't be sure about anything. *What do I do next?* He came to the conclusion to keep his head down, get on with his work and que sera, sera.

This plan lasted barely two days.

Stephen drove the company van into the car park for what he expected would be another day on 'planet tedium', as his old hero had described his future. He looked in envy as a black Porsche pulled up next to him. The driver's window opened, he was younger than him and looked vaguely familiar.

"You must be the legendary Steve Ross." The young man smiled.

"Legends are normally dead," Stephen replied.

"Jump in Steve."

The passenger door opened, he climbed in and admired the mean machine. "Nice motor mate."

"Twenty first birthday stroke first class honours degree present," the driver boasted in a cut glass public school accent. "Hi Steve, I'm Sam, Sam Saltzman."

The prodigal son, Stephen remembered, the eldest with the non-negotiable future. "Hi." They shook hands.

"I'm sure you've had it up to here with us Saltzmans, not least my sister." Samuel was obviously in the loop. Stephen noticed his eyes were red as if he'd been crying.

"Are you running the company now?" Stephen chanced.

"God no. I'm helping out for a few months before I return to Cambridge to do a masters. Daddy's given me responsibility for moving offices to our new HQ in Mayfair."

"Wow." Stephen was impressed.

"Well, daddy insists you get your own office as I hear you currently reside in the 'hole in the wall'."

"Sounds great, thanks."

"He greatly appreciates everything you've done in your brief but lively career thus far." Stephen warmed to Samuel's sincerity. "Some difficult news however, which is why I'm here Steve. Sadly uncle Harvey passed away last night."

There was a long awkward pause. Stephen was shocked, he recalled Maurice Saltzman's words just a week or so earlier, *He's dead to me.* "Blimey, I'm so sorry. How old was he?"

"Fifty two."

"Heart attack?" Stephen asked.

"Maybe," Samuel shrugged, "anyway you are aware that there's been a bit of a rift in the family and daddy insists we are not going the funeral today."

Stephen was bewildered to say the least.

"He'd like you to pick up Auntie Trudie and drive her to the cemetery and then back home, but not in that." He pointed at the company van.

"Harvey's wife?" Stephen had heard she was difficult.

"Yep, poor Auntie Trudie. You ever driven one of these?" Samuel asked offering the keys.

"Only in my dreams."

"Well you better get some practice, you can drive me home later and then pick Auntie T up."

Stephen had never actually been given a job description save for driving the horsebox, which up to now he'd never seen. Today would be another string to his bow. There were even more surprises in store as he drove Samuel home.

"Okay Steve keep your eyes on the road, I'm going to guess the questions you're itching to ask me," he stated as Stephen gripped the steering wheel. "When and why is Rachel home? She arrived last week from Morocco, we think she ran out of money and was ill. Why is she working in reception? It's temporary because you are taking her and the elusive horsebox to Berkshire on Monday. What happened to her planned rendezvous with her American boyfriend? No idea, but we know their last communication mentioned London. Why has Cassandra left us? No idea, we know you like her but it's tied up with the issue between daddy and Harvey, poor Harvey. I'm sorry I can't give you an answer to that one. Anything I've missed out?"

Stephen was trying to make sense of the information. "Does your sister know I was out there looking for her?"

"Good question, I don't think so, but of course it's likely she will find out soon enough so bear that in mind because daddy has a new proposition for you."

Shit, Stephen thought, *what next?*

He arrived at the Saltzmans home, relieved the car was in one piece. Samuel gave Stephen details regarding the funeral.

"You mentioned a proposition Sam?"

"Pick me up from here tomorrow eight sharp and I'll give you the details, one last thing Steve, do not engage with Auntie Trudie. Get her there, get her home, enjoy the car tonight."

Stephen carried out his task as instructed; Auntie Trudie never said a word on the way to the burial grounds or the journey home. As he came to a halt in her driveway she turned to him and said calmly, "I suppose they told you Harvey killed himself."

Stephen shook his head, not knowing what to say.

"They killed him," she continued, "those fucking Saltzmans, they killed my Harvey." She got out the car, leaving Stephen stunned. He felt the scar above his right eye twinge and thought about Marvin and his gun, this was one dangerous job.

"Don't just sit there mate, you've got a fucking Porsche to play with tonight." Jonny Rotten was in the passenger seat. "Let's hit the Kings Road," he suggested.

Stephen gave him short shrift. "Fuck off a Rotten, I told you, you're history."

He picked up The Crow, they christened the car the 'Black Stallion' and drove around town until the petrol gauge hit empty. He'd decided he liked Samuel. Rachel, not so much.

23

TIDAL WAVES

"I appreciate the opportunity Sam, but in light of recent events and in addition to the restructuring of the company I feel it's best for all concerned if I move on."

Stephen had spent the night parked near Hampstead Heath because he didn't feel such a car would survive a night unscathed in Bethnal Green. Also he wanted to spend as much time with the 'Black Stallion' as possible. He'd practiced and refined his resignation speech over and over since the small hours, he'd had enough of the Saltzman family and would take his chances joining The Crow in his latest scam, something to do with a revolutionary carpet-cleaning product.

He arrived at chez Saltzman at eight sharp, he was surprised to see Samuel waiting in the road. Stephen got out and handed him the key.

"Thanks Sam, I'm going to miss that beast," Stephen said genuinely.

"Pleasure Steve, apologies I've got to meet Colin Davis at the new offices in half hour so I'm rushing off. The gate's open, pop in, daddy would like to see you."

Stephen watched him roar off, he had the resignation speech on the tip of his tongue. Oh well, he only had to change the 'Sam' to 'Maurice' and he'd be free.

As he walked through the gate into the circular driveway, hidden from the road by several large conifers, he was surprised to see a shiny new horsebox parked up. His boss opened the door himself, greeting Stephen warmly and taking him to the kitchen. They sat opposite each other on high stools at the breakfast bar. Mr. S poured him a fresh filter coffee.

"Before you offer your resignation Steve." He startled Stephen with his opening gambit. *Was he a mind reader? Was the 'Black Stallion' wired for sound?* "I have a proposition for you. But I'd understand if you've had enough of us Saltzmans."

He was very perceptive Stephen thought. He started his well-rehearsed speech, "Well I-"

"Let me cut to the chase young man, we are surprised and delighted our daughter is home, I'm aware this may be temporary, she could fly the nest at any time. As you know there are certain things I can't divulge." Stephen remembered the burning letter. His boss continued, "Rachel has negotiated her future and due to unforeseen circumstances I've had to compromise. So let me put this to you, obviously the five grand reward is null and void, but I can offer a lot better than that. Firstly, as of today, every month that my daughter remains within the faith you can enjoy your flat rent-free. On top of that I'll give you an extra twenty pounds a week cash whilst she remains at home. Lastly, if she marries within the faith I will give you the freehold to the flat with the proviso that when I say 'within the faith' I don't include converts Steve, with respect to your good self. Two Jewish parents is a must."

Stephen wondered whether Saltzman had lost his mind, there was no sign of him being drunk but it was only half eight in the morning.

"Even if you decide my business isn't for you and you wish to go your own way, I'm happy to shake on the proposition anyway."

Stephen quickly realised this was maybe a win-win situation, work with The Crow and keep an eye on the princess.

"I was hoping you'd drive Rachel, and her horsebox, to pick up her horse in Berkshire and take them to stables near Cambridge today, what are your feelings Steve?"

Steve tried to recall the resignation speech, now more confused than ever. "Do I tell your daughter about my trip to the Kibbutz?" He asked.

"You're free to employ any tactics you deem necessary."

"I have to clarify one thing that's troubling me Maurice."

"Harvey." Saltzman read his mind correctly again. "He took an overdose."

"Trudie said you were responsible." Stephen was frank.

"No Steve, he took his own life because he couldn't live with what he'd done. I don't want to hear his name again, end of!"

Stephen realised he would have to forever remain curious and decided to give his resignation speech and tell Maurice Saltzman where to stick his proposition, this was madness. Rachel Saltzman entering the kitchen bedecked in her riding gear interrupted his moment of clarity though. She headed for a low cupboard to look for some shoe polish, Stephen was transfixed by her skin tight jodhpurs.

"Okay Maurice you've got yourself a deal," he whispered, shaking his hand whilst feeling slightly ashamed that Rachel Saltzman's shapely behind was the deal clincher.

"Rachel darling, you've met Steve, he's going to drive you to collect Sunbeam."

"Sure, hi Steve, I've just got to get a few things and I'll be down," she said in a matter of fact fashion.

"One more thing Maurice, could Cass have her job back?" Stephen asked hopefully

"You can invite her back Steve but I'd be surprised if she wants to return. I'll put Colin in the picture on all matters, I'm going to join Hillary who's taking some time out in Herzliya. Best of luck young man."

There was little chitchat on the way to pick up Sunbeam, Stephen was frustrated the horse box had to be driven so slowly after racing around in the 'Black Stallion'.

He managed a few horsey questions on the way home but Rachel seemed distant and distracted.

He spent the next week either chasing rent arrears or driving Rachel to and fro. He had the small satisfaction of reflecting on the fact she was still Jewish!

The move to the swanky new offices in Mayfair arrived but Cassandra resisted both the temptation to return to the company and go on that elusive date with Stephen. He was quite enjoying life on 'planet tedium', until Samuel popped into his new office.

"Congratulations Steve on your first rent-free month and agreed bonus." Stephen was a little embarrassed as Sam handed over his pay envelope.

"Daddy called me last night a little concerned to report that our friend Avi has been suspended pending an inquiry."

"An inquiry, what for?" Stephen answered, feeling uneasy.

"We're not sure, daddy didn't want to elaborate, he will no doubt bring you up to speed but he specifically asked me to tell you."

Stephen had had a bad feeling since he left the 'silent assassin' in the mortuary. Samuel sensed his disquiet.

"Daddy did mention that the family of the chap who my sister was caught up with are kicking up a fuss, apparently they've not heard from him since he left Jerusalem."

"Wayne?" Stephen offered.

"That's the chap, I understand you met him Steve, what did you make of him?"

"Yeah I met Wayne, cunning, he's very cunning." Stephen paused for reflection. "Avi told me he'd been deported back to the States."

"Do you think he's on his way here Steve?"
"Maybe," Stephen replied, "I'll find out soon enough."
"How?"
"Simple, I'll ask your sister."

A couple of days later Stephen drove Rachel up to the stables, it was a long boring day, he'd hung around for hours whilst she put Sunbeam through his paces. They were on their way back, winding through a picturesque village, when Stephen made his move, swerving the van into the car park of a country pub.

"What the fuck are you up to Steve?" Rachel protested.

"You're clearly not happy with life Rachel, I'm going to treat you to a drink, maybe some pub grub. Anyway, I'm starving."

"Excuse me, your job is to simply drive me around. Now get back on the road please."

"I just think you need to lighten up," Stephen suggested.

"Now listen and listen carefully. You will take me home immediately, you are way out of your league." Rachel was now furious.

Stephen decided to throw some bait. "Is it because I'm only half Jewish Rachel?"

"What the fuck are you on about, fucking drive!" She screamed.

"The fact that my mum's not Jewish." Stephen was enjoying this, Rachel was at the point of exploding.

"Drive or I'll make sure you're fucking sacked you idiot!"

Stephen feigned to turn the ignition but stopped in half turn, just as Rachel assumed she'd got her own way.

"I know why you're so miserable Rachel and I understand totally."

She was so angry she could no longer find the words, her cheeks were red with rage. "What-"

"You're worried that you've not heard from your boyfriend for ages." He stared into Rachel's green eyes and tried not to flinch as she slapped his face.

"What did you fucking say?" She could barley comprehend what she'd heard, Stephen calmly decided to play his ace card.

"You've not heard a word from Wayne for weeks."

Rachel stared at him with her mouth wide open, her cheeks, red with rage, instantly turned a ghostly white.

"You need to calm down Rachel, let's go in for a drink and I'll tell you all about my meeting with Wayne in Jerusalem."

Rachel was clearly confused and Stephen could see tears in her eyes. He made his way out the van and came round to open the passenger door. Rachel climbed out in a trance and followed him into the pub.

They found a discrete alcove and Stephen purchased a bottle of red. As he filled Rachel's glass he recalled The Crow claiming that Jewish girls couldn't take their drink. He explained how her parents were out of their minds with worry and asked him to help find her. He tried to be honest, allowing for one or two omissions.

He told her about the road trip and how he ran into Wayne by coincidence. She tried to listen calmly but couldn't contain herself. "Wayne was really worried about Hank and Marvin, he was paranoid about them, you don't think they've hurt him do you?"

"You haven't heard?"

"Heard what?" She said frantically.

"About Hank and Marvin?" Stephen remembered that it turned out they were using aliases and even though the bombing made the BBC news, their real names were used.

"What about them?" She repeated.

"They're dead."

Rachel stared at Stephen for several seconds, tears began streaming down her cheeks.

"The bombing in Rosh Pinna, that was them, the two Americans, it was Hank and Marvin. They're not their real names." He was about to tell her he saw them in the mortuary but held that info back.

"My God, I can't believe it." She started sobbing.

Stephen got her to have a gulp of wine hoping it might calm her down.

"Are you sure Wayne was deported, how do you know?" She said, trying to compose herself as some regulars entered the bar.

Stephen didn't want to mention Avi. "That's what they said on the kibbutz, the authorities told them." He tried to sound convincing.

Rachel was knocking back the wine, she suddenly grabbed Stephen's hand. "Steve you've got to help me find Wayne, you have to."

"What can I do, I've no idea where he lives, you know more than me, where were you supposed to meet him?"

"Firstly Morocco, then he said Delhi, but my money ran out and I was ill, I had to get home. So he said he'd come to London, but that was weeks ago and…"

Stephen noticed she was as desperate to find Wayne as her father had been to find her. It was funny how a family that seemingly had everything was so miserable.

"Well maybe he's lying low after all the drama and will be in contact shortly." Stephen tried to be positive.

"Maybe, Wayne doesn't realise Hank and Marvin are dead, maybe he's worried they're looking for him."

"It's possible, but I still don't know what I can do to help."

"You were happy to help my dad, why can't you help me?"

"Your dad is my boss, he pays my wages," Stephen replied.

"I'll pay you more Steve."

"What with? You just said you ran out of money."

"That was before I told him about, about…" She hesitated, deciding not to finish the sentence.

Stephen realised it was time to play another ace. "Before you told your father about your uncle?" He waited for the explosion, it wasn't short in coming, Rachel got up and stormed out of the pub.

Stephen wasn't sure where she'd run to but he was confident she'd return to the van so he waited calmly in the driver's seat.

Five minutes later she climbed into the passenger seat. "Take me home please."

Stephen had seen everything he needed to know in the anguish in Rachel's eyes at the mention of Harvey. He decided there and then he wouldn't mention his name again, there was no need, he didn't need to read those burning pages to know why her father would give his daughter anything she desired to ensure her silence.

They drove home in silence until they reached the Saltzmans home. "I can't stay here tonight Steve, please let me stay at yours."

24

PLANET TEDIUM

Stephen sat with his back to the wall as Rachel slept soundly in his bed. He thought about the last time he was in this position, surveying the post orgy mayhem in the Leeds hotel. She lay face down fully clothed, Stephen was turned on by her figure hugging jodhpurs. *Is there was any tactical benefit in taking advantage*, he thought. *Probably not, not yet, but who knows.*

"You going to just sit there then?" Rotten sat on the edge of the bed. "How many chances does a civilian like you get to fuck a princess," he jibed.

"I thought I told you to fuck off," Stephen replied.

"Well I don't see any of your other heroes about so you're stuck with yours truly."

"Just wait and see mate." Stephen blinked and the 'has been' was gone.

Where was Wayne? Why hadn't he been in touch? If he was going to keep Rachel Jewish he needed to find out.

He spent the next few months chasing debts from his plush new office, driving Rachel and Sunbeam to and from competitions and writing letters to various different places looking for info on Wayne.

He'd plotted with Samuel to try and find Rachel a nice Jewish boy but all attempts failed miserably. With every passing week Stephen enjoyed the status quo and Rachel got more desperate.

'Planet Tedium' rotated slowly until he received a letter, hand delivered to his bedsit. The Hebrew writing on the A4 sheet looked horribly familiar and he noticed an official looking seal in the right hand corner. Under the line where he'd twice signed his signature was written in red pen.

HOW TO KIDNAP A STRING QUARTET

Saturday, Brighton Pier, 11.00 Am.

Shit, Avi. Stephen was worried, but at the same time excited, he'd not heard anything about the 'silent assassin' since Samuel had told him he'd been mysteriously suspended.

He phoned The Crow and arranged a weekend on the south coast. They enjoyed a Friday night of drinking, clubbing and general mayhem. Stephen woke up in their sparse B&B with a massive hangover and no sign of The Crow who'd disappeared with a young lady he met on the dance floor.

A cold shower, a fry up and a bracing walk along the promenade brought Stephen back to life. He reached the pier dead on eleven. He felt nerveless due to recent experience and because he'd taken a couple of 'blues' he'd scored in the club.

He strolled past the arcades and seafood stalls, the wind was so strong it was difficult to walk. He reached the funfair at the end of the pier but there was no sign of the silent assassin in his trademark sunglasses. He strolled back towards the promenade stopping at an empty bench and waited for what seemed an age. A young woman appeared, she was wearing a parker with the furry hood protecting her from the weather. She sat down beside him. "You're disappointed," she said, taking the wind literally out of his sails.

It took a few seconds for him to recognise the accent. She removed her hood. "Hi Steve. You're disappointed it's not Avi," she said again.

Steve continued to sit dumbstruck. "Marci, what the fuck you doing here?" He wasn't expecting to ever see the Canadian again.

"Don't worry I'm not here to burn the pier down," she joked casually.

"Well this is an unexpected pleasure Marci."

"I hope so Steve, let's get our business out the way then maybe we can have some pleasure." She winked.

"What the hell you doing here Marci?"

"Laying low, hiding." She replied.

"From Avi?"

"No, from Neville."

"Where is he?"

"On the run."

"Who from? Why?"

"The Police. He's a fanatic"

"Fanatic about animals?" Stephen assumed.

"Everything, I thought it was animals, which is why I colluded with him but he's basically an anarchist, he's an attention seeker."

"You've fallen out with him then?"

"Big time."

"Why?"

"I was happy to help him burn my parents factory down but I couldn't abide his next plan, it's a step too far."

"What was he planning?"

Marci shook her head and paused a few seconds. "To kidnap a scientist from a animal testing lab and conduct experiments on him."

"Fucking hell! That's what the Nazis did. What was your roll to be?"

"Film it." Marci was very matter of fact.

Stephen couldn't get his head around this scenario. "So how'd you get out of it?"

"Someone tipped off the police." She looked Stephen in the eye, he didn't need to press her on this.

"So where's Neville now?"

"He scarpered before the authorities could get to him, I think he's in Europe somewhere, that's one of the reasons I wanted to meet you." Marci winked.

"Go on," Stephen prompted her.

Before she could continue a passerby interrupted them. "Stevie boy!" The Crow shouted as he strolled along the pier with the previous night's conquest.

There was an exchange of small talk and introductions (vague in Stephen's case) before Marci suggested they adjourn to her B&B.

After reacquainting in bed for a couple of hours they shared a couple of beers and a joint. "So apart from missing my body why did you lure me to stony Brighton?" Stephen asked.

"First, how's your search for Rachel, Steve?"

Stephen told her the whole story including the 'proposition'.

"Good God Steve you should marry her, you'd get a property, bonus for life and a sexy Jewish princess."

"And a horse," Stephen added, "problem is I'm not a hundred percent kosher."

"You've had the snip." Marci laughed.

Stephen paused for thought, "Two questions Marci, where the hell is Wayne and why is Avi suspended?"

"That's why I'm here Steve," Marci answered cryptically.

"I haven't a clue where Wayne is but I have a feeling Neville does," she added.

"Neville?"

"Neville had a call from Wayne a few months ago, Wayne was terrified, I don't know what happened between Avi and him but according to Neville, Wayne was going to lay low for five lifetimes."

Stephen reflected on Avi's interrogation of Marvin. "Avi is very persuasive, I can vouch for that."

"I don't know why Avi's been suspended, but I would guess it's something to do with Wayne, or possibly me," Marci stated.

"You?"

"Avi recruited me to keep an eye on Neville because of some kind of the Irish shit and then we go off and burn my parents factory down. I know he's seriously pissed off with me, Avi's not the kind of man who would take betrayal lying down."

"Yep, you're not Avi's favourite," Stephen confirmed, "What's with the Irish shit?"

"Can't go there Steve, not important. I need you to help me." She put her hand on Stephen's heart. "I need you to go and talk to Avi, I need you to return to Tel Aviv."

"What?" Stephen was taken aback.

"I'm wanted for arson so I can't go there myself. I need you to go on vacation and explain to Avi I didn't betray him."

"Who's going to pay for my holiday and well, yes you did betray Avi," Stephen pointed out.

"Firstly Steve, you tell your Jewish princess you have a lead that her Wayne is back in Israel and you need some funds to go check it out. Secondly, I didn't betray Avi, my parents did!"

****

Three weeks later Stephen found himself on his usual spot on Tel Aviv beach, appreciating how much sandier and hotter it was than Brighton. He thought about Marci, so sexy but so devious. He wouldn't trust her as far as he could throw her but he was grateful to her for disrupting 'planet tedium'. He had no trouble convincing Rachel he needed funds to globe trot in the hunt for Wayne. He was so successful that he managed to persuade her he'd need to take a minder.

He'd arranged to meet Samuel in a cocktail bar in Soho to discuss a particularly bad debt and to confirm holiday dates.

Whilst sat deep in conversation Stephen noticed a familiar face at the bar, when the opportunity arose he'd excused himself and made his way over to where two smartly dressed pretty young ladies were chatting.

"Hi Cass." Stephen put his hand on her shoulder, his heart was beating faster than normal.

"Steve, how you doing?" Cassandra smiled. They engaged in some small talk whilst her friend visited the 'small' room.

"How's Toby?" Stephen cheekily enquired.

"He's in Singapore for three months, taking care of a merger."

"That's good, we can have that date then." Stephen chanced his arm.

"Technically I'm still going out with him," she laughed.

"I think you'll find that according to the Queensbury dating rules, anything longer than two months renders the relationship temporally null and void." Sometimes even he believed his own bullshit.

"Is that right, well you better come up with something special after so many crushing disappointments." She cheekily suggested.

"How about a week in the sun?" Stephen explained he was being sent to Tel Aviv by the Saltzmans and was being given enough money to take a guest. "If you turn me down I'll have to take The Crow," he protested.

"Let me sleep on it, I'd have to tell my mum that I'm going to Greece or something," Cassandra said.

Stephen was a little surprised she was capable of deceit. "Why's that Cass?"

"Because my mum wouldn't be happy me going to Israel."

"I can assure you Tel Aviv is perfectly safe, we won't be going anywhere near the Lebanon border," Stephen reassured her.

"It's not that, she just hates Israel and Jews."

Cassandra's reply shocked him. "Wow, what does she think about the Saltzmans?"

"I won't go there."

"Perhaps I should invite your mum instead," Stephen joked.

"That would be ironic. I'll call you tomorrow."

Despite the drama and intrigue Stephen had experienced since starting his new career nothing got his heart pounding more than being in the presence of Cassandra. He hoped he'd sleep well so tomorrow would come quickly, but he didn't, too much was happening. Rachel, Marci, and now Cassandra, it was messing with his mind.

Morning came slowly but the postman brought an unexpected surprise in the shape of a wedding invitation from the 'Big A'. A weekend in New York, wow, that's a thought.

The accompanying letter was full of tittle-tattle from the big man's last days at the kibbutz, Stephen felt guilty he'd left without saying goodbye after the mortuary business. He was relieved there was no reference to any of the craziness.

He was still plotting and planning about replying positively to Alberto's invitation when Cassandra called him to confirm their first date.

He sent an acceptance to the wedding invitation. A few days later he received a letter from his old roommate asking Stephen to come over and stay with him and his wife-to-be for a couple of weeks before the wedding, so he could show him around the 'Big Apple'. Alberto also mentioned he'd sent an invitation to Wayne via the 'post restante' in Casablanca and his family address in Oklahoma. He'd also had word from Ronnie that his book 'Around The World by Lambretta' had been published and that he'd moved to Boston. This was manna from heaven to Stephen who having persuaded Rachel to finance his (and Cassandra's) trip to Israel now had multiple possibilities open to him.

A new hero suddenly joined him. "How you doing buddy, looking forward to showing you around New Jersey." What a nice guy 'The Boss' is, Stephen thought, though he wasn't looking forward to Rotten finding out about his new friend.

25

DATE NIGHT

Not many first dates start with a 4am pick up. Stephen and Cassandra had made a pact they wouldn't strike up a conversation until their flight took off at 7. Stephen was looking forward to really getting to know Cassandra during the five-hour flight, but during take off she announced, "I don't do mornings," closed her eyes, and slept for the entire flight.

However, Stephen had the rest of their day carefully planned. His cousin Mark would pick them up from the airport and deposit them at Stephen's favourite spot on the beach. They would then enjoy some lunch, go home for a siesta and head out for a night on the town. It had been a good idea, but the best laid plans...

They approached a female passport control officer who looked casually at Cassandra's passport before stamping it. She seemed to study Stephen's more cautiously, constantly referring to a folder with a seemingly long list of names. "What is the purpose of your visit Mr. Ross?"

"Holiday, visiting my cousin," Stephen answered, half true.

She asked where they were staying and made a note of the address before asking him to wait a moment. She disappeared and returned with an older women in plain clothes.

"Could you follow me Mr. Ross," she said politely but sternly.

Cassandra followed nervously, the woman said she was free to go if she wanted but Stephen explained they were together. Cassandra was to wait on a bench outside a side room, the same room Stephen was taken to before. He was told to wait and wait he did, locked alone in the room, more concerned about Cassandra than himself. He wondered if Mark would be pacing up and down outside in the arrivals lounge.

It was a good hour before the women returned, telling him someone would be along immanently and that she'd explained to his friend there was a problem with his passport and had escorted her to the luggage belt. He was relieved when she confirmed Cassandra had found his cousin Mark.

"What's wrong with my passport?"

"Nothing," she replied locking the door as she exited again.

Half an hour later the door opened and a familiar figure entered. It was the thickset soldier with the fancy epaulets, who made him sign the 'gooly chit' when he exited the country previously. "We meet again Mr. Ross."

Stephen saw a telephone on the desk and demanded to phone his cousin. To his surprise his inquisitor gestured to the phone. "Be my guest."

Stephen spoke to Mark who'd just got home, he reassured Stephen they would take care of Cassandra. Stephen gave some bullshit about problems with his passport.

"Sorry to keep you, but I was wondering if you've seen or heard anything of my friend who you never saw at the Haifa Hospital?"

"No," Stephen replied honestly.

"He's been suspended from his duties and has disappeared, I thought you might know where he is."

"I haven't got a clue," Stephen confirmed.

"He's my friend Stephen," the soldier said in a sincere voice, which reassured him.

"Why has he been suspended?" Stephen asked.

"Politics," the 'general' replied, "a missing American's family have kicked up a stink and the embassy is on our case, so the powers that be have made my friend a scapegoat as he was the case officer."

"So why am I here?" Stephen protested.

"In case you have any information that can help our friend."

Stephen paused, he thought briefly about the third body in the mortuary. "No I can't but I suppose the answer is to find the missing American," Stephen suggested.

His inquisitor concurred and offered him a lift to his cousin's, which Stephen gladly accepted.

They discussed various scenarios on the half hour journey to his cousin's. As they came to a halt Stephen weighed up whether this important soldier was truly on Avi's side.

"Where do you think your friend is?" He asked.

"Well, the powers that be have confiscated his passport, but that wouldn't hold my friend back, he's very resourceful. Maybe he's looking for the American or maybe the Canadian chick, who I believe you know. She seriously pissed him off."

Stephen paused before taking a chance. "Yes, Marci, I know her and if you by any chance hear from your friend please be sure to tell him the fire has nothing to do with animal rights, it was arranged as an insurance scam by her parents."

Stephen's cousin explained he'd dropped Cassandra at the beach (usual spot) so he jumped in a cab, wondering what the chances were of his pretty date not being chatted up by a local. *Bees round a honey pot*, he thought. He walked around for a good ten minutes as the sun started to set, but there was no sign of Cass. He started to get concerned as different scenarios went round in his head. *Had she got fed up and headed home? Maybe a fit young Israeli beach guy has taken her for a drink?* His last thought was Avi. *Had his friend from the airport tipped him off? Had Avi decided to ruffle his feathers?*

He spotted the Danish waitress that normally served up his cold beers at his favourite beach bar. He described Cassandra, particularly her long dark brown hair, the waitress acknowledged him immediately.

"Yes, very nice pretty English girl," she confirmed, "she was pestered by guys from the moment she sat on that deck chair over there. In the end an older guy who'd been sitting nearby cleared some guys off and I saw him apologising. They left together about half an hour ago."

"What did he look like?" Stephen asked frantically.

"Late thirties, slim, dark, sunglasses."

"Shit!" Stephen cursed and legged it from the beach in panic.

He decided to head for the trendy bar area he knew Avi liked to frequent, it was only a few minutes walk away. *What was his game?* Until his meeting with Marci in Brighton he'd had no angst with him. Stephen was sweating by the time he reached the north end of Dizengoff Street. He checked out bar after bar, with no luck. He spotted a cab and wondered if he should head back to cousins but decided to phone Mark instead from a phone box. There was no answer. *Why didn't I take Cass for a drink in Covent Garden?*

He had walked almost half mile out of town when he saw a trendy café across the street. He could see all the outside tables were taken by young couples. His heart missed a beat as he noticed Cassandra sitting on a corner table engaged in conversation with a man. He hesitated for a second before crossing the road, the man had his back to him. When he got to the café he caught Cassandra's eye. "Stephen!" She shouted in a mixture of relief and guilt.

He ignored her as he was closing in on Avi. The man turned casually in his chair and extended his hand whilst removing his shades. "Hi, I'm Yakov," he said, as Stephen realised it wasn't the 'silent assassin'. He was so relieved that he didn't particularly care about their excuses as they explained how she'd been harassed by the beach bums from the moment she'd arrived and that Yakov had decided to rescue her.

"I'm going to go and see friends now," he said offering his seat, "Cass is a very nice girl my friend, I'd keep her close if I was you." He winked as he said his goodbyes.

"I should have taken you to Covent Garden for our first date. What a day." Stephen laughed.

They spent a few moments reflecting on what had been a very strange first date. Stephen claiming he was the victim of mistaken identity at the airport. "I'll have to draw my scar on my passport photo," he joked.

They dined in a 'Yemenite' restaurant, the conversation flowed easily from the Saltzmans to Cassandra's racist mother and Stephen's difficult relationship with his father. "So I take it Toby knows where you are and who you're with?" Stephen asked eventually.

"God no," Cassandra replied. "I haven't technically dumped him yet, you are on trial and so far I'm far from impressed," she said matter of factly.

"The night is but young, besides what's he got that I haven't?"

Cassandra paused for thought and pretended to count her fingers. "Well, where do I start, you have a company van, Toby drives brand new BMW soft top." She threw down the challenge to Stephen.

"That means he must have a very small penis," he joked.

"Well if yours is half the size of Toby's I'll be impressed," she replied without her expression changing. "Plus he has an apartment overlooking the Thames."

"So apart from his kick ass pad, super car and massive cock, he's no match for me," Stephen exclaimed.

Cassandra smiled and took his hand. "You've got five days to persuade me to cancel my next trip, which is to Singapore."

They took a taxi to the beautiful old city of Jaffa where they strolled hand in hand along the narrow streets. They found a bench with a panoramic view of Tel Aviv, lit up like a Christmas tree. They sat there for a couple of hours enjoying the view and both discussing their angst with their families. Cassandra never knew her father and wished she didn't know her mother. Stephen couldn't imagine how such dysfunctional parents could have produced someone so lovely.

Their was a natural pause in the conversation, Stephen glanced at Cassandra and she looked back at him. He took his chance and leaned in for their first passionate kiss. Stephen felt dizzy whilst they kissed, he'd never wanted something to work so much. In that moment he briefly forgot about why he'd come back to the holy land in the first place.

It was almost three in the morning when they decided to get a taxi back to Mark's. "I'll get this," Cass said as they sat in the back of the cab, she rustled through her handbag. "Shit," she cursed, "my purse is missing!"

"Yakov," Stephen guessed.

"You think?" She didn't rule the idea out of hand.

Stephen suggested they go back to the café on the off chance it was still open and instructed the driver accordingly. The cab cruised down the maze of back streets that linked Jaffa and Tel Aviv.

"Are you on holiday?" The driver enquired.

"Yes, why?" Stephen asked.

"Because I think there's someone following us."

Stephen and Cassandra looked round and saw a car some thirty metres behind, just as the cab reached the café and parked outside. "Shit," they said in unison. Stephen noticed the car behind had come to a halt, there were two men inside. They decided to go on to his cousin's and return the next afternoon on the off chance she'd dropped her purse.

"What was in it?" Stephen asked.

"Around hundred pounds in cash and two hundred in travellers cheques."

"Bastard," he said. He noticed the car behind was on the move. "Do us a favour mate, pull up again and see if that car stops."

The cabbie slammed on his breaks and a few seconds later the car passed, Stephen sighed with relief but then they were alarmed to see it park at a bus stop further up the road. He noticed a familiar bar adjacent to where they'd stopped, Club Exotic's garish neon sigh flickered above the black door. He recalled his previous visit to this decadent establishment with The Crow.

"Fancy a drink Cass, this place is open all night."

They paid the driver and rang the buzzer. Stephen glanced up the road, the mystery car was still parked at the bus stop.

"I must warn you Cass this place is full of pimps and prostitutes, The Crow was here for days."

Cassandra gave a knowing eyebrow raise. The bouncer led them down the steps into the seedy basement bar. Within seconds an excited patron embraced Stephen. "Stephen, how are you?"

Cassandra stepped back as the young woman pressed her exposed ample cleavage against him. He managed to break from the clinch. "Sylvia, what the hell you doing here? This is my friend Cassandra."

They said there hellos and Sylvia offered to buy them a drink. "Pimps and prostitutes hey," Cassandra repeated sarcastically.

He explained about Sylvia's big shot music producer father, he guessed she was not in a good place. She brought the drinks over.

"What the hell you doing in this dump Sylvia?" He asked frankly.

"Well I came back to my boyfriend's apartment earlier than expected and found him with someone else," she explained.

"Oh dear," Stephen said with genuine sympathy.

"Yes, he had another man's cock in his mouth," she said matter of fact.

"Oh dear," Cassandra chipped in.

"He threw me out on the street without any of my stuff," she continued sadly.

The bouncer interrupted them, demanding Sylvia go and look after a couple of Russian businessmen.

Stephen told Cassandra about the road trip, well the first part, and how he felt sorry for her. *She should have stuck with Ronnie*, he thought.

"Shit." Cassandra interrupted his thoughts. "Look over there, it's him, Yakov!"

They saw him on the other side of the circular bar, sitting on a bar stool talking casually to a barmaid.

"What should we do?" Cassandra pondered.

Stephen noticed Yakov's jacket hanging on the chrome stand on the back of his stool. "Okay Cass, you go and chat to him and deflect his attention whilst I search his jacket."

"I can't do that!"

"Why not? He doesn't know you know your purse has gone."

Cassandra paused for a few seconds. "Come on then, but be subtle."

They shuffled through the throng and separated as they neared the suspected thief. "Hi Yakov," Cassandra put her hand on his upper arm and smiled, "fancy seeing you again."

"Cass, hi, what you doing in this dive?" He seemed surprised and a little nervous, embarrassed even.

Stephen waited till they were deep in conversation, slipping behind his stool and gingerly searching the inside pockets. He felt a chunky wallet and nervously yanked it out struggling to stuff it in his shorts pocket before shuffling to the toilet where he was greatly relieved to see the solitary cubicle empty.

Meanwhile in the bar Cassandra was inventing a story about how she and Stephen enjoyed an open relationship, which more than caught Yakov's attention.

A young Israeli girl interrupted them. "Excuse me, you were in the café I work in before." Both of them recognised the waitress and confirmed that they were indeed her customers. "I'm so pleased I've run into you. I don't know if you've noticed your purse is missing but I found it on the floor where you were sitting."

Cassandra felt hot and confused but made a fair job of looking in her bag and feigning surprise. "My God, thank you so much." Cassandra hugged the waitress but felt a surge of panic remembering Stephen had taken Yakov's wallet, albeit with honest intentions.

"It's in the till, you can come for coffee when we open," the waitress said.

Meanwhile Stephen sat on the toilet seat and emptied the contents of the wallet. There was approximately two thousand shekels in cash, he tried to do a quick conversion but decided to take back half, which he stuffed in his jeans pocket. There were no travellers cheques. He started to put everything back in the wallet, credit cards, receipts, some photos.

He briefly glanced at one of Yakov, with what he assumed to be his father. He was careful not to crease it. He came across what looked like a warrant card, on examination he was sure the crest on the corner was the same as the 'gooly chit'. Last was a handwritten note in Hebrew with two photos stapled to it. He wished his father had sent him to Hebrew classes when he was younger, he felt such an outsider not knowing the language of his ancestors, but then again he was the only boy to fail his French GCSE at school. He glanced at the two photos and panic took a hold of him. He wiped his eyes in disbelief, one was of him showing his passport at Tel Aviv airport, the other was of Cassandra taken from the same security camera.

26

FAVOURS

"Where the fuck is he?" Stephen yelled as he re-emerged into the bar area.

"Steve, you won't believe it." Cassandra explained about the waitress and said Yakov had gone outside for some air.

"Hang on here Cass, I'll tell him he dropped his wallet, it happens," he smiled.

He could see the car that had followed them parked some fifty meters up the road as he exited the bar. He walked briskly towards it, as he drew nearer he could make out three figures inside. They obviously noticed him and started to pull away into the traffic, which luckily was too heavy for a quick get away. Stephen got to the curb and waved Yakov's wallet frantically in the air. Just as the car was slipping away, it slammed its breaks on and the cars behind hooted in unison. Stephen crouched down and placed the wallet over a drain, waving it precariously between the grills. Yakov stepped out of the passenger seat holding up his hands in a calming gesture.

"Don't come any fucking closer!" Stephen shouted placing his foot over the wallet.

"Avi said you were good Steve," Yakov stated, confirming Stephen's suspicions that they were linked.

"I want to see him now!" He shouted.

"He wants to see you."

"What the fuck were you doing with Cassandra at the beach, she's nothing to with any of this shit, she's on holiday."

"My boss asked me to keep an eye out for any problems."

"Avi's your boss."

"He is indeed, he will meet you tomorrow, we have no interest in your girlfriend, I'd really appreciate my wallet back Steve."

"Where do I meet Avi?" Stephen asked, whilst picking up the wallet.

"My colleague will pick you up ten thirty in the morning, we've arranged for Cassandra to go on a sightseeing trip. I can assure you everything is kosher."

Stephen hesitated then threw the wallet at Yakov, who caught it and placed it in his pocket.

"You want a lift anywhere Steve?" He asked as a got back in the vehicle.

Stephen shook his head, he noticed Cassandra exiting the bar. "Wait!" He shouted and ran towards the car. Yakov wound down his window. "This is yours." Steve handed him the photos and the cash had taken. "You need to be more careful," Stephen teased him.

"Too busy watching your back to worry about mine, see you tomorrow."

Stephen returned to Cassandra and explained he'd told Yakov he'd dropped his wallet. He shivered as the memory came to him of displacing his wallet in Jan's bedroom in deepest Dewsbury.

It was now getting light and they'd have to be up in a few hours so he flagged down a taxi, realising he'd have to wait another day before they could consummate their relationship.

"Well that was quite a first date," Cassandra laughed.

"You wouldn't have that much fun in Singapore eh?" Stephen replied.

Cassandra pulled a beer mat out of her handbag and showed it to Stephen. "Your friend Sylvia gave it to me, look she's written something in Hebrew."

The taxi pulled up outside Stephen's cousin's block, he handed the driver his money and asked him if he could translate what Sylvia had written.

"Azer Lee," he read. "Help me."

"Shalom Steve, we've spoken on the phone." The smartly dressed young lady greeted Stephen as he was waiting for Avi.

"Have we?" He queried.

"You called Avi from the Skanda hostel in Jerusalem, I found him for you."

"Right yes, Clara, I remember, thanks."

"I'm going to look after your girlfriend for a couple of days, we can tell her you have some business for Mr. Saltzman who insists he treats Cass to a private tour. I'll show her Jerusalem, the Dead Sea, she'll have great time whilst you and Avi can get together."

"Sounds good Clara, Cass will be down in a minute, we had a late night."

They stopped off at the café to pick up Cassandra's purse, Clara gave non-stop commentary as they drove to Jerusalem. She and Cassandra seemed to instantly hit off and aside from history there was also the promise of retail therapy.

They parked up near the Jaffa Gate, opposite the hotel where Wayne did his runner. "Okay Steve, Avi's going to meet you in one of your old haunts, the Star restaurant, usual table," Clara announced.

Stephen felt uneasy. He kissed Cassandra on the cheek, wished her a good trip and disappeared into the souk. He reached the shop where the 'Big A' had hidden after seeing his old roommate. The passage was busy with tourists and vendors. He looked up at the bedroom window in the Star hostel where he had hidden from Marvin and thought about Boris, his guardian angel.

The Star restaurant was almost full, he noticed a group of loud Scandinavian UN soldiers enjoying a meze and a few beers. There were two Israeli guys sitting at Wayne's table, where he was supposed to meet Avi. He hesitated before they both stood and vacated the table, walking past him without making eye contact. *A coincidence? Not likely,* he thought as he moved to one of the vacant seats.

The boss came over and gave him a long stare, "You been in here before," he commented as he cleared the table.

"Yes, I've been here to change money, I'm a friend of Wayne's," Stephen chanced.

"Not seen him long time, nice man, you want something?"

"A Carlsberg please."

He noticed the boss motioning towards him as he spoke to a couple of his staff. He felt uneasy, wishing the 'silent assassin' would arrive quickly. A few moments passed, suddenly there was shouting out in the passage, he saw a border guard blowing a whistle as everyone's attention was drawn to the street.

"So you're here to tell me your nympho girlfriend is a common criminal and not a double agent?" Avi was standing beside him as if he'd been beamed there from the Starship Enterprise! He sat opposite Stephen, went to remove his shades but thought better of it.

"Hi Avi, how are you?"

"Pissed off. So it was an insurance job."

Stephen realised Avi wasn't there for small talk, he related the conversation he'd had with Marci on Brighton Pier. "She's not my girlfriend Avi, Cassandra, my travelling companion, is and she has nothing to do with any of this so please make sure everyone knows that," Stephen implored.

"Well you should make a better effort of keeping her close," Avi chided him.

"Marci was very keen for me to come and tell you the truth, particularly about Neville."

"Not sure she's capable of telling the truth, which is one of the reasons I recruited her in the first place. So Neville clearly is motivated by money rather than activism, be it political or animal." Avi mulled over his own sentence before continuing. "She wants me to tell you where I think Neville is."

"Yep," Stephen nodded.

"I know exactly where he is," Avi said casually, as a waiter brought a mint tea over.

"You do?" Stephen was surprised.

"Yes, but I'm more interested in where he's going."

"So where's he going?"

"I'm officially suspended Steve," Avi changed the subject.

"So I hear."

"The Americans have made a fuss, I've been made a scapegoat."

"I take it the family have complained," Stephen surmised.

"No. Wayne," Avi stated.

"Wayne?"

"Things got messy after the Iraq attack, even the Saltzmans were suddenly an irreverence. I reluctantly had to let Wayne go, so I had him deported immediately back to the States where he told the authorities about Marvin."

"What about Marvin?"

"Apparently there was a gap of a few hours between me releasing Wayne and him going to the airport. He decided to visit Marvin in hospital, he claims to have seen him at ten thirty in the evening. He was in the room on his own, he claims Marvin was dead! He panicked and ran out of the hospital, getting a cab to the airport. Then of course he saw the news that Marvin was killed by the rocket attack at Rosh Pina."

"What?" Stephen was totally lost. "He was, I saw his body on the slab," he confirmed.

"I know you did but I'm going to tell you something you will never ever repeat, I mean never."

Stephen had never seen Avi look so serious. "Go on."

"I went to the hospital at ten fifty, I must have literally passed Wayne on the stairs. When I went in the room Marvin was indeed dead."

"What the fuck?" Stephen interrupted.

"Boris had given him one hell of a blow, I wasn't going to let our Russian friend get involved in any shit so I called in some colleagues and we got Marvin out of there. When we heard about the business at Rosh Pina I took advantage of the situation and to cut to the chase the American embassy want to know how one of their citizens died twice."

"Fucking hell, what a mess, Avi please tell me there's no surprise about the third corpse."

"No surprise, just a poor Arab worker who was unlucky. Anyway we told the Americans Wayne must have been mistaken and that Marvin, who after all was wanted in the States for manslaughter, slipped out of hospital and headed north with dubious intentions." Avi sipped his mint tea, looking Steve in the eye. "So I need a favour Steve."

"A favour?"

"You need to find Wayne for me, tell him Marvin's intention was to kill him, leaving the path free for Hank to claim Rachel for himself."

"Wow. So where's Wayne now?"

Avi stood up and cleared the table. "I'm not a hundred percent sure where he is but I know where he's heading," he said, turning the table over. Stephen looked in amazement at the graffiti on the underneath. *'DELHI'* was scrawled in red felt tip and a drawing of a drum.

"No idea what the drum is about Steve, but we are pretty sure Wayne plans to meet Neville there and possibly Rachel."

"So you want me to go to India?"

"I want you to find Wayne and persuade him of Marvin's intentions. My job could depend on it."

"And Marci?" Stephen added.

"She's all yours, you want to find Wayne and she wants to find Neville, you might as well team up, besides it seems someone else wants to employ you."

"Employ me, who?"

"We are heading up north to meet the Goodmans."

"Who the fuck are the Goodmans?" Stephen pleaded.

"Who do you think the Goodmans are?"

"Sounds like they are related to the Saltzmans."

"Well yes, they probably are if you subscribe to Maurice Saltzman's theory that Abraham is the father of all us Jews Steve. The Goodmans are your nympho Canadian arsonist friend's parents." Avi smirked.

"Marci's parents, what the fuck do they want from me?" Stephen mused.

"I guess they want you to find their daughter, or Neville, or both, and let's not forget the money from the safe."

Stephen sat quietly weighing up the situation. The Saltzmans were paying him to keep Rachel away from finding Wayne. Rachel was paying him to find Wayne. Avi was desperate for him to find Wayne and now Marci's parents were about to pay him to find their daughter, which wouldn't be too difficult as he knew exactly where she was. Neville and the loot, that might be trickier.

"So where's Neville?" Stephen couldn't recall if he'd asked Avi.

"Denmark."

"Denmark, you sure Avi?"

"Yep, my sources are keeping an eye on him in the hope he leads us to Wayne, maybe you should go on a European rail holiday Steve."

"I'm off to New York for Alberto's wedding shortly," Stephen confirmed.

"And what do you think about your friend?"

"Mad but not bad, but who knows." Stephen felt bad doubting his friend. "I've got a favour to ask you Avi."

"Go on."

"A friend of mine, Sylvia, an English girl, Jewish, works in the bar where I stole your man Yakov's wallet. She's in some kind of trouble, gave Cassandra this." He showed Avi the beer mat with 'help me' written in Hebrew.

"Not the kind of bar for a nice Jewish girl to work in," Avi commented.

"Who said she was nice," Stephen joked.

"Will Yakov know who she is?"

"I'm certain he would, Cassandra introduced her to him."

"Then consider it done, I'll send Yakov and the boys there for a few drinks tonight."

27

THE VALLEY OF LIES

Stephen had hoped he would get a chance to know Avi the human being, the family man, but he was to be disappointed. The five-hour drive was tedious, apart from some plotting and planning for the first hour Avi was back in his shell. Stephen thought about mentioning the third body but sensed it would be inappropriate. The revelation about Marvin was enough for one day. At least this time Avi drove him right into the heart of the kibbutz and didn't dump him on the road. He promised this would be the last meeting and there after it would be a time for action, whatever that meant.

He was surprised that Avi didn't join him at the meeting and instead went to the dining room. Stephen was pleased to see Avaram and Cheryl and they seemed delighted to see him. The other guests he wasn't so keen on. He was introduced to the Goodmans who sat opposite him, the hosts sat at each end of the dining table. There were no pleasantries, Jack Goodman got straight to the point.

"Avaram has told me that you have experience in looking for missing wayward daughters."

Stephen smiled and nodded.

"And that you were successful with reuniting her with her family."

He nodded again glancing at his hosts, *what had they been told?*

"And you met my daughter here in this house?"

"That's correct, I met Marci here, she was my kibbutz sister."

The Goodmans looked at each other then at their hosts then intensely at Stephen, who suddenly felt hot.

"Have you had any contact from her recently?" Betty Goodman spoke for the first time.

Stephen could see who Marci took after physically. Her mum was well put together, Marci had her lips, he wondered whether her mum was as skilled with them, he briefly imagined her in nothing but one of her mink coats. "No, she disappeared from the kibbutz and I've busied myself looking for Rachel Saltzman." He felt slightly ashamed at his natural talent for lying. He'd honed his skills in deceit in his early teens when he discovered his father would say no to everything, so he invented a world of subterfuge so he could get up to mischief without incurring the wrath of his father.

"We believe she's in the UK, Stephen," Jack said.

"We have some leads, we were hoping you could follow them up, we will reward you obviously. We don't want you to confront her, just locate her and contact us."

Stephen remembered Avi's plan and with his reply gave it the green light. "I don't think she's in England," Stephen said casually. The Goodmans looked confused. "I think she's in India," he continued.

"What!" Jack Goodman was startled.

"She told me she wanted to earn some money so she could travel to India." Stephen was in full flow.

"Why India?" Betty Goodman said.

"She told me it was a long standing ambition, but she also wanted to follow a boyfriend there."

"Fucking Neville," Jack whispered to Betty.

"Neville?" Stephen tried to sound genuinely surprised. Then he played his ace. "Neville from Liverpool, I don't think she'd follow him anywhere. No, she told me…" he hesitated inviting the Goodmans to react.

"Carry on Stephen, you can be up front with us, nothing can shock us when it comes to Marci."

Stephen took a sip of his beer and continued, "She told me she couldn't stand Neville, no, she was totally in love with Wayne. He was here on the kibbutz, but disappeared, apparently to India."

The Goodmans sat dumbstruck, Stephen looked at Avaram and Cheryl who were still keeping their own council. He wasn't sure if they were in on Avi's plan.

"Do you know this guy?" Jack turned to Avaram.

"I remember him, quite a charismatic guy as I recall." Stephen guessed his kibbutz parents were with the programme.

"Would you go to India? We'll pay you generously." Betty sounded desperate.

How much money was in that safe? Stephen pondered. "I'll have to think about it, I've got to go back to London, I have a job and I've got a wedding in New York looming."

"How much?" Jack Goodman snapped.

"Have you seen the 'Godfather' Mr. Goodman? Make me an offer I can't refuse."

Stephen never imagined he'd spend a night with the 'silent assassin', he was grateful the kibbutz guest accommodation had twin beds. Avi slept soundly, Stephen stared at the fan, reflecting on his current life situation. He'd spoken to Cassandra from the kibbutz office, claiming he'd been sent to Haifa by the Saltzmans to photograph various properties. She didn't seem bothered which upset him a bit, she told him what a great day she had and how lovely Clara was. She was very excited about swimming or floating on the Dead Sea the next day. Stephen wondered if he'd ever get his wicked way with her.

So he was now going to be looking for Marci, though he knew exactly where she was. He guessed she'd be looking for Neville. He was supposed to be looking for Wayne for Rachel but didn't want to ever find him for her. He was also looking for Wayne for Avi and didn't want to let him down. No wonder he couldn't sleep, *Too many lies*, he thought. Just as he was drifting off, his new hero appeared in the rocking chair beside the window. "Stay strong buddy, do the right thing, I've got your back."

"Cheers mate, appreciate your support mate." Stephen closed his eyes as 'The Boss' disappeared.

He awoke with a start, Avi was nowhere to be seen, he heard the rocking chair as he wiped the sleep from his eyes.

"You've got to be shitting me." His old friend Rotten was back and far from happy. "You have to be fucking joking, you've sacked me for the fucking self proclaimed 'Boss'. Weller or Strummer I'd gladly move aside for but that bloody yank Ross, go fuck yourself, we are history."

Stephen found Cheryl in the dining hall, she told him that Avi would pick him up at midday and that the kibbutz had managed to root out the 'cultists'. The war just across the border had helped to put a dampener on the movement. She also informed him of the rumour that a Saudi Arabian sheik had financed the operation and offered generous commissions to anyone that could produce a convert, particularly if they were Israeli. "War without weapons." She shrugged.

Avi picked him up and they drove south, he seemed preoccupied, though that wasn't unusual. "Forget about the money," Avi said suddenly.

"What money?" Stephen was lost.

"The money from the Goodmans safe, forget about it."

"I wasn't considering the money." Stephen was telling the truth for a change.

"No but Marci is, that's the main reason she asked you to come and see me. She wants me off her back, she's a manipulative bitch." Avi was clearly still pissed off with her. "You might want to tell her that if she does have any designs on the eighty-seven thousand, three hundred and twenty-one dollars taken from the safe, she'd be best to forget it."

"Wow, that's a lot of money to forget about," Stephen said.

"Trust me Steve, even I won't be trying to track it down."

"Who's got it?" Stephen was curious.

"You don't want to know, end of."

"Sounds like you've been busy this morning Avi," Stephen guessed, correctly.

"Considering I'm supposed to be suspended, yes I've had quite a productive morning."

"Squeezing some poor Palestinians testicles?" Stephen teased.

"You're right about squeezing testicles, but not Palestinian, English!"

"Neville?" Stephen guessed.

"Yep."

"He's here in Israel?"

"No, he's with some friends of mine in Copenhagen," Avi teased. "They squeezed enough to find out what I need to know."

"So what now?" Stephen pondered.

"Enjoy the rest of your trip. One last bit of advice, don't trust Marci."

"I don't and I won't," Stephen confirmed.

Stephen stood for a few seconds before pressing the buzzer outside his cousin's apartment block, All he wanted now was to concentrate on true love, he had unfinished business cementing his relationship with Cassandra.

Mark greeted Stephen with a finger against his lips, signaling that he should be quiet, he ushered him into the kitchen and closed the door.

"Everything okay Mark?" Stephen whispered.

"Cass is under the weather, she came back from her trip last night and has been alternating between the loo and bed since then."

"Shit," Stephen cursed before excusing the pun.

He spent their last day nursing her, fortunately the bug passed and she was fine to fly. It had been a very strange and frustrating first date.

On his return to London, Stephen met up with Rachel, he told her that he'd had a productive trip and had learnt that every clue pointed to Wayne making his way to Delhi, but Neville reckoned Wayne was in communication with Alberto and that he could end up the 'Big A's' wedding. Rachel told him he'd simply have to go to New York and do some digging. *If I must*, he thought.

Marci made contact with him. She'd moved from Brighton, just in case Avi had persuaded Stephen to betray her. He relayed the conversation he had with her ghastly parents and she agreed to meet him before his trip to New York, suggesting he contact her parents and claim she was invited to the big man's wedding and they should forward funds to finance her trip. "Remember fifty fifty," she reminded him.

Avi was right, she was a slippery bitch alright, but she was hot.

He had phoned Cassandra a few times however she seemed to be playing hard to get, he wondered if she suspected he was up to all this skullduggery and was far too unreliable. He couldn't blame her, yet he still felt guilty meeting Marci at a hotel in Bloomsbury.

She was disappointed to have been refused a visa to enter the States due to being wanted for arson in Israel. They discussed the possibility of going to India together, but decided to see how his trip to the States panned out. They spent the night together and Marci discussed finances over breakfast in bed. She was very precise in what Stephen owed her, it was after all her idea to crucify her parents who were paying him with what was ultimately her inheritance.

"When you return from the States, you can help me find the money Neville stole and then I'll help you track down Wayne," she plotted.

Stephen decided not to mention Avi's warning re. the money from the safe, realising it was better to bury his head for now, which he did in Marci's ample cleavage.

28

THE SIGNATURE DISH
(1983)

"This car isn't really built for me is it!" The big man laughed as they drove over the Kennedy Bridge. The big man filled the driver's seat and his right thigh was pressed hard against the hand break.

"I'll invest in a roomier model in the near future but this wedding is killing me financially. At least it's black!" He roared.

Stephen was both excited and intimidated by the sheer height of Manhattan's skyline, which obscured the night sky. Alberto drove along all the legendary streets pointing out the different venues where he'd seen various bands.

"We're going take a ride out to New Jersey at the weekend, do the 'backstreets tour'." Stephen noticed 'The Boss' giving a thumbs up in the back seat. They continued to Central Park where Alberto parked and led Stephen to a huge apartment building. "On behalf of the people of this great city I'd like to apologise," he said, tears welling in his eyes as he pointed to the pavement where John Lennon had been shot dead some three years earlier. "The world's gone fucking mad," he said, giving his ex roommate a hug.

As he was lost in the big man's embrace, he noticed Springsteen cross himself and look to the heavens.

Back in the car Alberto produced a hip flask, he gave it to his English guest. "Welcome to the 'Big Apple' Stevie boy." He swigged the neat brandy as the tour continued. "125th Street, guess what's across the other side man?" Alberto asked.

Stephen noticed the decrementing quality of the buildings.

"We are entering Harlem," the 'Big A' announced with an air of menace. It was almost midnight and the streets were pretty much deserted. "I won't be stopping at any red lights Stevie and if there's any trouble check the glove compartment."

Steve opened the glove compartment and was shocked to discover amongst the discarded sweet wrappers a small pistol. "Fucking hell Al, it's not real is it?"

"Locked, loaded and fully legal, just exercising my rights under the constitution to defend myself."

Stephen shook his head and was relieved when they survived 'badlands'.

They drove over the Brooklyn Bridge and ten minutes later arrived at Alberto's brownstone studio flat.

"Stevie, say hi to the soon to be Mrs. Susan Canavaro." Stephen had wondered why his roommate hadn't shown him a photo of his intended, he know realised why. She was wider than he was tall and her hair appeared unwashed.

"Hi Steve," she said as if it was a struggle to acknowledge him. "Where the fuck have you been Al, you never told me you'd be this long," she snapped.

"My fault," Stephen interjected, "I demanded Al take me on a tour."

There was an awkward silence as Susan went to the bedroom, which was separated from the living area simply by a curtain.

Alberto opened a couple of beers. "She's a bit stressed out about the wedding, her parents are still on her case, they're learning to love me."

"So you've converted then Al?"

"I'm one hundred per cent kosher man."

"And do you think Susan's family appreciate your sincere efforts?" Stephen asked.

Alberto reflected on the question for a few seconds. "Nope," he replied honestly, "I'll always be a 'wop' to them, even if I become a Rabbi!"

"And what about your family?"

"My family have never understood me, they are still living in the old country, I guess they think I'm mad and a traitor," he replied sadly. "Except for my cousin Dino, who's a real old school guy, rumoured to be a bit of a hombre, but he's been real supportive to me. You'll meet him at the bachelor party, he's the only member of my family coming. Anyway, you left the kibbutz in a hurry, what a bunch of shit with poor Hank and Marvin, unbelievable man."

"Yep, I'm sorry I disappeared but I was scared of that Wayne guy," Stephen lied.

"Wayne?" Alberto laughed.

"Yeah, everything was very weird when I met him in Jerusalem, I kind of got paranoid about him, he reacted very badly when I mentioned Rachel Saltzman." Stephen paused not knowing what his host knew or didn't know about his involvement. "Funnily enough I've caught up with her in London through a mutual friend, nice girl, desperate to catch up with Wayne." Stephen said, chancing his arm.

"There was a lot of heavy shit around Wayne and Rachel, I liked them both, but that mad fucker Marvin, he seriously worried me," Albert confessed.

"What did Wayne make of you converting Al?"

"Very weird, he didn't have a problem with me converting but he banged on about me being Jewish but still believing in Christ." Alberto took a swig of beer. "I sent him an invitation to the wedding, not sure it was such a good idea."

"Where did you send it to?"

"Wayne left a list of post restantes, Cairo, Casablanca, Istanbul, New Delhi, and I sent one to his home in California."

"California?" Stephen was surprised. "I thought he was from Oklahoma?"

"He's from Oklahoma but has been living in Mendocino, a small hippy town in Northern California."

They chatted for another hour before a travel weary Stephen dozed off where he sat. He was woken by Susan's shrill voice castigating Alberto over something trivial. The apartment was damp and stunk of something Stephen couldn't put his finger on. *I've got another ten days in this dump before the wedding*, he thought to himself.

Susan rushed off to work shouting orders at the big man, Stephen smiled to himself reflecting on his roommate trading with the delectable Sonia from France.

Alberto emerged with a cup of coffee in a chipped mug. "I'm off to the office, working for the man. Listen I've left a map of how to get to the nearest Metro station, it's only a five minute walk away. What're your plans?"

"I'll probably do the touristy stuff, Empire State Building, Central Park etcetera," Stephen replied.

"Sounds good man, Susan is going to cook Chinese tonight, it's her signature dish. In fact it's her only dish. Anyway she's serving up at nine so gives you plenty of time. I'll catch you later."

Stephen followed his host's handdrawn map to the subway, which also included instructions on which subway routes to Manhattan he should take. He thought he should memorise the info before going underground so as not to look like a lost tourist. He noticed a bar across the road, it was only eleven in the morning but his body clock was five hours ahead so he decided to have a livener before going into town.

The bar was like every one he'd seen in the movies, long, with bar stools stretching along its entire length. There was only one punter in there, sipping coffee and reading the Wall Street Journal.

"I'll have a 'Bud' please." Stephen nodded at the bottles.

"Australian eh?" The bar tender nodded.

"English," he corrected him.

They exchanged some banter for the twenty minutes it took to neck the bottle. Just as he was about to leave a couple of Irish guys came in, obviously regulars.

"Set em up Vince, usual please." They nodded at Stephen, he guessed they were a few years older than him.

"Our friend here's from London, it's his first day in New York." Vince the bar tender said.

"First beer eh, good man, give our friend another," the bigger of the two insisted. "I'm Eamon and my friend here is Declan."

They shook hands as Stephen introduced himself. He told them about the wedding and the uncomfortable atmosphere at his hosts. Declan bought another round so Stephen felt obliged to get his round in. It was now twelve thirty and he was feeling slightly merry. Having told them his plan to hit Manhattan they invited him to join them on a courtesy bus to Atlantic City that stopped right outside the bar.

"We'll be there in a couple of hours," Eamon said optimistically.

"Come on Steve, a bourbon for the road."

Why he joined them on the bus he wasn't sure, he'd never set foot in a casino. He remembered Susan's signature dish, "I've got to back for nine lads," he pleaded.

"The magic bus leaves every hour on the hour, we generally get the six o'clock one, back by eight, no sweat."

They arrived and strolled along the Boulevard until they entered a casino straight out of the Wild West. The Irish lads sat Stephen in the courtesy bar telling the bar tender, a fellow Irishman, to look after their guest, before sitting at a black jack table.

Stephen hit the JD's and was offered the biggest burger he'd ever seen, all on the house as long as his new friends were gambling. He decided they were very dodgy characters but he wasn't about to get involved in any more complications.

"That sure looks a great burger buddy, welcome to the promised land," 'The Boss' said, joining Stephen on the adjacent bar stool.

"Cheers mate, not a bad first day in your manor," he replied.

"Anytime you fancy a tour you know where to find me," 'The Boss' added.

"Beneath the giant Exon sign that brings this fair city light," Stephen confirmed.

'The Boss' slipped away as the Irishmen joined him and ordered a bottle of expensive champagne with three glasses. Stephen tripped twice on his way to the toilet, he suddenly felt very drunk.

He lost all sense of time whilst as bus battled through the traffic back to Brooklyn. The lads insisted they have a last bevy back in Vince's bar, he was about to agree when he looked at his watch, it was almost ten. "Shit!" he shouted. He couldn't recall where Alberto lived, he searched his pockets for the map but he must have lost it.

"Shit!" he shouted again. He found the pay phone at the end of the bar and was very relieved when the 'Big A' answered.

"Stevie where the hell are you, where you been?"

Stephen explained that he'd lost both the map and his bearings.

Alberto met him by the subway entrance, Stephen tried to sober up enough to manage the five-minute walk back but it was a struggle.

Alberto explained they'd eaten but there was a plate in the oven for him. Susan sat solemn faced on the sofa as her fiancé put the plate on the table in front of Stephen, who still couldn't quite place the dreadful smell in the apartment. The room was spinning, his host was talking to him but he couldn't take in what he was saying. He took a mouthful of Susan's Chinese feast, spat it out and ran to the toilet, where he spent the next two hours throwing up.

Stephen woke mid morning with a throbbing head and a huge sense of shame, his hosts had long gone off to work. He found a note from Alberto with details of the evening's bachelor party. He needed to get himself together starting with a cold shower and a black coffee.

He tried to find a clean mug in the filthy kitchenette, which didn't make him feel any better. He collapsed back on the sofa eyeing the telephone, reaching for his pocket notebook he picked up the red handset, the 'bat phone' as Alberto called it. He felt guilty making international calls without his host's permission but he had twelve days to go before the wedding and he was sure as hell the 'Big A' and his intended would be pleased if he disappeared for a while.

He phoned Rachel, explaining he had a lead but would need funds to book return flights to San Francisco. He called Marci's parents and told a similar story. He then spoke to Ronnie and congratulated him on his Lambretta book getting published. He received an open invitation to Boston and was given the address of Ronnie's younger brother who was living in San Francisco.

Next he navigated the subway system to Manhattan, where he found a 'bucket' shop selling cheap flights. He managed to take in the Empire State Building and the Lower East Side, before getting a cab to the Midtown bar where Alberto had hired a room for his stag night.

He was a trifle embarrassed to see the big man after disgracing himself the night before, but nothing was mentioned as the twenty-nine friends, plus cousin Dino, gathered in the hip bar.

Alberto stood on a small stage and spoke into a microphone, "Great to be spending the night with you guys, I love you all, well some more than others. To be honest there are at least five of you who I've invited because I had to. Love you? I don't even like at least five of you."

"Fuck off big man, I fucking hate you!" A colleague bellowed with a throaty laugh.

"I'd like to say a big thank you to my best man Richie, who is only my best man because he works for a brewery!" The crowd cheered. "Then there's my honorary best man who's come all the way from London." Alberto pushed a button on the tape deck and 'London Calling' blasted out from the speakers. "Take a bow Stevie."

Stephen put an embarrassed hand up in acknowledgment.

"He's only been here thirty-six hours and he's drunk Atlantic city dry and vomited on my beloved Susan's signature dish!" Laughter filled the bar until Alberto raised his hands. "Lastly I'd like to thank my cousin Dino who has stood by me in tough times, you know the old saying, 'You can choose your friends but not your family'. Dino is the exception, I thank you man from the bottom of my heart."

Dino just nodded and tilted his JD.

They drank to the early hours as the big man's favourite tunes blasted out. He drunkenly led the sing a long to 'Born To Run'. 'The Boss' nodded to Stephen in approval from a barstool. Best man Richie went round collecting thirty dollars per man for the wedding present. Stephen was too drunk to work out the total, but he guessed it wasn't far short of a grand.

A colleague of Alberto, one of the five wankers Stephen surmised, engaged him in conversation, spitting with every word as he patronised him with a mock English accent.

"Fancy a joint buddy," he spat. Stephen declined, having caused enough trouble just through drinking he didn't want to chance going back to his friend's apartment stoned.

"You fucking English are so fucking pompous, so fucking straight, whatever happened to the 'Great' bit of Britain?"

Stephen wiped some spittle from his cheek and paused for thought when an old friend popped up beside him. "You going to let that yank cunt take the piss or what?"

For once Stephen agreed with the has-been Sex Pistol and put his face up against his tormentor. "Listen pal, we gave the world Shakespeare, Dickens and the Beatles. You've given us fucking herpes, tomato ketchup and you shot the Beatles, so go fuck yourself!"

Stephen heard Rotten clapping at his retort as the yank's fist connected with his nose. Stephen felt the unbearable sensation between his watering eyes, despite the alcohol. He launched himself at his attacker, they both fell onto a table knocking over bottles and glasses.

Richie managed to pull them apart and Dino grabbed the wanker's collar and dragged him outside. He re-emerged a minute later blowing on his sore knuckles.

29

THUNDER ROAD

Ronnie's brother Jacob was everything Stephen imagined a resident of San Francisco should be, an out and out hippy. He spent the night on a beanbag in Jacob's ramshackle Ashbury Heights abode. Unlike his hosts in New York, Ronnie's brother and his girlfriend Candy were so laid back they were horizontal. He shared a spliff and some veggie food with them, they'd never heard of the Pistols or The Clash and played endless west coast pre '72 records. Jacob was happy to lend Stephen his battered compact car, not concerned any paperwork or insurance. They gave him a tour of the bay, he was relieved to be away from the happy couple and was pretty certain they were relieved to be shot of him for a few days. The sun was warm and apart from his sore nose he felt in fine fettle.

He was nervous as he drove the borrowed car across the Golden Gate Bridge and not just because of what he might discover at his destination. Jacob had apologised for the car's first gear, which was a trifle temperamental, and he had been warned the coastal road heading north was hilly in the extreme.

Driving and navigating at the same time was a challenge and he managed to miss the turnoff for the coastal road. He studied the map Jacob had given him, "One oh one, then the one two eight," he confirmed aloud. He felt a sense of relief as he turned onto the latter road that would take him directly to the coast and Mendocino. The road became more winding and treacherous as he reached 'Redwood' country. He found himself crawling round uphill bends, with giant logging trucks right up behind him, first gear had completely disappeared. He'd lost a few pounds in sweat when he eventually hit the straight road to the coast.

He stopped at a small town by a diner and could sense the locals' stares as he entered and ordered a coffee and burger. He noticed the natives watching him eat all had red hair.

He wondered why he was going on this pilgrimage and where would it end. What if he ran into Wayne, what would he do? What would he say? What would Wayne do? For a moment he even considered turning back.

An old man came and stood by his table muttering something that Stephen didn't understand. He paid his bill and got out of the strange town as quickly as second gear would allow.

Mendocino Population 879' the sign announced as he entered the town. There seemed to be only five roads, he figured the street facing the sea would be Main Street and turned out to be correct. He parked right outside the Mendocino Hotel, which resembled a saloon you would find in 'Dodge city'.

The sign above the door confirmed its Wild West roots, *'MENDOCINO HOTEL EST. 1878'*. He pressed the bell at the tiny reception, a couple of minutes later a rotund woman appeared. "Hi sir, how you doing today?" She said with a welcoming smile.

"I'm hoping you have a vacancy."

"I do have a single room with a fine view of our garden," she confirmed. She asked Stephen to fill in a form and he committed to three nights.

"Where have you come from today sir?" She asked.

"San Fran."

"That's a mighty long drive, did you stop for refreshments?"

"Boonville," he confirmed.

"Boonville sir, you don't want to be stopping in that hillbilly town, they're all related!" She confirmed what he'd already suspected.

"Is there a bar in this town?" He enquired.

"Our bar is closed for redecoration but there's Red's place next door, but it's a bit wild to be honest."

Twenty minutes later Stephen stood outside Red's, a sea mist had enveloped Main Street. A few hobos gathered around the small bar through the door. "Come in, don't be afraid." A woman in her late twenties was sitting on a bench on the veranda, she held a bottle of wine in one hand and a spliff in the other.

"Afraid? I'm from East London love, why would I be afraid?" He answered.

"Wow," she sighed, "I love London. Come on I'll introduce you to everyone." She staggered up and beckoned him inside.

The bar in 'Star Wars' meets 'Easy Rider', Stephen thought, as he acknowledged the regulars.

"This hombre is from London," his new friend announced.

The collection of hippies and mutants nodded and grunted their greetings.

"I'm Pie, come sit." She led him to a small table in the corner.

"Interesting name, I'm Steve." He shook her hand, noticing a ring on each finger.

"My father reckoned I was as sweet as apple pie, so he called me Pie."

"Nice one."

"He died when I was three in a motorbike accident."

"Oh, how sad."

"So, what brings you to Mendocino?" She said, quickly changing the subject.

Stephen hesitated but decided to be honest for a change. He told her about his misbehaviour in New York and how he wanted to see something of the real America and was hoping to run into a friend who'd been living in the area.

"What's your friends name? I know everyone of drinking age in this town," she laughed.

"Wayne." He realised then his 'friend' probably used an alias.

"Nope, don't know no Wayne. I've been to London I'll have you know."

"Really, when?"

"When I was sixteen, I was a ballet protégé, I went with the North California company on a tour of Europe, London was our first port of call. I loved it, especially your River Thames."

"Sounds a great trip," Stephen said.

"It should have been," she said, "but on our last night in Rome, my ballet teacher raped me."

"Wow, I'm so sorry Pie." Stephen was taken aback by her sudden revelation.

"Yeah, would you believe my middle name is Lucky." She laughed ironically. "So that was the end of my glorious ballet career."

"So what do you do now Pie?"

"Grow weed," she replied matter of factly. "Everyone round here does, even the local doctor grows it in his garden. Strictly for medicinal reasons."

"So it's legal is it?"

"Not really, but we don't see many cops here."

Stephen got a photo of Wayne out of his pocket and showed it to Pie.

"Ha Jeez," she laughed, before holding it up for the crowd to see, "fucking macaroni, that cretin owes me two-hundred dollars." One of the mutants cursed.

"You know him?" Stephen pressed Pie.

"Of course I know him I'm sort of his mistress, well, I was until he upped and left again a couple of weeks ago."

"Mistress," Stephen was taken aback. "What do you mean mistress?"

"Well things are quite free and easy round here, Christopher's wife Carol is okay with it," she said casually.

"Wait a minute Pie, this fella here, who I know as Wayne, and you know as Christopher, is married?"

"Sure thing, Chris is married to Carol, they have a year old baby, the fucking Jesus freak left her when she was pregnant to go on what he said was a holy mission to the holy land."

"That's where I met him, in Jerusalem. So he's been back here?" Stephen's adrenalin was flowing.

"Too fucking right he's been here, turned up on a fucking 'Harley' flashing cash all over the place, promised to take me to Florida but then said he had one more spiritual road to walk."

"Spiritual road?" Stephen queried.

"To India, he left for India two weeks ago. Does he owe you money or are you one of his disciples?"

"He doesn't owe me money and no I'm not a disciple but I think he'd like me to be."

"Are you a Jew?" She asked.

"Half, why?"

"When he wasn't womanising he banged on about introducing the Jews to the love of Jesus," Pie confirmed, "of course his greatest triumph was marrying Carol."

"His wife's Jewish?"

"Sure is, he wooed her in her native LA, poor little rich girl, she's a Hebrew Jesuit now."

"And Wayne, I mean Chris, has just upped and left her?" Stephen remarked.

"Yep, do you want to pop and say hi to her?"

"You mean she lives nearby?"

"Sure does, just round the corner above the pharmacy."

Stephen didn't sleep well in his hotel bed because his mind was racing. He thought of Rachel and her obsession with a married man, who had at least one mistress. He was however relieved that Wayne wasn't the third body back in the Haifa mortuary.

He was amused to see the mid-morning queue of hobos outside the pharmacy, waiting for their medicinal weed. He found the iron staircase at the back of the wooden building and there was a vintage pram parked at the bottom so he guessed he was in the right place. A baby's cry confirmed the inhabitants were in, he knocked on the door unsure of what he'd say. Carol appeared with her baby daughter on her hip, her beauty took his breath away.

"You must be Carol," he stuttered before rather clumsily explaining who he was and how he came to be in Mendocino. He claimed to be on a tour of California and had been seduced by Christopher's romantic description of the town. She invited him in, unlike Pie she didn't seem to harbour any bitterness towards her wandering husband. Stephen mentioned that he was about to embark on a tour of the Indian sub continent himself and it would be great to catch up with his old friend. She claimed she had no clue to his itinerary, except she was fairly certain he was flying to Delhi via Amsterdam where he planned to catch up with his English friend from Liverpool. Carol said he'd hoped to go to a wedding in New York on route!

She showed him a calendar with a hand drawn picture of the Taj Mahal on the date he left. He also noticed a drawing of a drum underneath and recalled the same illustration under the table in the Star restaurant. There was also a capital 'A' penciled in on Alberto's wedding day. It turned out to be a strange but brief meeting.

Stephen couldn't see any benefit in staying any longer in this weird town, he checked out of his hotel and belted himself into Ronnie's brother's compact car, that now had no first gear at all. He said a silent prayer and headed back up the long and winding coastal road.

30

LOVE, DRUGS AND MARRIAGE

Dear Rachel,

There is no easy way of telling you this but I have it on good authority, as of two weeks ago, Wayne is travelling in India.
I also have to inform you he has a wife and baby in north California!
See you on my return after the 'Big A's' wedding.

Love Steve

Stephen pondered on Rachel's reaction to this news, he hoped she'd go bonkers in the short term then calm down and realise her infatuation was history.

Dear Mr. & Mrs. Goodman,

I have been to see Wayne's family in north California and they've confirmed that he and Marci are travelling in India. I must inform you that he has a wife and baby back in the States. What would you like me to do?

Kind regards,
Stephen

P.s. Will be back in London end of next week.

Stephen had a good idea what their response would be, hopefully another cheque. He studied the third letter making sure the truth and lies were all in the right places.

Dear Marci,

Wayne (who is married and has a baby) has just gone to India, I've told your parents you are with him. Fancy an exotic holiday?! Will speak to you on my return after the 'Big A's' wedding.

Lots of love,
Steve

He wrote and then tore up four letters to Cassandra, before posting the others, which he guessed would only just beat him home. He spent a day hanging out with Ronnie's brother and girlfriend, before reluctantly catching a flight back to New York the day before the big mans wedding.

Alberto was waiting at LaGuardia airport. They were both relieved Susan was staying with her parents. Stephen told Al about Carol and the baby as they headed back to Manhattan. "Jesus H fucking Christ, that Wayne is a fucking love machine man."

"He's a player alright," Stephen agreed.

"Was she, was she…" Alberto hesitated.

"Jewish." Stephen answered.

"Wow, he's fucking seriously spreading the word Steve."

"And getting well rewarded for it," Stephen added as an afterthought.

"What?"

"Nothing Al, just overthinking."

"You don't think I'm part of these crazies do you Stevie?"

"Of course not Al, you're giving up Jesus aren't you."

They continued in silence till they got back to the Brooklyn brownstone. They wouldn't discuss Wayne together, or for that matter Christ, for another twenty-seven years.

Alberto was in total meltdown, Richie, the best man, had phoned from an emergency room at seven on the morning of the big man's wedding day to explain he'd broken his leg messing about on his nephew's skateboard.

"Stevie, I'm upgrading you to number one best man, you've go eight hours to prepare your speech man."

"What about Dino, surely he's your man," Stephen protested.

"Dino's a man of action not words, bit like your mate The Crow, besides I've got a couple of pick me ups for you." Alberto handed a couple 'blues' to his reluctant best man.

Stephen spent the rest of the day, including the long drive to Susan's parent's local temple, feverishly trying to pen a humorous but sincere speech. Both at the temple and at the reception, back at a giant marquee in Susan's parents kickass home, he noticed that the two tribes were keeping well apart, Italians on one side, Hebrews on the other. Alberto gave Stephen a ten-minute warning, asking him to tell the guests the buffet was open at the end of his speech. He swallowed the 'blues' with a swig of beer and re-read his speech.

Susan's father said a few words that went over Stephen's head, but he was grateful for his last words, "So Al's best man Richie was so worried about following my good self he broke his own leg, so give a big hand for Stevie who is stepping in with a best man's speech which has been hastily written in the Queen's English."

Stephen nervously stepped forward to the microphone, he hoped the booze and pills would see him through.

He surveyed the Catholics to the left and the Jews to the right, opposite a long table housing the sumptuous buffet staffed by African Americans. Three cultures within the same tent but never the thrice should meet.

He looked at his friend and his less than sumptuous bride and thought of starting his speech by describing how he first met the big man whist he was getting a blowjob from the lovely Sonia. The speed was clearly beginning to kick in. "If I may start by quoting Marx, that's Groucho not Carl, 'Marriage is a wonderful institution, but who wants to live in an institution'."

There was a ripple of laughter but it wasn't worth the eight dollars he'd spent on a book of quotes he'd bought in a local bookshop.

"Of course this marriage brings together two of New York's great cultures and funnily enough I saw loads of photos of your grandparents when I was doing the tourist bit at Ellis Island the other day." There were knowing nods on both sides of the divide, Stephen relaxed and continued to describe his roommate in glowing terms. He concluded his hastily prepared speech on a roll. "Having ruined Susan's signature dish and caused a rumpus at the bachelor party I'm hoping not to destroy their big day. I will conclude by declaring the buffet open!"

The ripple of applause was quickly replaced by the stampede towards the buffet as the two tribes collided. The Canavaros and the Cohens devoured the corn beef, pastrami, chicken legs and smoked salmon.

Dino patted Stephen on the back in approval and told him the bachelor party guys were going to meet in the games room in fifteen minutes to give the groom his present. Stephen was curious to what his thirty dollars had contributed to.

Stephen was one of the first in the games room and chatted to a couple of Alberto's colleagues. He saw 'The Boss' sitting the corner, "I'm looking forward to your tour of New Jersey," Stephen whispered.

"You know where to meet me, nice speech man."

Dino entered last with a package that he hid behind a sofa. He made sure everyone had taken a beer from the covered pool table before he started. "Okay everyone I'll go and get the big man," Dino grunted.

A few minutes later the door opened and Dino led his cousin in to cheers, then someone put 'Born To Run' on the Hi-Fi. 'The Boss' gave Stephen a thumbs up as Dino locked and bolted the door. Alberto stood at the pool table facing his friends whilst Dino fetched the package and placed it on the sofa, raising his hand for the boys to quiet down whilst the music was turned off.

"Al, cuz, your buddies have got together and bought you a little something we hope you'll appreciate." Dino placed the package on the pool table and motioned for the groom to open it. Stephen was at the back of the mob and struggled to see his friend rip open the brown paper. Alberto held the contents up and gave out a primal scream. It was an ornately framed mirror approximately a metre square. Alberto was staring at the back of it and tears of joy were rolling down his cheeks. He placed the mirror glass down on the table and the boys crowded round in a two deep circle. Pink Floyd's 'Comfortably Numb' emitted from the speakers, "My god, I love you guys!" He screamed.

Stephen caught sight of the object of his friend's joy. Encased between the mirror frame was a cellophane cover, a corner of which he ripped open exposing a healthy portion of cocaine. Dino scooped a handful into an envelope and stuck the cover back on, he turned the mirror over and poured the white powder onto the mirror.

"Enjoy!" Alberto shouted. As the crowd formed a queue Stephen hung back feeling uneasy as one by one Alberto's mates indulged.

"Not my scene man," 'The Boss' mouthed and disappeared. Everyone had partaken except for Stephen, who hovered around the back of the queue.

"Go on, don't be a fucking wanker, don't let your fucking country down," Jonny Rotten snapped having gatecrashed Stephen's thoughts.

The best man stepped forward as the mob sang in unison to the music, "I have become comfortably numb…" He sniffed at the powder, hoping he'd looked the part without actually managing to snort any but it turned out he was a natural. The crowd stopped singing and cheered the Englishman.

Stephen vaguely remembered making his way into the garden for some air and a diner with a crowd of black guys in garish velvet jackets mocking his accent. He knew for sure he was in Penn station, so he was pretty confident he got to Washington by train, but he couldn't remember any other details. He woke up on Ronnie's sofa, staring at a giant painting of a Lambretta. He'd lost thirty-six hours.

Ronnie claimed he'd got a phone call from a pay phone with a rambling Stephen babbling on about coming to see him.

He was in total panic at the thought he was literally loosing the plot. He checked his wallet, everything was in order, but he suddenly wondered what Alberto would be thinking of him going AWOL. He tried phoning but got no reply.

Ronnie later took him on a tour of the capital, he enjoyed the Smithsonian but his thoughts kept returning to Brooklyn. Eventually he got through on the phone, Susan answered saying that Alberto was out of his mind with worry but had gone to see an aunt who was too sick to come to the wedding. She said they'd had a phone call from his friend in London, Dave The Crow, saying he'd read in the paper that the cheap airline Stephen had booked with had gone bust!

He returned to New York the next day on a Greyhound bus. He was relieved to find a note from Alberto saying they were at work, although he'd taken the next day off to take him on the Springsteen tour.

He looked at The Crow's postcard and called the company he booked with but got an unattainable tone so he packed his bag, left a note for his hosts and took a cab to JFK.

'The Boss' appeared beside him. "I've been waiting 'neath that giant Exon sign man."

"Sorry mate things got a little messed up."

"No sweat man, next time."

"Do me a favour, keep an eye on the 'Big A' for me," Stephen asked 'The Boss'.

"Will do man."

Stephen managed to book a flight that night on British Airways, spending his last two hundred dollars. He looked out the window as Manhattan's dazzling lights disappeared behind him. He wondered how long Alberto's marriage would last and if he'd ever see the 'Big A' again.

PART FOUR

31

'BRISTOL'
(1984)

Stephen's meeting with Rachel on his return from Alberto's wedding didn't go well. She seemed more upset at Stephen for breaking the news of Wayne's domestic circumstances than at the actual revelations.

Cassandra was dating Toby again, who'd invested in a swanky Islington apartment and, unlike Stephen, was reliable. He had a terrible row with his father who thought he was wasting his time seemingly swanning around the world. He was also deeply troubled by the lost thirty-six hours between New York and Boston and had decided to keep clear of all substances for the foreseeable future.

On a positive note Marci was very keen to join him on a trip to India, financed by her gullible parents. She joined him for the injections and was very proactive in planning the trip. She also suggested she give Stephen a crash course in Israeli hand to hand combat skills, Krav Maga, which she'd learnt whilst working for Avi.

Her old boss, in the meantime, was seeing plots everywhere, convinced it was only a matter of time before Wayne tried to blackmail him, possibly encouraged by some sinister Saudi source.

A month to the day of Alberto's wedding, they flew to Delhi. They spent their first night in a decent hotel before hitting the backpackers trail.

The only clue to Wayne's whereabouts on arrival in Delhi was the drum symbol that had surfaced a couple of times back in Israel. It didn't take

Marci long to solve this riddle. The discovery cam whilst she was flicking through the cheap accommodation in New Delhi section in the 'The Lonely Planet'. "I've got it!" She shouted. "Look!"

"Ringo's hostel," he read aloud, immediately seeing the connection.

They spent a couple of hours discovering the madness and heat of Connaught circus, before returning to take advantage of a decent room, where Marci spent an hour coaching her fellow traveller in the art of breaking an opponent's nose with a swift upward strike with the palm of a hand. After beating each other up, they went through the Karma Sutra for the rest of the evening.

The next morning they made their way to Ringo's, which was on a fairly quiet road not too far from the centre. Their room was tiny, situated on the roof, it reminded Stephen of A6 back at the kibbutz, it probably contained a similar amount of asbestos.

It was blisteringly hot and the fan wasn't working properly. They'd requested single beds but were given a double, which didn't look sturdy enough for Marci's strict daily regime of Martial arts and sex.

They made their way down to the garden where backpackers tended to hang out and quickly mingled with the collection of travellers from around the globe, Swiss, Columbian, Mexican, French, Australian and Israeli. *Israeli, interesting*, Stephen thought whilst talking to a young couple from Tel Aviv. *Were they genuinely on their post uni tour of the subcontinent or could they be working for Avi?* Avi's paranoia was clearly catching.

Marci mingled with the strange assortment of travellers whilst Stephen showed photos of Wayne and Neville to the staff. Both spun the same story, that they were supposed to meet their friends but had been delayed in Europe and desperately wanted to catch up with them. The two met back in the garden where they realised they had both been given the same information. "Speak to 'Bristol', he knows everything about everything," the manager said. "'Bristol' will know," a Dutch backpacker confirmed, adding he could be found in the Raj Hotel bar most evenings, if he didn't pass by Ringo's with his bag of goodies during the afternoon rounds.

They returned to their room for a siesta but Marci insisted on a half hour of Krav Maga. Stephen protested but she put her foot down, literally. "Steve you've already cheated death at the hands of Marvin, who knows what Neville will do to protect his loot and Wayne could be equally as disappointed to see you."

Marci slept like a baby that afternoon, Stephen, when not staring at the slow motion fan above the bed, was making frequent visits to the communal toilet.

By the time she had woken from a restful siesta, Stephen was clutching his stomach in agony. "You've only been here twenty-four hours and you have Delhi belly already," she chided him without sympathy. She decided to leave him to suffer whilst she went to look for 'Bristol' at the Raj.

Stephen spent the evening running between his bed and the hole in the ground.

Marci found an empty bar stool and ordered a gin and tonic insisting on no ice, having deduced it was the ice in last night's drink that had done Stephen in.

"I'm looking for 'Bristol'," she said to the smart barman. He nodded to a suave feller a few stools down. He stood out in his linen suit, pink shirt and ivory fedora hat.

"I'm looking for 'Bristol'," she repeated as he acknowledged her by tipping his hat and then moving to the seat next to her.

"M4 all the way from Chiswick, past Reading and Swindon, should be there in three hours," he responded.

"You're 'Bristol'," she said knowingly.

"At your service," he said in his distinctive West Country accent. "You've only just arrived haven't you darling?"

"Is it that obvious?"

"You've still got plenty of meat on the bone," he was eyeing her cleavage, "anyone who is here too long looks like they've been in Belsen."

An unfortunate term to use to a Jewish girl, she thought. "I'm looking for a couple of friends." She placed the photos on the bar.

"Clients, yes I've met them, what's a nice girl doing with a couple of dodgy geezers like these?"

"Supposed to be travelling with them but I was late getting out here, do you know where they might have gone?" She asked.

"Indeed I do, I've got their itinerary pinned to my bedroom door."

Stephen didn't think it was possible for the human body to produce so much waste. He reckoned such illness was commonplace at Ringo's as no one seemed perturbed by his retching and moaning. He eventually dozed off late in the evening, waking with a start as light filled the room. He looked at the small travel clock, 5am. *Where the fuck was Marci?* He lay, staring at the pathetic fan, getting seriously concerned about her whereabouts. He considered getting a rickshaw to the Raj but couldn't lift himself from his sweat soaked bed.

He tossed and turned feeling weak and tired but grateful his urgings to rush to the hole in the ground had passed.

"You look like shit," Rotten smirked, standing against the room door, "you smell like shit too."

"Fuck off," Stephen replied without enthusiasm.

"You're just pissed off your bird's spent the night with a low life drug dealer." Rotten touched a nerve.

"Fuck off Rotten, I thought I told you you're history."

"Well you're stuck with me mate, your fucking 'Boss' is still waiting for you 'neath that fucking Exon sign in fucking 'Jungleland'. What a wanker."

"He's history too," Stephen confirmed.

"So, who's the new one minute wonder?"

"Have you heard The Smiths?" Stephen lit the fuse.

"The fucking Smiths, are you fucking joking, please don't tell me your not sucking up to that fucking hearing aid wearing, flower waving, moaning diva."

Stephen smiled knowing he'd got the better of his bitter ex hero. "He's a charming man and you're fucking history Rotten." Before the Pistol could reply, the door opened and a weary looking Marci staggered in.

"Where the fuck have you been?" Stephen snapped.

"You're still alive then," she replied, collapsing on the bed beside him.

"I spent most of the night in the loo. Where the hell have you been?"

"Bristol," she confirmed.

"You found Bristol?"

"I sure did."

"And?"

"And he told me where Neville might be and exactly where Wayne is."

Stephen sat up, he felt like shit. "And how exactly did you acquire this information?"

"I spent the night with him, we did a trade, besides you wouldn't be much use in your state," she said casually.

"You did a trade?" Stephen said, thinking of the 'Big A' and the French volunteer.

"You got a problem with that?" She replied coldly.

Stephen appeared to sulk.

"For Gods sake Stephen, we are on a mission, we are both consenting adults and it's not like I'm your girlfriend or anything, you should be grateful I'm such a accommodating travelling partner."

"How about your self respect?" Stephen asked.

"Fuck you Stephen, this isn't a fucking holiday."

"So where are they?"

"Neville is en-route to Jaslemere via Jodhpur and Jaipur. Wayne is in the Imperial Hotel, Hyderabad."

"Where the fuck is that?"

"Middle of India, twenty-four hour train journey apparently, you'd better get your shit together, I'm going to look for Neville," she confirmed.

"We're splitting up." Stephen was taken aback.

"Well you can join me if you like, but my priority is Neville and the missing money." Stephen thought about Avi's warning, he thought about the Saltzmans and Mendocino. "And how does this Bristol feller know all this?"

"He sorted out their drug and currency needs, he's a one man Mr. Fixit."

"Suppose we go together and look for Neville and then Wayne?" Stephen suggested

"A waste of precious time, besides Bristol's joining me, not sure you two will get on," she added coldly.

Stephen stared at the door feeling betrayed.

Marci put her hand on his shoulder. "You'll be fine Steve, just keep practicing the upward palm into the nose movement I taught you."

32

HALF A PERSON

Marci was packed and gone within a couple of hours. Stephen lay sweating on his bed feeling sorry for himself, he was relieved the trips to the toilet had subsided but he felt weak, lonely and angry. This fucking 'Bristol'. *How could she trust him? How could she sleep with him? How could she travel with him?*

He slept for hours before slushing himself down with dodgy water and forcing some chapatis down. He decided he'd go to the train station in the morning via the post restante just in case there were any messages. It was a long lonely night, he thought about Marci with Bristol and wondered if Cassandra was still seeing Toby. He hadn't met either man, but he didn't like them.

He was up and away early, but the traffic in the centre of town was ridiculous. The post restante sat in the middle of a huge roundabout and it took him twenty minutes to cross the road. He was desperate for a drink by the time he eventually reached the post room. He purchased two Campa Cola's at a small kiosk and downed them in one.

He showed the man behind the grill his passport and waited whilst he disappeared into the bows of the building. He returned with a solitary telegram that Stephen read over and over, eventually having to sit on a vacant bench opposite. The telegram had been sent the afternoon he'd left the UK.

FOLLOWED YOU TO AIRPORT BUT MISSED YOU STOP
GETTING NEXT AVAILABLE FLIGHT STOP

LEAVE DETAILS OF YOUR WHEREABOUTS STOP
HAVE YOU FOUND WAYNE STOP
CATCH UP ASAP RACHEL

Stephen felt queasy again and very confused. He purchased some notepaper and envelopes from the kiosk and pondered what to write and do next. His stomach cramps and dizziness suddenly returned and he quickly dropped the paper on the bench and ran to the public toilet.

The stench emanating from the hole in the ground was overpowering. He squatted above trying to make sure his shorts didn't touch the soaking floor. Just as his bowels emptied, a fat rat climbed out of the hole and scurried away. *I give up*, he thought, *I want to go back to phoning poor tenants for Mr. S.*

Jonny Rotten crouched down beside him holding his nose. "Well you wouldn't get the 'pope of mope' hanging around here would you my old china, heaven knows I'm fucking miserable now eh. Anyway I've got good news and bad news."

"What's that, you've retired," Stephen laughed.

"The good news is you've got company out there, the bad news is there's no fucking loo paper!"

Stephen swore as he realised there was only an empty slosh bucket. He decided on drastic action and removed his sweaty smelly socks and wiped himself with them.

He felt faint as he returned to the bench but he started to write a note for Rachel Saltzman.

Dear Rachel,
I've had enough, I feel ill, I'm going home asap.
Sorry.
Good luck,
Steve

He placed the note in the envelope and wrote Rachel's details on it. He didn't have the energy to get up and cross the hallway to the man behind the grill. He closed his eyes and slumped on the bench not caring if security came and moved him on. He dozed off for a good couple of hours but woke with a start, at first he thought he was dreaming, he recognised the voice, then the back of those legs. "Rachel," he croaked, then cleared his throat and tried again. "Rachel!" She was speaking to the postmaster behind the grill but at his shout turned to face him. She looked immaculate, her green eyes gleaming amongst the greyness of the building.

"Steve," she said as she came towards him and then recoiled when she saw the state of him.

"I know, I look and smell like shit."
"You look ill Steve."
"That's because I'm actually dead."

He stood under the shower in Rachel's en-suite bathroom in her five star hotel room. He'd been under the powerful jets for at least twenty minutes using an entire bottle of shampoo. He wrapped himself in a fresh towel and emerged a new man. "That, Rachel Saltzman, was the best twenty minutes of my life."

Rachel treated him to a 'European meal' at one of the hotel's seven restaurants. At first she brought him up to date with the latest tittle-tattle from the Saltzman property empire. Then she told him of her growing trophy cabinet due to her blossoming partnership with her horse, Sunbeam.

"So where's Wayne?" She said, getting to the point.
"Hyderabad."
"Where the hell is that, how do you know?"
Stephen brought her up to speed with recent events. "So what now Rachel, what exactly you doing here?"
"We go to this Hyderabad place and find him," she said as if it were the obvious thing to do.
"And if he's there, what's your plan Rachel?"
"My plan is to marry him."
Stephen blinked and paused before replying. "But he's married, he has a baby."
"So you say, but I have a plan Steve. I won't give up on him."

They both spent the first few hours of their journey south reading books they'd taken from second-hand book libraries in their respective hotels. There were no first class tickets available so Rachel had to suffer second class reserved, which meant sharing with four others. This would have been unimaginable a year previously but Rachel's kibbutz experience now held her in good stead, though Stephen wondered what she'd make of her second class toilet experience.

After reading, they both closed their eyes for a few hours. Stephen awoke to find a new occupant opposite him, long unkept hair, incredible beard and dressed only in a loin cloth.

Stephen thought at first Jethro Tull's Ian Anderson had replaced Rotten, but the stranger introduced himself. "Good afternoon, I'm Trevor the 'Sadhu'."

"Hiya," Stephen mumbled as Rachel stirred.

"You may be wandering why I'm dressed in this strange attire sir," Trevor stated.

"I'm more mystified by how you got the name Trevor," Stephen replied.

"Good question sir, my father was a teacher at an international school in Bombay, the headmaster's name was Sir Trevor Wilcox. My father named me after him, said it was a distinguished name."

"And I guess you're not a teacher Trevor?"

"No sir, I'm a civil servant, or should I say was, before I became a sadhu."

"A sadhu?" Rachel questioned.

"A sadhu is one who forsakes the material world and follows the spiritual path. I worked in the Ministry of Agriculture for over twenty-five years and one day I came home from work and told my family I had decided to travel the path of the sadhu. I went upstairs and removed my expensive pinstriped three piece suit, set fire to it and wrapped myself in a sarong, wished my family well and hit the road."

"How long have you been on the spiritual path?" Stephen asked.

"What do you do for money, for food etcetera?" Rachel added.

"Just over two years. The good people I meet on my travels sustain me and tell me, are you two handsome people on honeymoon?"

"God no," they both answered in unison.

"We're looking for a mutual friend," Stephen explained.

"Well I wish you both luck but I think you have both found what you're looking for," Trevor said mischievously.

"I don't think so," Rachel confirmed with a firmness that troubled Stephen, who winked at the sadhu.

"I like you Stephen."

"You don't know me."

"I can see you have a good soul and you have spirit."

"Thanks Trevor, you've made my day."

The sadhu leaned forward and clasped Stephen's forearms. "Most of us climb the stairway of life holding firmly onto the hand rail, a few of us, not many, are brave enough to let go, you my friend have let go."

"So have I," Rachel interrupted, "I rebelled."

"No my dear, rebelling is not letting go of the hand rail, you have the luxury of rebelling and that luxury stops you from falling back down those stairs. Young Steve here hasn't got that safety net."

Stephen thought he understood but Rachel shook her head in confusion and disappointment. Trevor closed his eyes and mumbled a mantra to himself.

After a period of silence Stephen turned to Rachel, "So when we find Wayne what's your plan?"

"I'm going to pay you a healthy finder's fee and wish you the very best for the rest of your life." Rachel's green eyes glowed with sincerity.

"What if Wayne confesses to his domestic bliss back in California?"

"He's here isn't he, he's not in California, we all make mistakes."

"I think you are making a big mistake Rachel."

"You've met my family Steve, my father's a control freak, Wayne is my future."

"Your father loves you more than anything on this earth Rachel, your mother is lovely, your brothers are charming, you don't know how lucky you are. They are all there for you."

Rachel's eyes watered, Stephen thought he might have struck a chord. "So where was my lovely family when Uncle Harvey raped me?" Rachel's steely tone shocked Stephen. She stared at Steve for a few seconds before continuing. "Thank you Steve but fuck my family. I have to think of myself, you've no idea how shit it is being me."

"I'm sorry Rachel, I can't possibly imagine your pain." He considered his next words for a few moments. "Do know what it's like to be half a person though?"

"What, what do you mean half a person?"

"Half Jewish, half Christian, equals nothing. I'm not considered a proper person. Your children with Wayne could be half people like me, I wouldn't recommend it."

"Well I'll accept Christ for Wayne, so it won't be a problem will it." Rachel replied coldly.

Shit, Stephen thought, *this isn't going well.*

33

WHITE GIRL IN THE TROPICS

Rachel had fallen asleep again with her head on Stephen's shoulder. It was getting dark outside, long shadows spread across the endless featureless plains of central India. Trevor the sadhu snored loudly whilst Stephen cogitated on Rachel's rant. Surely half a person was better than a non-person, that would be her father's view. Well, half a chosen person maybe. At the end of the day it was probably Wayne's magnetic personality and looks that had won her over.

He had to face defeat, short of drastic measures, he'd have to accept that tomorrow Rachel and Wayne would be reunited and in all probability spend the rest of their lives together. No bedsit, no more monthly handouts from Mr. S. He could however convince Wayne that Avi was a good guy and had saved both their lives, that at least would be a victory to savour.

He spent an hour writing letters, first he took revenge for Marci's betrayal with 'Bristol', which hurt him more than it should. He thought of Marci travelling through the glorious cities of Northern India giving this geezer regular sex and possibly Krav Maga lessons. He disliked this character almost as much as Toby. He shuddered at the thought of him wining and dining Cassandra.

He wrote to the Goodmans explaining that he'd tracked their daughter and Neville to New Delhi and gave details of their travel plans. He guessed they would contact the Canadian or Israeli embassies and the matter would soon be closed. One last cheque from the Goodmans, but no more spectacular blowjobs that's for sure.

He wrote a brief letter to the Saltzmans just to put their minds at rest that he was with their daughter and all was well. Lastly he wrote a frivolous ditty to Cassandra.

A train guard put his head in the compartment and announced it was lights out The sadhu's neighbour stood and pulled down the fold up bunk bed then did the same above Stephen, who gently lay Rachel down on the seat, covering her with an Indian Railways blanket before he climbed to the bunk above her. He peeped down admiring her good Semitic looks. *Should I be wooing her?* He pondered. He could convert fully, so the Saltzmans would be happy, and he'd get something much grander than a bedsit.

Jonny Rotten suddenly appeared at the end of the bunk. "Don't even think about it matey, you're batting way above your station."

"Fuck off," Stephen mouthed.

"Well you ain't going to get any advice from that gladioli wielding idiot are you."

"I wouldn't bother him over such a trivial matter, so just fuck off."

Rotten disappeared. Stephen closed his eyes and thought about Cassandra. He hoped this adventure would soon be over so he could see her again.

He slept well, interrupted only by Trevor gently shaking his hand in the middle of the night to tell him he was getting off at a village containing a holy shrine. "Good luck to you my friend, may God bless you. We will meet again one day, somewhere in a faraway place." The train came to a halt in the middle of nowhere and the sadhu was gone.

They arrived in Hyderabad during rush hour, he'd heard 'Bedlam' was a town in India this could have been it. Rachel held onto Stephen for dear life, they were both alarmed by the apes that ran freely around the station. They headed to the taxi rank where a scene of complete mayhem met them.

There was a line of taxis as far as the eye could see. The drivers were all outside their cabs thrusting placards in the air and chanting loudly. In the road was a sea of bicycle rickshaws and thousands of commuters. In the middle of this scene was an auto rickshaw on fire and the driver being beaten by a mob of taxi drivers with large sticks.

"They are on strike sir," a stout businessman exclaimed.

"Why are they attacking that poor man?" Rachel asked looking alarmed.

"He's a strike breaker madam, the taxi drivers won't allow the auto boys to work, only the bicycle boys are allowed. Where are you going?"

"Hotel Imperial!" Stephen shouted.

The local ushered them through the mob towards a vacant bicycle rickshaw and wished them good luck.

Stephen started to barter with the driver but Rachel interrupted, "We can give you American dollars, how much do you want?"

"Twenty," the driver replied.

"That's more the my train fare from Delhi mate."

"I just want to get out of here, go get another one if you want to be stupid," Rachel chided him, he felt foolish. He relented and took Rachel's rucksack off her back and then his own.

As Rachel was climbing into the rickshaw she turned and started screaming at a young man standing directly behind her.

"What's up?" Stephen shouted.

"He touched me, he assaulted me!" She cried pointing at the accused. "He put his hand between my legs," Rachel said, distraught.

Stephen dropped the bags on the floor and strode round to confront him. A crowd had developed amongst the general mayhem outside the station.

"Did you touch her?" Stephen yelled.

The young man was a similar age to himself, he stood his ground and smirked.

"I said, did you assault my friend you fucker?"

The fella continued to smile, Stephen thought he might be simple, possibly crazy. It was almost ninety degrees, the taxi drivers were getting more agitated. Stephen's head was throbbing, he looked at Rachel who was crying. A high maintenance bitch she might be, but seeing how desperate she was to get to the hotel he couldn't see any way she'd make this up.

"You fucking touched her didn't you!"

The young man just stood there smirking. All those lessons in Krav Maga were forgotten as Stephen hit the guy with a good old-fashioned right hook straight in his nose, sending him dazed and confused to the dusty floor. Even allowing for the Leeds incident, the business with Marvin, and the fracas at the bachelor party, this was the first time Stephen had thrown a proper punch. His knuckles stung as he went to retrieve the bags the rickshaw driver was struggling with.

From nowhere two police emerged and grabbed Stephen telling him he was under arrest. Rachel started yelling at them, the driver joined her, one of them blew a loud whistle and within seconds police who had been trying to help the auto rickshaw driver came swarming to assist their comrades, who wrestled Stephen to the ground where they handcuffed him. A couple of others assisted the abuser whose nose was clearly broken and covered in blood. The situation was totally out of control.

A siren could be heard in the distance. Rachel clung onto Stephen, protesting his innocence. Suddenly the businessman who'd shown them to the rickshaw emerged through the mob that had gathered. "Officer, officer, I saw everything, this lunatic here did very bad thing to tourist lady, this man defended her."

The police looked at the bloodied 'lunatic' who still seemed to be smiling despite his obvious discomfort. The bicycle rickshaw driver confirmed the facts. The police removed the handcuffs from Stephen and put them on the 'lunatic', they beat him with their truncheons as they dragged him to the nearest police car.

Stephen helped Rachel into the back of the rickshaw and was relieved as they sped towards the centre of town.

Stephen felt nervous as they entered the Imperial hotel, after the last forty-eight hours he wasn't ready to face Wayne. Rachel turned to Stephen and, to his relief, suggested they rest and have a wash before finding Wayne.

Stephen lay on his single bed, too tired to consider his next move. Rachel had gone to the communal bathroom to freshen up, she returned to the room wrapped in a towel and lay on the other bed staring at the ceiling.

"You nervous?" Stephen enquired.

"A little," she answered.

He closed his eyes and drifted off for the next three hours. He woke to a frantic Rachel shaking him. "He's ill Stephen, he's in hospital!"

"What, what you on about?" He saw she was dressed, though not, in his opinion, appropriately for a predominantly Muslim city. He thought she looked stunning but quickly realised her efforts were not for him.

"I went down to reception and asked about Wayne and he confirmed he'd been staying here. He went to hospital in a taxi the day before yesterday. Stephen we have to go and find him, make sure he's okay."

"Did he say what's wrong with Wayne?"

"Acute stomach pain was all he knew."

"I know the feeling," Stephen muttered.

The manager confirmed which hospital he'd gone to and suggested they take a bus as the strike was still in place. The heat was stifling, the pavements crowded, both felt dizzy with stress. The bus stop was only a short walk away but they were exhausted and thirsty by the time they got there. At least two hundred souls thronged around the stop, it was not a queue in any shape or form. A bus arrived and the crowd surged forward, Stephen held Rachel's arm and tried to get on but barely a quarter of the crowd made it. Ten minutes later and another bus arrived, the same story. The heat was stifling and Rachel was getting frantic. "I've got an idea, give me some rupees, fives if poss."

Rachel did as he asked emptying her money belt. Stephen saw another bus in the distance fighting through the chaotic traffic.

He ran into the road shouting at the crowd, which seemed to have grown even bigger. "Who wants some, who wants some!" He yelled whilst releasing note after note into the dusty air. A couple of the throng followed him, then more, until the bus was almost at the stop and he flung a wad of Rachel's cash in the air. A riot ensued as the city's poor fought each other for the money, he grabbed Rachel and pulled her onto the bus.

A conductor pushed Rachel towards a section at the front reserved for 'ladies'. Stephen was in a terrible sweat but still strained to catch sight of Central Hospital.

Twenty minutes later he saw the Art Deco building ahead, Rachel nodded, she'd seen the giant red H as well. They exited through separate doors and were relieved to meet up on the pavement. They made their way to the grand front entrance and were shocked to see a mass of doctors shouting slogans about pay and hours.

"The fucking doctors are on strike," Stephen exclaimed as they barged through the white-coated mob.

The reception was another scene of chaos, with nurses, relatives, and patients all screaming at each other. "Come on Rach, let's just look in every ward till we find him."

They headed towards what seemed to be a surgical ward but when they entered they were confronted by rows of dental chairs full of patients with their mouths open, waiting for a solitary dental consultant to examine them. They ran out straight into a bearded man dressed in a long white robe, who they both assumed was an imam. "Slow down my friends, who are you looking for?"

"For my friend," Rachel said, exasperated.

"Okay, do you know what's wrong with him?" The man asked.

"Acute stomach pains," Stephen answered.

"What is his name please?"

"Wayne, Wayne Richardson," Rachel said, hesitating for a second hoping he'd not used another name.

"Possibly Chris, Christopher," Stephen added.

"Wait here please, I will do my best to help you."

They stood against the corridor wall trying to calm down. "Thank you Steve," Rachel said taking him by surprise, "thank you for helping me."

Stephen breathed out a long tired sigh, "We're both fucking bonkers Rach."

She laughed and kissed his cheek.

A few moments later the imam returned. "Follow me, there is only one white person here in this hospital, I have a ward number, let's give it a go."

They followed the kindly man, he reminded Stephen of Trevor the sadhu. They walked through the labyrinth of corridors till they reached ward East 14. "This is where he's supposed to be, good luck."

"Thank you sir." Stephen shook his hand, wondering how there was so much goodness amongst the chaos in this crazy country.

Stephen tensed up as they entered the huge open ward full of beds and shabby curtains. The smell was shocking and there was a constant hum of moaning cries of pain. They walked around the ward but there was no sign of Wayne. They approached a nurse who was scrubbing her blood soaked hands. "Excuse me." Rachel was about to ask after Wayne but the nurse spoke first.

"You're here for the American," she said.

"Yes, yes we are, do you know where he is?"

"Yes, he's still in surgery."

"Surgery?" Rachel repeated.

"Yes, he had a burst appendix, he's very sick, they are operating now."

Tears started to fall down Rachel's cheeks. "Can we see him?" Stephen asked.

"You can wait in the corridor, they will bring him back down later this evening I would think."

They sat in the corridor on a bench with two other visitors. Stephen's eyes closed a couple of times but Rachel stared, wide eyed, up and down the corridor for hours.

Just before midnight, the double doors in the distance swung open, two porters were pushing a bed towards them. They stood together and watched in disbelief as a heavily sedated Wayne was wheeled pass them. He looked skeletal, his ponytail gone, Stephen didn't think it was possible for someone to look so pale.

34

A PLACE BEYOND HELL

Stephen and Rachel had been fidgeting for hours on two fold up canvas chairs either side of Wayne's bed. The ward was quiet save the odd cry of pain. They knew back home Wayne would be on a high dependency ward but this wasn't home and they were also in the midst of a doctors' strike.

It was 4am when Wayne regained consciousness. Rachel knelt beside the bed and held his hand, his wrist was so thin his name tag was falling over his knuckles. "Wayne, it's Rachel, I've come to look after you, I'm going to get you to a private hospital in the morning."

Wayne blinked, possibly in disbelief, and tried to speak but no words would come. Eventually he managed to croak, "Drink, I need drink."

Rachel looked at Stephen who gestured towards the door and slipped out to search for a shop. He found a concession near the reception but it wasn't open till seven so he stepped out to the street. A row of rickshaw drivers lined the pavement asleep in their passenger seats. He saw a boy, no more then eleven years old, sleeping against the hospital wall clutching a box of Fantas. Stephen gently woke him, "How much for the box?"

The boy stirred amazed to see a westerner. "How many cans sir?"

"All of them."

They negotiated for couple of minutes before they shook hands and he returned to the ward with a dozen cans. Wayne gulped two straight down, it was as if he hadn't had a drink for days. "You," he mumbled, "I know you." He made eye contact with Stephen.

"Yes, it's Stephen, we met in Jerusalem. I've helped Rachel find you."

Wayne looked confused and slightly agitated. Stephen guessed he was trying to equate their previous meeting with him being with Rachel.

"It's a long story Wayne, don't worry yourself now, you need to recover. Is there anything else I can get you my friend?"

Wayne tried to sit up, he became agitated and took another gulp of Fanta. "Mendocino, you were in Mendocino," he grunted clearing his throat.

"He was helping me find you," Rachel interrupted, trying to calm him. "Don't worry about anything, all that matters is that you get well."

Wayne clutched Rachel's hand. "I'm so sorry, may the Lord forgive me."

"Can I get you anything darling?" Rachel asked.

"My bags, I need my bag, the manger has it, at the hotel. Please get my wash bag, you must fetch the wash bag!" He closed his eyes and drifted off.

They decided the best plan of action was for Stephen to go back and get Wayne's bag and provisions, whilst Rachel stayed and kept an eye on him.

By the time Stephen got back to the hotel it was the morning rush hour, he was relieved to see the taxis back on the road and hoped the doctors would be back on duty as well.

He collected Wayne's backpack and took it back to his room. He found the wash bag in the side pocket and pulled it out before lying back on his bed. Stephen drifted off for a few hours and was woken abruptly by the sound of the door closing. He sat bolt upright, it took about thirty seconds to realise Wayne's backpack had gone. He looked down the passage and then ran to the bedroom window. Two Arab looking guys were getting into a taxi, the driver was putting Wayne's bag in the boot.

Stephen had been wondering why on earth Wayne had come to this city, a strange choice for a traveller. He wasn't about to go chasing after what wasn't his business. He bent down to put his shoes on and saw Wayne's wash bag still lying on the floor. He emptied the contents on the bed but there was no washing paraphernalia. There was however an envelope containing five thousand pounds in cash, another envelope containing three thousand dollars, a letter handwritten in Arabic and a sealed airmail letter addressed to Carol Berkovitz in Mendocino. *The wife*, Stephen thought. There was also a box of plasters, which Stephen thought was a stroke of luck as his heels were red raw where he'd scratched mosquito bites.

Suddenly he went into panic mode. *Shit, whoever took Wayne's stuff was probably after the contents of the wash bag*. He put everything back, placed the bag in Rachel's rucksack and quickly packed both their things.

The manager was surprised by Stephen's request to check out and pay the bill. "What about your friend in hospital?" He enquired.

"I'm sure he'll be okay, I'm going to Bangalore today," Stephen lied.

"Please, if you take this, it's boiled water, it's going to be extra hot today." The manager gave Stephen a large metallic flask, he felt guilty lying to such a decent man. Stephen hailed a taxi and the driver threw the baggage in the boot. "Station?" He guessed.

"No I need a hotel near the Central Hospital, not too expensive but not to shabby either."

"Leave it to me sir."

Stephen noticed the pavements were less crowded now the strike was over, the city seemed less claustrophobic than the previous day. He looked round several times to see if he'd been followed but saw no one suspicious. They arrived at a reasonably quiet avenue outside a functional old building.

"This is the old post office sir, it is now a hotel, only five minute walk from the hospital."

Stephen handed the driver a generous wad of cash. "Is that enough to hire you for the rest of the day?" He asked.

"I'm yours till midnight sir, what now?"

"Help me carry the bags to my room then wait for me."

He checked into a double room overlooking the avenue and told the taxi driver to keep an eye out for the two Arabs, to hoot three times if they enter the hotel. The room was as basic as the Imperial but it did have its own facilities. Stephen looked out the window and saw Mohamed, the taxi driver, in his cab reading a newspaper. He thought back to the Star hotel in Jerusalem when he was keeping an eye out for Marvin.

He sat on the edge of the bed, "Shit." He realised it was a double bed. *Rachel won't like this*, he thought. He took Wayne's letter to Carol out of the wash bag and carefully opened it.

Dearest Carol,

I pray you and Chris junior are in fine fettle. I'm currently in Hyderabad, which is a hellhole but I'm taking care of business. Delhi was fascinating, Agra spectacular. I met my Saudi friends and everything's ready for the 'end game' with Rachel who, as expected, has arrived in Delhi with the English guy who called on you. Rachel wrote to me on hearing about you and our son, declaring her love was undimmed and she would organise a lawyer to obtain a quick divorce (ha ha). She also reckons the English guy is in cahoots with the Saltzmans and that Israeli lunatic that I think killed my friend Marvin.

Anyway once we have enjoyed our 'sham' marriage in Thailand my friends will take over and then we can enjoy the big fat pay cheque. It's a win win, double commission plus contributions from the Saltzmans to stop me going public re. their nasty family secret.

Best contact me at the Bangkok 'post restante'.

You know I'm doing this for us and the love of Jesus.
God protect us.

HOW TO KIDNAP A STRING QUARTET

All my love,
Christopher

Stephen read the letter five times. "Fuck!" He shouted, trying to come to terms with the implications. He wished Avi were there.

Suddenly he heard three blasts from a car horn. He looked out the window, Mohamed was gesturing frantically towards the front entrance. Stephen stuffed the letter into his shorts back pocket, grabbed the wash bag, placing it under his sweat stained shirt, and ran into the corridor.

He reached the stairs and could hear two sets of footsteps running up the two flights of stairs. He froze for a second and then decided there was nowhere to run, the mystery visitors reached the landing below Stephen. "Give me bag, give me bag!" One of them demanded.

"What bag?" Stephen replied.

The two men were about to climb the last few stairs when there was a shout from below. "Police, stop, police!"

They hesitated not knowing what to do next. At that exact moment Stephen produced the wash bag and threw it towards his attackers.

Stephen ran back to his room and managed to bolt the door, he was expecting a repeat of the 'Marvin' incident and frantically searched for anything he could use as a weapon. A couple of moments later there was a knock on the door. "Mr. Steve, are you okay sir? It's Mohamed."

Stephen opened the door flushed with relief. "The Arabs have scarpered sir," he confirmed.

"Where's the police?" Stephen asked.

"That was me Mr. Steve." Mohamed smiled and winked.

"I need a phone Mohamed, urgently, I need to make an international call."

"Mr. Steve this is India, 'backsheesh' will get you everywhere, be nice to the hotel manager and your wish will be his command."

A handful of ten rupee notes and Stephen was phoning an old friend. "Clara!" Stephen shouted down the mouthpiece, nodding to the manager to vacate his own office. "Clara, it's Steve, Steve Ross, I need to speak to Avi urgently."

"Steve, hi, you in trouble? Where are you?"

"Hyderabad, southern India, I'll give you my number, he needs to call me back urgently." He felt an acute sense of deja vu.

"Okay, it's early morning here, Avi should be at home still. Stay by the phone."

Four minutes later Avi phoned back, Stephen tried to calmly explain the recent events and particularly the contents of Wayne's letter. Avi, after a brief pause whilst he took in Stephen's revelations, was unusually agitated.

"Listen Stephen, from what you're saying, I think Wayne has Saudi backers whose main interest is embarrassing the Saltzmans and fucking up the charity Hilary Saltzman heads. It's also possible they could be planning to kidnap Rachel. Wayne's illness has put a spanner in the works. The Saudis wanted their money back and now they have it they might just disappear. They might be concerned that you have the letter, the one written in Arabic, I'm guessing it's incriminating. You need to go and get Rachel out of that hospital and get the hell out of there, get yourself back to Delhi. Go to the Danish embassy and ask for Lars. Tell him Benjamin wants to see him. He'll look after you."

Stephen ran up the steps of the hospital and through the chaotic reception area. He carried a bag full of drinks and food for Wayne but he wasn't carrying any plan. How on earth could he persuade Rachel she had to get out of town and Wayne's life, other than show her the letter. She was a spoilt pain in the backside but Stephen had a modicum of sympathy for her, particularly for her family troubles.

He entered the ward, the smell hit him in a way he hadn't encountered since his introduction to the turkey house. He saw a doctor standing in the middle of the ward with a mop, cleaning up fresh vomit. "Nice," Stephen said sarcastically.

"The nurses are on strike today, someone's got to do it."

Fucking hell, this town is hell on earth. Stephen was now focused on getting back home and back to normality. He made his way to where he'd left Wayne and Rachel but to his surprise the bed was empty, save for a pile of filthy sheets. He called the doctor over and asked where his friends had gone.

"I'm afraid the American developed a nasty infection so has been moved to isolation."

"What kind of infection, where's the girl?" Stephen asked frantically.

"Your friend had very major surgery, infection is not uncommon, he has septicaemia, he's very poorly. I presume the young lady is looking after him. Come, I'll show you where he is."

The doctor led Stephen through the maze of corridors whilst explaining the complexities of the infection. Eventually they came across a line of rooms, a sign saying '*Isolation*' hung on chicken wire from the ceiling. They stopped at room Y8 and the doctor gestured to a small window in the centre of the door. Stephen peered through, he could clearly see Wayne's face, it was paler than Hank's was on the slab back in Haifa. There was a drip going into both his hands. "Is the infection catchy?" Stephen asked.

"Not for you, but you could be a danger to him as his immune system is not good right now."

"I have some drinks and food for him," Stephen mentioned.

"Grab a chair and wait here, someone will come and check on him soon, they will put it by his bed."

"I'm concerned about the girl, where is she?" Stephen asked.

"Maybe she's gone for some air or food," the doctor suggested. Stephen thought he was probably right.

He paced up and down for a good half an hour and grew more anxious with every passing minute wondering where Rachel could have gone. "Fuck it," he said and opened the door to Wayne's room. He noticed his clothes dumped on the floor beside his bed. Stephen picked up the trousers and found Wayne's wallet, which he rifled through. It was empty except for a scrap of paper that Stephen placed in his own pocket.

"The bastards have stolen my money."

Stephen jumped out of his skin as Wayne croaked with his eyes wide open. "The fuckers have taken my money," he repeated.

"Keep cool Wayne, you look like shit, save your energy. I've brought you some drinks and stuff, where's Rachel?"

"I'm fucked man," Wayne whispered. "I think I'm dying."

That would be a result, Stephen thought guilty. "Marvin intended to kill you," Stephen said instead.

"What?"

"Marvin planned to kill the both of us and then help Hank claim the prize."

"What prize?" Wayne coughed as he spoke.

"Rachel, the reward from the Saudis, I've got the letter you intended to send to your wife. I know everything Wayne and so does our Israeli friend Avi. He saved both our lives, you have to believe me, if it was wasn't for him we'd both be long dead."

Wayne tried to speak but only managed a cough. He whispered, but Stephen couldn't hear him. He noticed some fresh blood on Wayne's gown that he'd coughed up but reluctantly put his ear close to Wayne's mouth. "It's not the Saudis," he moaned.

"What?" Stephen was perplexed.

"The money, it's not the Saudis. Yes they want to fuck up the Saltzmans but they didn't fund my team."

"What are you on about?"

"He's a fucking old Nazi." Wayne coughed blood into Stephen's face, he recoiled at both the blood and Wayne's revelation.

"Slow down Wayne, who's a Nazi?" He gave Wayne a bowl to spit out some more blood and then gave him a fizzy drink through a straw. He finished half the drink and grabbed Stephen's forearm, his wrist was now so thin his name tag fell off.

"Our sponsor is a fucking old German Nazi, I went into this with pure belief but I confess the money seduced me. The Saudis are working for him, not their government. There's no conspiracy, it's nothing to do with Middle East politics, it's an old Nazi millionaire still trying to fuck the Jews." He motioned for the bowl and wretched so violently Stephen thought his ribs would snap.

Stephen looked at the note he'd removed from Wayne's wallet. *'Klaus the German. Koh Samet'.* "Thailand?" Stephen guessed.

Wayne nodded. "I've never met him, I'm supposed to marry Rachel in Bangkok, a sham marriage. Then we'd have our honeymoon in Koh Samet where I was told the old Nazi lives and he would personally reward me."

"And Rachel?" Stephen asked.

"I don't know, I was only told I could go back to the States with the money, I'd have done my bit."

"It's a fucking kidnapping," Stephen growled.

Wayne grimaced as he cleared his throat and shrugged under the sheets.

Stephen momentarily considered pulling the drips out or worse, but there was a question he wanted answered, or possibly he didn't. "Ask the cunt," Jonny Rotten snarled from across the room, "you've got to ask him the fucking question."

Wayne's eyes were closing and his breathing was shallow.

"I don't want to know, I can't," Stephen told his ex hero, who shook his head and disappeared only to replaced by 'The Boss'. "Do the right thing man, you're going to regret asking the question but you're sure as hell going to regret not asking it."

"Wayne, Wayne." Stephen tried to stir him, as he seemed to be loosing consciousness. He splashed some stale water on his face. "Fuck it," he said, as Springsteen rolled the Sex Pistol out the room. "Has the big man been rewarded?"

Wayne rallied, his eyes were now wide open. "The big man?" Wayne repeated confused.

"I was at Alberto's wedding to his fat ugly American Jewish princess. Is he up for a prize?" Stephen waited, feeling a terrible sense of betrayal but confident the answer would be no.

Wayne grabbed at Stephen's arm again pulling him as close as possible. "I'm dying Steve, please get a doctor."

"Answer the question Wayne and I'll sort everything out."

"There's only one thing you need to know my friend," Wayne spluttered and then started to choke. "She's gone to Thailand, I sent Rachel to Thailand ahead of me."

35

THE LUNATIC EXPRESS

Stephen had lost two days. Not in the same way he had between the 'Big A's' wedding and Washington though. He could recall every torturous second he sat beside Wayne.

He'd rushed down to the exit when Wayne told him Rachel had long hit the road. He hoped to see Mohamed's familiar face, but was confronted by a sea of striking nurses and orderlies, chanting their mantras with gusto. He stopped in his tracks as his conscience dragged him back to Wayne's room. He sat watching the doctor change the drips and give various injections, struggling to find veins fat enough.

Fuck Rachel, Stephen thought, *Fuck Avi, the Saltzmans, Marci, the Goodmans, fuck them all.* Wayne was a nutter but he was human and Stephen decided he couldn't leave him in that hellhole alone. If Rachel had made it to Thailand then so be it, wherever she went, she wouldn't be marrying Wayne, sham or legally.

After a forty-eight hour vigil Stephen dozed off for just a few moments, sitting upright on the canvas fold up chair that had been his home for his entire visit. He dreamt Avi had slipped into the side room and disconnected Wayne's drip.

"Mr. Steve, Mr. Steve," he woke to a doctor shaking him roughly, "I'm sorry." Stephen was completely disorientated but relieved it was the exhausted Indian doctor and not the Israeli 'silent assassin'. "I'm sorry Mr. Steve, but your friend has gone."

"Gone, gone where?" Stephen mumbled, rubbing his bloodshot eyes.

"Mr. Wayne has passed away, just a few minutes ago."

It took a few seconds for the words to sink in. He looked at the American's ghostly white face, eyes and mouth wide open. "Is it okay if I close his eyes?" The doctor asked.

Stephen gestured positively, not quite believing that he was looking at another dead person, thinking of Hank and Marvin and the third body in the Haifa morgue.

The doctor helped him call the American Consulate in Bombay but he quickly discovered there's no point dying at two in the morning during a weekend. He tried the British Consulate but got no joy there either. He returned to the side room to say goodbye. He thought of Wayne's wife sitting on her wooden veranda in misty Mendocino, Wayne's dysfunctional family dotted around the plains of Oklahoma, and of Rachel. "Shit, Wayne," Stephen addressed the corpse. "Well at least you survived Marvin's plan, at least you got to see the Taj Mahal. What the fuck am I going to do about Rachel?" He suddenly had dark ideas, Rachel Ross, it had a ring to it.

"Don't even think about it you devious cunt," Jonny Rotten smirked in the corner. For once Stephen agreed with him.

Stephen held Wayne's hand and fumbled through the Lord's Prayer, before the orderlies came to take his corpse to the morgue.

He slept through the first twelve hours of the train journey and woke as they pulled into a chaotic provincial station. Dusk was falling on the endless flat terrain that dominated central India. Stephen was in no mood to engage with any of the fellow passengers who shared his compartment.

Suddenly, a mad eyed guy burst in and sat opposite him, roughly pushing a businessman along the bench seat. He stared wildly at Stephen, who tried to look away, but ten minutes after the train continued northwards he found the wild man still staring and more alarmingly he had placed his hand inside a filthy hold-all. The other passengers looked worried, Stephen thought the lunatic might have a knife in the bag and tried to recall his Krav Maga lessons from Marci.

He mistakenly made eye contact with him and the two stared at each other for a good three hours. The lunatic's hand remained in his bag, Stephen locked his fists in attack mode, deciding his left elbow would be used to attack the hand holding the knife and his right closed fist would thrust upwards into the nose, hopefully disorientating his foe. He hoped the fellow passengers might assist him but he wasn't confident. The ticket inspector entered the compartment and broke the stalemate. "Out!" The lunatic screamed, tensing his arm that was half submerged in his hold-all. The inspector fled in fright, slamming the door behind him. Stephen wondered what action the inspector would take but half an hour later the train was still hurtling into the night and they were still eyeballing each other.

Stephen was now considering a pre-emptive strike, smash his nose, two fingers thrust into his eye socket. Marci was very enthusiastic about that one. The lunatic was sweating profusely, Stephen thought of Trevor the sadhu, he had definitely let go of the handrail. *Which eye, left or right?* He pondered.

The train stopped at a tiny, remote station and the lunatic suddenly stood up, "Goodnight sir," he grunted and gave Stephen a friendly pat on his shoulder. "Please take this," he passed him a rolled up magazine from the hold-all, "enjoy sir, I wrote it, enjoy." The four other passengers collectively sighed with relief as the man left the train.

"Thank God for that," Stephen announced as he looked at the magazine.

"What is it?" The businessman enquired. Stephen shook his head as he showed him the cover. It was a trade magazine specialising in sewing machines. Stephen wanted to grab the handrail and go home.

As mad as the traffic was in Delhi, Stephen found the wide roads a refreshing change from Hyderabad, also no one seemed to be on strike. The embassy area was literally a breath of fresh air. The Danish embassy seemed pretty laid back like its people who he recalled fondly, having enjoyed a boys trip to Copenhagen a few years back.

"Hi, I'm here to see Lars, I believe he's expecting me."

The reception manager looked Stephen up and down, he knew he looked and certainly smelt like shit. "Tell him it's Benjamin, Stephen Benjamin Ross."

He was invited to sit in the plush leather chair that dominated the waiting room. He sat, admiring the grand paintings that adorned the colonial style interior for a few minutes, before Lars appeared. "Steve, hi I'm Lars, I'm a friend of Avi, how you doing?"

Stephen shook his hand, he was surprised at Lars' hair, he looked like a Viking or possibly a rock god with his long blonde locks. "I need a shower and some food and I need to speak to Avi."

"Okay, your wish is my command," Lars pointed to the door, "let's go to my place and take care of all three wishes."

"Plus I need to go to the post restante," Stephen added.

They exchanged small talk as they made their way through the rush hour madness. Lars smoked a pre-rolled joint as he drove, he offered Stephen one but he declined, all he wanted was food.

He received two letters and opened them as Lars swerved around vehicles and cows that littered the suburban streets. "Fuck!" Stephen shouted as he read through the first letter.

"You okay?" Lars could see his passenger was shocked.

"My father had a heart attack, fuck, I need to get home as soon as possible." He checked the date on the letter. "Shit, it was eight days ago!"

"You can phone home from my place, it's no problem."

The second letter was from The Crow, it was brief and diverted Stephen from the bad news.

Dear Stevie,
How's India, how's your arsehole?
Ran into Cass up west last night, that posh twat Toby proposed to her.
Enclosed is a present
Crow

Normally Stephen would have appreciated the single sheet of toilet paper his mate had sent but he was in no mood for joviality anymore.

Lars' apartment was in modern block housing that was almost exclusively occupied by diplomatic staff. Stephen showered for the first time in days and put on reasonably clean clothes. Lars had prepared a spread of Danish meats and cheeses, which normally Stephen would have wolfed down, but his appetite had disappeared. He felt a pang of guilt that it was the second letter that dominated his thoughts.

Lars pointed to the phone on the neat Danish teak wall unit. "Please call home, then I will see how quickly we can send you back." Stephen tried his home number but got the answerphone, he left a message confirming he'd just heard the news and he would be home as quickly as possible. He tried his brother but had no joy there either.

"Is it okay if I phone Avi in Israel Lars?" He shouted to his host, who was digging some cold beers out the fridge. He waited for permission whilst Lars placed three beers on a glass coffee table. "Okay if I give Avi a call Lars?" Stephen repeated.

"He's not at home, come have a nice cold Carlsberg."

"I'm sorry?" Stephen wasn't sure he heard correctly.

They were interrupted by the intercom. "Come on up." Lars pressed the entry button before opening the beers, inviting Stephen to sit.

"Avi's not at home."

"How do you know?"

"Because that's his cold Danish beer." Lars nodded at the third beer.

"Avi's here?" Stephen asked quizzically as the doorbell rang.

"Come in the door's open!"

A few seconds later Avi strolled casually into the living room shaking Lars' hand and then offering his hand to Stephen, who was too surprised to shake with any conviction. "What the fuck are you doing here?" Stephen exclaimed.

"After your phone call we decided the situation was too serious to ignore, we came as quickly as we could, where have you been for the last three days?" Avi asked without any warmth.

"With Wayne." Stephen replied sharply.

"How is he?" Avi asked.

Stephen was taken aback that he hadn't heard the news, he wondered if Wayne's body still lay unclaimed in the hospital ward. "Not good," Stephen understated.

"Is he still in hospital?"

"I would have thought so." Stephen decided to hold off on telling him and to see where this was heading.

Avi removed his sunglasses, "Is it worth me paying him a visit?"

"To do what?"

"Have a word with him regarding his intentions."

"Intentions?" Stephen laughed.

"Towards Rachel Saltzman," Avi offered.

"And yourself," Stephen added.

"Did you tell him about Marvin's plan?"

"I did indeed."

"And?"

"He was too ill to be bothered."

"So he really is very ill?"

"He couldn't be more ill." Stephen was enjoying this.

Avi sat forward. "Any chance he could die?" He asked hopefully.

"That would be helpful?" Stephen queried.

"Very." Avi was always to the point. "So is it worth me paying him a visit?" He continued.

"I'm hoping the American Embassy have already been to see him," Stephen teased.

"What, why would the Americans be involved?" Avi was agitated.

"Because I called them."

"You what?"

"Avi," Lars interrupted, "I think you should know Steve's had some bad news from home."

"Why did you call the fucking American Embassy?" Avi repeated ignoring his Danish friend.

"Because Wayne's dead," Stephen confirmed, stunning Avi into silence. "I fucking watched him die."

Avi took a gulp of his beer whilst staring at Stephen, he didn't like being played.

"Well that's saved me a trip," he said coldly. "Who's going to tell Rachel the good news?"

"Rachel, where is she?" Stephen asked, suddenly on the back foot.

Avi turned to Lars,"Any chance of a lift to the Raj Hotel Lars?"

36

THE A TEAM

Avi gave the highlighted events since Stephen's phone call from Hyderabad as Lars drove them to the Raj hotel, where Stephen recollected that glorious shower after his 'Delhi belly'.

Avi's team were convinced Rachel and Stephen were in real danger and got over to Delhi as soon as they could. In the meantime Lars, who owed Avi a favour, discovered Rachel was planning to get to Bangkok via Delhi and managed to delay her after chatting her up in the hotel bar. Stephen was dismayed to learn Lars spiked her vodka and lime with a sedative and laxative that led her to believe she had food poisoning. The result was Rachel was still in Delhi and Avi hoped the news of Wayne's death would persuade her to go home.

Two old friends met them in the hotel lobby, Stephen was delighted to see Clara, who had looked after Cassandra so well. He was less pleased to see Yakov, who had chatted Cassandra up on the beach. "Blimey Avi, you've brought the A team, I'm honoured."

"Rachel's wellbeing is very important to our bosses, or should I say the Saltzmans reputation is." Avi winked.

"Not forgetting your reputation Avi," Stephen added.

"I'm not bothered about my reputation just my job," Avi replied matter of factly.

"Shall we go and tell Rachel the bad news?" Avi ushered Stephen to the elevator.

"I'm really surprised you've taken this so seriously, bringing your troops all this way." Stephen commented as they entered the elevator.

"Those fellows who visited your hotel in Hyderabad are known to us, they are dangerous and they have followed Rachel to Delhi."

"Really?" Stephen was concerned.

"With respect Steve you've swam way out of your depth, we need to get you and Rachel home and sort this problem out."

They exited on the top floor and he followed Avi down the plush corridor to a suite. "I have another surprise for you," Avi said as he tapped the door four times and stared into the spy hole.

The door opened slowly. "Hi Steve, how are you?"

Stephen's jaw hit the floor. "Marci, what the fuck you doing here?" He said, dumbfounded.

"Marci's back onside Steve."

"Come in, Rachel's sleeping in the bedroom." Marci beckoned them in to the small reception area and offered drinks from the well stocked mini bar.

"I'm going to keep an eye out in the corridor, good luck with the bad news Steve," Avi offered as he left the two old lovers alone.

Stephen realised he'd be explaining events on his own. "How, when, why?" He addressed Marci.

"'Bristol' led me to that mad idiot Neville in the middle of Rajasthan, he's now totally under the influence of a 'Guru'."

Stephen laughed. "Well he's not the first Scouser to fall under the influence of an Indian Guru. What about the money?" He asked.

"The mad fucker has given every last cent to his 'Guru'!" Marci exclaimed.

"Well, I hope they've given him his own sitar," he quipped.

"I've never been anywhere as hot as Rajasthan so if his Irish friends come calling they better wear hats."

"And Avi?" Stephen enquired.

"I felt I should let him know about Neville and what with your and Rachel's situation he suggested we let bygones be bygones, so here I am."

"What does Rachel know?" Stephen nodded towards the bedroom.

"Not a lot, Lars did quite a number on her. I told her I was your friend and you've asked me to look after her till you get here."

"Impressive," he concurred.

Stephen entered the bedroom, Rachel was lying in the fetal position on top of the luxurious silk sheets. He kneeled beside her and touched her hand. She opened her eyes, they had lost a little of the their green sparkle.

"Stephen," she whispered, sounding pleased and relieved to see him.

"Hi Rach, you feeling better?"

She sat up and sipped a glass of cola. "Wow, I've had quite a bug," she said.

"Who hasn't, our western bodies aren't tough enough for this part of the world."

"He's gone hasn't he?" Rachel's words surprised him, he could interpret this two ways. Before he could answer Rachel clarified what she meant. "He died a couple of nights ago didn't he?"

"I'm sorry Rachel, I stayed with him till the end."

Rachel squeezed his hand in a gesture of appreciation. "Where is he now?"

"The American Embassy took care of everything, I guess they've arranged for his body to go back to the States." Stephen hoped this was the case at least.

"I knew he died Steve, I felt his presence two nights ago."

Stephen smiled sympathetically. "I've got to get home as soon as possible Rachel, my father's had a heart attack. Will you come with me Rach?"

A tear rolled down her cheek as she nodded. "Take me home Steve, I want to see my horses."

Clara confirmed she'd organised flights for the next morning. Avi stalked the corridors all night, Yakov was stationed in the lobby, Stephen lay on the sofa and Marci spent the night 'on call' in the room next door with Lars! Stephen had given up any lingering jealousy, accepting Marci was a nymphomaniac who he'd shared some good times with and had learnt a few moves from.

The night passed without incident, Avi treated Stephen to breakfast and briefed him on the logistics of getting to the airport. He also asked Stephen for one last favour before he returned to his normal life chasing tenants.

Rachel, still feeling the effects of being unwittingly poisoned by Lars, was unusually quiet on the flight home. Stephen pondered on the monthly payments continuing for sometime, plus a juicy bonus for getting her home safely.

As the captain informed the passengers they should prepare for landing, Rachel placed her hand on Stephen's knee. "I can't believe my father involved the Israeli Embassy in tracking me down," she sighed. "I can't face my parents Steve, can I stay with you tonight?" Stephen felt a sense of déjà vu.

"He loves you," Stephen confirmed.

"Maybe you're right Steve, but he's so overbearing."

"Because he loves you," Stephen repeated.

Stephen's bedsit was freezing, it was in the same mess he left it in when he'd rushed off to India. Rachel ablated in the bathroom whilst he busied himself tidying as best he could.

Rachel emerged in a negligée that didn't leave much to the imagination. She climbed into the bed. Stephen took his turn to freshen up, feeling slightly awkward.

"I hope you're going to sort the princess out this time matey," Jonny Rotten sneered from his perch on the laundry box.

"I told you Rotten, The Smiths are my friends now so fuck off!"

"Well you ain't going to take any advice on matters of a carnal nature from that flower wielding loser are you."

Stephen emerged from the bathroom in shorts and his old 'Clash' t-shirt. Rachel was on top of the bed, the negligée discarded on the thread born carpet.

Don't be stupid, I could regret this for the rest of my life, she's a princess for God's sake, he told himself.

An hour later he lay entwined with his bosses wayward daughter, having enjoyed the best sex of his life. The next morning he put her in a taxi to Hampstead Garden Suburb. He wouldn't see her again for fourteen years.

37

THE ALL IMPORTANT SECOND DATE

Although lying and scheming had become second nature to Stephen, he didn't enjoy the skullduggery involving Jimmy the locksmith and The Crow that resulted in him procuring Cassandra's passport. He found the stalking particularly uncomfortable but within a few days he had built up a pretty good idea of her and Toby's routine.

The hospital visits to see his father were, of course, a distraction, but he seemed to be making a good recovery. He met up with Rachel's brother Samuel who handed him his bonus for getting Rachel home safely and with the Saltzman bloodline intact. Stephen's brother pleaded with him to help with the family business whilst their father was recovering. Maurice Saltzman gave him a massive contract to update the glazing across his portfolio. He also had a surprise call from Marci, who told him she was staying in London and working for a Canadian bank, which he didn't believe, but he did tell her he might need a favour.

Operation 'second date' started with a short phone call from Stephen to Cassandra, which was friendly enough, but his pleas for her to join him for a drink weren't successful. After plotting and planning, including the aforementioned highly unlawful breaking and entering by his mates to acquire Cassandra's passport, D-day arrived.

Stephen got the green light from Marci that her honey trap had worked a treat and plotted up on a bar stool in the trendy wine bar Cassandra and her colleagues favoured for Friday after-work drinks. He'd travelled half way round the world and cheated death but he couldn't control his nerves as he watched the entrance. After what seemed an eternity she emerged with two friends. They headed for an alcove that was luckily was near the gents toilets. He knocked back his large scotch and headed to the loo where he splashed cold water on his face, breathed out and went to make his move.

"Hi Cass," he feigned surprise, "what you doing here?"

"Steve, hiya, after work drinks, what you doing up west?"

He was concerned she'd notice his heart pounding. "I'm stalking you," he laughed, telling the truth.

"Very funny." She introduced him to her work mates, "Steve is my jet setting friend." They indulged in some small talk, he was delighted when she asked him to join them but was concerned about the time. He brought a round of drinks and Cassandra told her friends how much she enjoyed her trip to the 'holy land', apart from getting the shits. Stephen looked at his watch and decided he'd give it five minutes and then ask her if he could speak to her in private. He was mightily relieved when her mates made their excuses and left them alone.

Cassandra noticed Stephen had a sports bag with him, "Off on another jaunt Steve?" She enquired.

"I'm going away for the weekend," he confirmed, "so how's your fiancé Toby?" He added, getting to the point. He noticed she looked a little tearful.

"Ex fiancé Steve, the bastard went missing on Tuesday, spent two days with some Canadian tart he met in here."

Stephen decided Marci would be his last lie to Cassandra. "I'm sorry Cass, but I have a confession to make," he gripped her hand, "since Israel I haven't stopped thinking about you. Don't go mad but I stole this," he placed her passport on the table, he thought Avi would be proud of him.

"How the hell did you get hold of my passport?" Cassandra shouted.

"I stole it from your house."

"What the hell for?"

Stephen put airline tickets next to the passport, "Because without it, these would be useless."

"What the hell are they?" She snapped.

"Okay Cass, this is the plan, you have two choices, you can join me in a cab to Heathrow where we'll take the eleven o'clock flight to Paris, I've booked a hotel for two nights near Montmartre."

"And the alternative is?" Cassandra interrupted.

"You tear the tickets up and tell me to fuck off, marry Toby, if he's still available."

She sat and stared at him for a few seconds. "You actually stole my passport?"

Stephen nodded.

"Steve you are a complete nutter."

He nodded again.

"Twin beds?" She enquired.

This time he shook his head. "We've got unfinished business Cass." Stephen chanced his arm.

"That's true," Cass confirmed. "Have you stolen some of my clothes?" She asked looking at the bag.

"No, I thought we could hit the Parisian shops."

They kissed and departed, hailing a taxi to take them to the airport.

The hotel was wonderful, fantastic location, well-stocked mini bar, comfy bed on which, after demolishing a bottle of champagne, they consummated their relationship. Stephen decided his hour with Rachel was not so glorious after all.

"I hope your shady capers are over Steve, I've given up a life of luxury for you," she teased.

"Come on Cassandra, the holy land and Paris for our first two dates, not bad eh."

"So what's next, New York?" She laughed.

"I think I'll best keep clear of there for a while," Stephen pondered.

"Perhaps we should try and do normal girlfriend boyfriend type stuff like go to the cinema, bowling, gigs, that kind of thing."

"Gigs, now you're talking."

"Yes, but I'm going to decide which gigs, in fact I'm going to take you to one next week," she stated.

"Really, this could be a deal breaker, who is it?"

"I was going to take Toby, but it looks like you'll have to do."

"I'm truly honoured, so who we going to see?"

"They're not everyone's cup of tea, I can find a someone on 'date line' if you aren't impressed."

"Come on, New York's off, where's our third date?"

"The Smiths." She waited for his response.

"I'm going to marry you Cassandra." He kissed her with an intensity that he'd never mustered before.

"You like The Smiths that much?"

"Where do you want to go on our honeymoon?" He whispered.

Cassandra dwelled on the question for a good minute. "Thailand."

"That's handy, an old friend recommended an exotic Thai Island called Koh Samet."

"Sounds good but you've got to meet my racist mother first."

"That's okay, I'll keep my cock in my pants and she will never know my dark side."

"So are you proposing?"

"I can't stand rejection, depends on your answer."

"I'd need to know your prospects, you'd need a proper job and a vow you'd never lie to me."

"Wow, I'm going to settle down into the boring family glazing business."

"So you've totally finished with the Saltzmans?"

Cassandra put him on the back foot, Stephen was about to lie but paused and did the right thing. "Not quite, I've got to meet a man about a dog tomorrow."

"Tomorrow, here in Paris?" Cassandra was puzzled.

"Got to deliver a message to an Irishman in a bar off the Arc de Triomphe tomorrow. It's a favour to Avi."

"Is the bar near the designer shops?" She asked mischievously.

"Absolutely, and that will be it, you have my word." He didn't mention the bedsit and commission arrangement with Maurice Saltzman.

"Well let's see how the weekend goes, let's see if you've got as much stamina as Toby." She teased him as she pulled off the bedspread.

"Blimey, you've thrown the glove down." Stephen laughed. He wondered if Toby was man enough to satisfy Marci.

Paris was bathed in sunshine as they walked along the Seine hand in hand. They had eggs for brunch, then visited the Eiffel Tower before winding their way towards the Arc de Triomphe area. The map Avi had given him was a little basic and they ended up revisiting the same side streets, struggling to find the bar donated by a felt tip blob. Cassandra eventually saw the sign down a tiny alley. She found the clandestine meeting very exciting and was impressed with how nonchalant Stephen was about it.

The bar was surprisingly busy, Stephen ordered two small beers and asked the barman if Liam was around, he told him to tell the Irishman Benjamin wanted to say hi. The barman pointed at a thickset man in his forties reading the Wall Street Journal on a stool at the end of the bar. Cassandra sat on a bench that ran under the window as Stephen headed towards him.

"Hi Liam," Stephen greeted the Irishman.

"And you'd be young man?"

"Benjamin, Avi asked me to give you a message."

"I'm all ears."

"Your friend is at a small village thirty minute taxi ride from Pushkar Station in Rajasthan. You need to ask for the Guru Shami, all the taxi drivers know him."

"Pushkar Station, Guru Shami I've got it. Thank you, have a good life." The Irishman returned to his newspaper, Stephen swigged his lager down and gestured to Cassandra to do the same.

"So is that it?" Cassandra asked as they walked hand in hand along the Champs-Élysées.

"That's it, I'm in the glazing business now," Stephen laughed. "So, should I propose to you now?" He chanced.

"Well, before you do and give up your lies and deceit forever, I'm going to give you a get out of jail card." Cassandra grabbed his arm and looked him in the eye, oblivious to fellow pedestrians who walked around them. "Have you slept with Rachel Saltzman?"

Stephen looked towards the Place de la Concorde in the near distance. His first reaction was to deny it but he had decided no more lies. "Yes, once."

"Recently?" Cassandra pressed.

"Yes, on our return from India."

"I thought you said you were desperate to see me?"

"It was research," Stephen teased.

"Research?"

"Yes I'm desperate to find her a suitable husband, I needed some background info." He tried to sound serious.

"So what conclusion did you come to?"

"She's fine in the bedroom department but she makes a crap sandwich," he laughed.

"And what kind of husband are you looking for her and why?"

"Just got to be totally Jewish, then I get my commission."

Cassandra looked at him quizzically.

"I'll explain all over lunch, I'm starving."

Stephen gave Cassandra the edited highlights of Maurice Saltzman's incentive package to keep the bloodline pure.

"So your bedsit could actually be your bedsit?"

"Yep."

"And you have risked your life chasing religious maniacs half way round the planet for that shitty little hole." Cassandra chided him.

"Well it may seem like a shitty little hole to you but I see it as a deposit on my three bedroom semi with a lovely garden for our kids." Stephen stared into her hazel eyes, she smiled and then sought one last confirmation.

"So apart from trying to find Rachel Saltzman a nice Jewish hubby, your life of deception is over?"

"Ha, the world of glazing is full of deceit, but yes I'm done with the Saltzmans, all of them."

"In that case Stephen Benjamin Ross, the answer is yes!"

38

STEPS FIVE (AND SIX) (2011)

Irene spat, bit, scratched and screamed. The rain was so heavy Stephen couldn't see a metre in front of him. The wind was so strong it was as if he was running the wrong way up an escalator. He felt a complete idiot for describing the hurricane as 'heavy drizzle' an hour earlier.

He turned to see the bar window but could only make out a blurred light in the distance. It seemed to take an age to reach the station entrance where the 'stooping man' continued his demented dance. Stephen tried to engage with him but to no avail. He turned and faced the closed grill, behind which were a group of policemen and security guards. Holding onto the grill he pressed his face up as close as he could. "Officers, I'm a tourist from London, I think I saw you arrest my friend Alberto!" He shouted, surprised that weather could be so loud.

"The station's closed sir, get off the street," an officer replied.

"I'm staying in the hotel next door, my friend came to help him," he nodded towards the 'stooping man'.

"I suggest you return to the hotel sir."

"I just want to know what's happened to my friend, why was he arrested? We saw him being led handcuffed into a patrol car."

The officer pressed his face up against the grill, Stephen was almost eyeball to eyeball with him.

"Your crazy friend was arrested for possession of a Class A drug sir and for threatening behaviour whilst resisting arrest," the policeman confirmed.

"Resisting arrest, my mate only wanted to help that poor man," Stephen said, desperately pleading the 'Big A's' innocence.

The officer gestured for his colleague to join him. "Show our English friend what his buddy was waving around."

The second officer produced a small bag of cocaine out of his pocket and then a handgun. "I'm afraid your friend is in big trouble, I suggest you go back to your hotel and dry off."

"What about him, you can't leave him out there, he'll die of hyperthermia!" Stephen protested and then watched aghast as the officers retreated into the station concourse.

'The Boss' tapped him on the shoulder. "You've gotta do the right thing man, I won't let this stand on my turf."

Stephen grabbed the 'stooping man', who was still going round in tiny circles. "Come on pal, I'm going to get you help." He dragged him back towards the hotel entrance wondering if Cassandra could see him. He reached the revolving doors but the hotel security refused to let the 'wretched street person' inside. "You've got to help him for fucks sake, he will die out here!" Stephen exclaimed.

After some deliberation they agreed the man could spend the night in a storeroom in the hotel basement. As one of the guards went to lead the 'stooping man' round to the back entrance, the poor man grabbed Stephen's hand and pressed something into it.

Stephen made his way into the lobby where Cassandra was waiting with a towel. After drying off Stephen decided enough was enough and retired for the evening.

Whilst Cassandra watched Irene's fury from the bedroom window, Stephen sat on the closed toilet seat fiddling with the mobile phone the 'stooping man' had given him. The phone was far more advanced than he was used too, but he managed to scroll the recent text messages. Within seconds he discovered whom the phone belonged to. *'Hi Louisa, meeting my old friend Steve in Manhattan. Keep safe xx Dad'.*

He clicked on the photo gallery and found himself searching through old photos as he tried to navigate to the most recent. He realised that Alberto had probably dropped his phone in the chaos and the 'stooping man' had picked it up. As he scrolled forward through the hundreds of photos the screen abruptly went blank as the battery died.

"Shit," he said, he placed the phone in his wash bag and rejoined his wife.

Post Irene New York was eerily quiet. Notwithstanding it was a Sunday, the transport wasn't due to return to working capacity until the following morning. Stephen had earned himself the day off, the girls and Luke decided they'd spend their last day in the Big Apple shopping but he gathered a lot of shops would be closed so he was free to try and make sense of the previous night's events.

His first port of call was to check on the wellbeing of the 'stooping man'. He made his way to the service entrance at the back of the hotel where he saw a queue of vehicles blocked by an ambulance at the front. A covered body was being loaded into the back. The security guy who'd helped out the night before saw Stephen and shook his head. "Sorry man, we found him this morning, I think his heart just gave up."

"Fuck," Stephen cursed, "poor fucker." He wondered if the 'stooping man' had a family, if he did they obviously weren't very close.

He made his way to a phone shop on Lexington where he managed to persuade the manager to charge the 'Big A's' phone whilst he had coffee next door.

At midday he sat on a bench in Central Park surveying deserted bandstand. The string quartets weekly concert was due in an hour, he felt guilty for hoping the hurricane would cause a postponement. *Was the big man still in custody? Had he been charged?* His friend's phone bursting to life interrupted his thoughts, the ring tone was 'Born to', 'The Boss' would be pleased. "Hello," Stephen answered gingerly.

"Al?" The caller hesitated.

"This is Al's phone, it's his friend Steve from London."

"Stephen, hi, how you doing? It's Dino, Al's cousin."

"Dino, yes I remember, been a long time."

"Sure has man, can you put me onto Al please, nice to talk to you Steve."

"Um…I'm sorry Dino, Al lost his phone last night, it's a very long story."

"Oh, don't worry Steve I know where he'll be, we have a meeting."

"Yes Dino I know, Central Park, I'm here now. I think your cousin's been arrested."

There was a pause before Dino answered, "Arrested, what for?"

"As I say, it's a long story, he told me about the string quartet, that's why I came here," Stephen explained.

"How much has he told you Steve?"

"Everything Dino, you know him, he's an open book, he's told me about steps one to four, but I think Irene's put pay to today's performance."

"No the performance is definitely on, I'm on my way, we won't need to take the steps Al had planned, I've got another alternative. I'll see you soon. If Al turns up tell him I've got everything under control."

Stephen ended the call and returned to the photo gallery he was studying before the battery died. He swiftly navigated to the most up to date entry, which turned out to be a video. He pressed the play signal and was shocked to see a shaky film taken inside what appeared to be the entrance to Grand Central Station. He could see the camera swing round from the police to the unmistakable figure of the 'stooping man', he searched the phone for the volume, finding the button as the clip ended, so he pressed play again.

> He could clearly hear Alberto's manic commentary, "I'm filming this you fucking arseholes. That poor guy will fucking die out there, you've got to do something!" The camera swings back towards the police.
> One of the officers, who Stephen recognised as the one who confronted him, steps forward, "Leave the area now sir, we are going to close the grill, leave now and take that freak with you."
> The chain of events repulsed Stephen and they were about to take an unexpected turn. The visual went blank as Stephen assumed Alberto put the phone back in his pocket. The next bit is inaudible, then he hears the big man shouting, "I'll put it down when you get him some help, this is fucking America man!"
> "Put it down, just put it down!" He hears chaotic screaming and shouting.
> "I will when you get him help!"
> "Put the gun down, you are in deep shit!"
> There's a loud almost primal scream and then a few seconds of muffled sound before a faint cry, "Stay still, you're under arrest, I've got the gun, turn him over."
> Suddenly the visual springs into life but all that can be seen is the ceiling, then the video ends.

Stephen guessed the phone must have fallen out of Alberto's pocket when he was arrested and was retrieved by the 'stooping man'.

"Fucking hell Al, you nutter," he muttered aloud. He noticed three figures in the distance heading towards the bandstand. His mind was racing, *why did he have a gun on him? Was it for something else?* The three members of the string quartet started to set up, Stephen decided he owed his crazy American friend a favour. He walked over to the bandstand, "Sorry to trouble you," he said.

"You're English," the female second soloist replied enthusiastically.

"I am indeed, I'm a tourist trapped here by hurricane Irene, I should be back in London now but the flight was obviously cancelled."

"Well it looks like you'll be our entire audience," she smiled.

"I'm honoured, but I must confess I have a hidden agenda for being here. I know my crazy friend has been driving you mad to play at his dying ex wife's bedside."

The three students looked at each other, the bassist appeared annoyed.

"Yeah, we know your friend, he's been on our case for some weeks, he has an attitude problem."

"I know," Stephen agreed.

"But I know him from old, we shared a cell together, he's a loose cannon, prone to extreme behaviour. He's been arrested again. I was rather hoping we could just get a taxi to Susan's place, a quick rendition of 'God

Only Knows' and everyone's happy." Stephen was rather pleased with his bending of the truth.

"Not everyone's happy," the bassist replied.

"I suppose if no one turns up to watch us we could make a quick visit to the poor lady," the young lady added.

'Born To Run' suddenly erupted in Stephen's pocket. "Hi Dino, I was just about to phone you, everything's sorted, they've agreed." Stephen didn't get the chance to explain the positive conversation he'd just had as Dino shouted down the phone. "Listen Steve tell those fuckers I've got the cellist tied up in the trunk of my car!"

"What!" Stephen yelled.

"Yeah, I tracked the fucker down, he's a student at NYU, and he's in my trunk, now tell them to get the fuck over to Elmhurst and 74th Queens, I'll meet you there."

That's step five out the window, so close yet so far, Stephen thought as he looked at the musicians. For once he couldn't come up with any bullshit. He considered the sensible option of wishing them well and heading to join his family in the posh shops of Fifth Avenue. He shook his head, took a breath and went for it.

"That was Dino, the big man's cousin, he's proper old school mafia. I won't lie to you, your cellist-"

"Marcus, what about him?" The young lady interrupted.

"Well there's no easy way of saying this, but Dino has him tied up in his trunk, I suggest we get over to Queens pronto."

"What the fuck!" The bassist yelled.

"I'm calling the police!" The violinist shouted.

"That's up to you, but it would be easier to join me in a cab, meet your friend, play 'God Only Knows', put a smile on Susan's dying face, fuck off and get on with your glittering lives." Not a speech he'd ever envisaged making but it had the desired effect.

The bassist stepped forward and moved closer to Stephen. "Okay, tell your maniac friend we will do it, but if we see any of you fuckers again we will not hesitate to call the police."

Stephen text Dino, *'On our way'*.

39

A SONG FOR SUSAN

Stephen looked at the three ashen-faced minstrels huddled together in the back seat of the cab dressed in identical black t-shirts and jeans, privileged hot housed kids, probably professional parents, not much older than his kids. Well, the girls for sure. He thought of his family laden with shopping bags heading to the Carnegie Deli for lunch. Meanwhile he was part of step six, kidnap! Possibly better than step four, definitely better than step four. But here he was on holiday in New York, a witness to an incident involving a gun and now body snatching. 'Buble' had a lot to answer for.

Suddenly his phone's 'London Calling' ringtone and Alberto's 'Born To Run' ringtone sang out in unison. He answered the former, "Hi Cass, how you doing?"

"You were right Stevie, not many shops are open."

"Oh what a shame." Stephen tried to sound genuinely sympathetic.

"We've booked to see a matinee on Broadway, can you entertain yourself?" She asked.

"No problem, catch you later love."

He then listened to the message left on Alberto's mobile. "Hi, this is Detective Mark Strader, if you are in possession of this phone you must call me back immediately as it's evidence in a serious crime enquiry and we will track it down."

"Shit," Stephen said aloud. His mind was in overdrive, whilst three quarters of the quartet sat in silence. He considered throwing the phone out of the window in case it could be tracked, but decided, whilst he was on a roll, to call the detective back. "Detective Strader?" He felt a little ridiculous putting on an American accent and drew some puzzled looks from his fellow passengers.

"Speaking."

"Yes, I found this phone."

"Where?"

"A strange guy who hangs around Grand Central Station gave it to me."

"Really, what did he look like?"

"He had a very pronounced stoop."

The detective paused before responding. "That figures, where are you now and have you activated the film?"

Stephen took his time before answering. "Yes, there's a very disturbing film on it, doesn't do you guys any favours?"

"Now listen to me buddy, don't fuck-"

"I must warn you officer this phone is on loudspeaker and my colleagues are listening."

"The guy pulled a gun, he threatened me and fellow officers," he replied defensively.

"With respect Detective, I've seen the film, you and your colleagues are a disgrace."

"The guy pulled a fucking gun," the officer snapped.

"And you and your colleagues are murderers," Stephen retorted with anger.

"What?"

"He died."

"Who died?"

"The poor 'stooping man', he was found dead this morning." There was a long silence, the musicians looked at each other shell-shocked by the conversation. "Okay, let me cut to the chase, we can easily put this whole sorry episode to bed officer," Stephen continued.

"How so?"

"You let your prisoner go and the film will be deleted. You and your colleagues will be able to carry on with your lives, as will your prisoner."

"And that crazy stooping man?" The detective's tone had softened.

"Sadly a victim of that bitch Irene," Stephen suggested.

"Give me an hour, I'll get our friend to call you on this number, but I warn you if that film sees the light of day you and our mutual friend will have the full force of the NYPD on your back."

Thirty minutes later the taxi arrived at the rendezvous, the passengers disembarked and found themselves on a residential street corner. Stephen saw a sign saying *'Flushing Meadows, 1 Mile'*, he knew the association with tennis, he guessed this would be a reasonably swanky area.

Stephen exchanged texts with Dino who claimed to be ten minutes away. He told the musicians the sad story about the 'stooping man', he could sense they were warming to him slightly. Eventually a large black saloon car pulled up and the unmistakable figure of Dino stepped out and warmly embraced Stephen. "You look good."

"Likewise."

Stephen briefly explained the situation regarding Alberto and was about to say how step five was going to be accepted when the bassist stepped forward.

"Where's Clive?" He shouted.

Dino engaged him aggressively, "Now listen up you fuckers, after I open the trunk I don't won't to hear a fucking word out of any of you, just follow me, show a dying woman some courtesy, play her favourite tune and then fuck off back to your ivory towers you cunts!"

Not a particularly motivating speech, Stephen thought.

Dino moved to the back of the car and unlocked the trunk, Stephen and the others peered in. *Goodfellas*, the Englishman thought, as they saw the young cellist tied up in the fetal position, gagged by a sock. Dino untied him removing the gag last then fetched the cello from the back seat. The cellist's friends helped him out of the trunk, unsurprisingly he looked unsteady on his feet.

"Your friend probably needs a swig of water," Dino suggested.

The young lady produced a bottle from her nap sac and the cellist gulped half the bottle down and then gave a throatily screamed, "Fuck you, I'm off!"

To everyone's amazement he sprinted down the road and disappeared into a maze of alleys that were part of a college grounds.

"Don't even think about joining that fucker, I will burn you fuckers alive if you try and join your friend." As Dino reached into his inside pocket, they all froze in terror, including Stephen. To their surprise he just pulled out a wad of cash. "There's a couple of grand here, 'step two' if you recall. You don't want to know about steps three and four believe me," Dino exclaimed.

"I can vouch for that," Stephen added.

"We can't perform without our friend," the first soloist chipped in.

"That's right, we're a string quartet," the bassist confirmed.

"No problem," Dino calmly added, handing the cello case to Stephen.

"What the fuck's he going to do?" The bassist laughed.

"Poor Susan has got a fucking brain tumour, she's half blind and almost deaf, my cousin promised he'd get her favourite quartet and that, with the help of our English friend here, is what's going to happen." Dino was incandescent.

"You three are going to play your hearts out. Stephen you're going to mime, you will be just fine as long as you make sure you don't make any contact with the strings with the stick thingy."

Three music students and a middle aged English tourist burst out laughing in disbelief.

"Come on, let's get this string trio and a half on the road," Stephen quipped.

They followed Dino through a newish development, he was about to press the buzzer to Susan's apartment when the strains of 'Born To Run' omitted from Stephen's pocket. It was the Detective. "How we going to do this?" Stephen asked.

"Ten thousand dollars bail, then I forget the gun and your friend and you forget the 'stooping man'."

"Seems reasonable," Stephen confirmed, though he was unsure if it was a good plan.

He conveyed the deal to Dino. "Ten grand, I suppose the mad fucker's worth it, he's bailed me out a few times, tell them I'll be over as soon as possible."

Dino pressed the intercom, after a couple of minutes a carer answered in a heavy Chinese accent.

"Hi I have a present for Susan!" Dino shouted.

"Who this?"

"I'm a friend of Susan's, can you let me in?"

"Who this?" She repeated.

"I'm delivering a present for Susan from Alberto."

"Susan very ill, she with doctor, I sorry." She said in accented English.

"It's very important she gets this present, please let me in," Dino pleaded.

"Hang on one minute Mr." She was gone for at least three. "Susan say leave with janitor and fuck off."

The janitor was sat at an oak desk speaking on the phone, Dino banged on the glass door to get his attention. He lumbered over to the door and opened it a little.

"I've got a surprise for Susan Canavaro." Dino smiled.

"We haven't got a resident by that name sir," the janitor replied.

The fucking stuck up Jewish bitch changed back to her maiden name, Dino thought. "Sorry I mean Susan Cohen."

"Oh, in that case you can leave it with me sir, I'll make sure she gets it sir."

Dino considered for a moment then ushered the 'surprise' into the lobby. Three quarters of the string quartet plus Stephen marched in armed with their instruments in cases. The janitor stood dumbstruck at the weird collection as Dino stepped forward. "Well here's the surprise, can you take these good people up right away please buddy."

"I'm going to have to phone up sir."

Dino looked agitated, Stephen sensed things were about to get messy. He put his hand on Dino's upper arm. "It's okay Dino, relax, I'll deal with this." He went over and lent across the oak desk, trying to recall the speech his old friend Avi would make about testicles, and whispered a threat into the janitor's ear.

"I'll escort you and your friends to Ms. Cohen's apartment sir."

Stephen winked at Dino, who had his hand in his inside pocket and then removed it. The elevator was crammed, Stephen stood toe to toe with the janitor. "You don't play the cello by any chance?" He asked.

His co-musicians giggled as the tension lifted. The janitor pointed out the door and wished them luck as he took the elevator back to the lobby, looking like he'd seen a ghost.

Dino pulled out a digital video camera from his pocket, Stephen was relieved, he was expecting a gun. "Probably best if I hang back and film the concert, I'm not too popular with the ex Mrs. Canavaro."

Stephen knocked on the door, a tiny Chinese carer opened it a fraction. "We're here to play for Susan, we're her favourite," he chanced.

"She with doctor, she not good."

"We just want to play one tune, then we will go."

"I'm sorry, she dying."

Suddenly Dino lost patience and pushed the door open, knocking the carer over. "We are all dying lady, now let us play please," he said, as he at least helped her up.

The doctor emerged from the room. "What's going on?"

Stephen decided he'd had enough of Dino's 'bull in a china shop' diplomacy, "How is Susan, doctor?"

"Are you relatives?" he asked.

"Dino here is, the rest of us are Susan's favourite string quartet, we are on her bucket list."

The doctor addressed Dino, "I suggest you contact any close family right away, I'd be surprised if she lasts the afternoon."

"Jeez, she has no close family Doc, parents gone, sister gone. Her Ex, my cousin, will soon be on his way."

"Well she's drifting in and out of consciousness, she has moments when she's lucid, but she's heavily sedated, I've told the carer to call me as soon as she passes. Good luck to you."

Stephen entered Susan's bedroom first, gesturing with the palm of his hand for the others to wait in the living room. Susan lay on a surgical bed, various drips hung from a rail above her. He approached the bed and noticed she was a different creature to the overweight overbearing bride he recalled all those years ago. *Skin and bones with a pulse*, he thought. He was shocked when she whispered something, he moved closer. "I'm thirsty," she croaked. He saw a plastic beaker with a straw and put it to her lips. A drop of water seemed to revive her a little. "Who are you?" Her eyes opened then closed shut in an instant.

"We're the string quartet from the bandstand in Central Park." He spoke in his fake accent, holding her hand whilst beckoning in the others. There was a slight smile on her face as they removed instruments from their cases. Stephen sat in the carer's chair, wedging the cello between his legs. The other three stood around the bed whilst Dino filmed. The musicians tuned up for a few seconds, pausing to collectively glare at Stephen who had decided to produce a few sounds with his bow. The three musicians then did a fair stab at a cello-less 'God Only Knows'.

It was over in just under five minutes. The second they played the final note they packed up their instruments, including the cello, and made a hasty exit, not bothering to claim Dino's cash. This meant he only needed another eight thousand for his cousin's bail money. "Well, that went well," he said, tapping his video camera, "Al will enjoy this."

"You'd better go get him," Stephen suggested, "I don't think there's much time." He nodded towards Susan. "I'm going to stay a while, here, take the 'Big A's' phone, I'll see you later. "

Susan's eyes were closed but she retained a slight smile, Stephen pulled the chair up close. After a few minutes with only the ticking of the clock for company, her eyes opened wide and she spoke clearly. "I guess Alberto arranged that?"

"He most certainly did," Stephen confirmed.

"I know you," she whispered, "you're from England, you were late for dinner."

Fuck Stephen thought, recalling the 'signature dish' incident. "I'm sorry Susan, it was a long time ago."

She closed her eyes again. Stephen was perturbed to think that her last mortal thought could be him vomiting in her Brooklyn studio flat. He stepped into the living room and saw the carer asleep on the sofa so he returned to Susan's bedside. She was making some gurgling noises and her breathing was noticeably shallower.

He text Cassandra to say, vaguely, that he was trying to track down Alberto. He presumed his family was enjoying a Broadway show. He considered heading back to the hotel but didn't feel it was right to leave Susan's side so he slunk back in the chair and wondered how a family trip could turn into such a performance. He thought of Wayne, the 'Buble', then Trevor the holy man, *I'd better grab hold of the handrail.*

40

THE FIFTEENTH UPLOAD
(2011)

Susan passed away a couple of hours after the string quartet/trio reluctantly serenaded her. The carer cried uncontrollably whilst the doctor certified her death. It jogged Stephen's thoughts back to Wayne and then his father, who'd succumbed to his third heart attack eight years previously. He text Dino to warn him of events, a few minutes later Dino text back telling Stephen he was going to drop the big man off at the bandstand and suggesting he get a cab over. He left a message for Cassandra explaining the situation and that he would be back at the hotel later in the evening.

Sat in the back of the taxi he reflected on the day's events, he was pleased with himself, no one was set on fire, Susan got to hear her favourite song and the 'Big A' got out of jail and some late brownie points from his ex.

The sun was disappearing behind the Manhattan skyline when the 'Big A' appeared in the distance. Stephen had claimed a bench, probably the very spot from where Susan used to enjoy the complete works of the string quartet. For a second Stephen considered disappearing into the rush hour throng and back to normality, but the closer the big man got, the stronger his sense of duty grew. "You look like shit," Stephen stated.

The big man shrugged and sat down next to his old buddy. "There was a time when a man would get a good beating and a hearty breakfast after spending a night in custody, now it's all fucking paper work."

"Well that was quite a twenty-four hours Al."

"This is New York City baby, all in a day's work. Outstanding cello work by the way, Dino showed me the film. Outstanding. I'd like to think Susan appreciated my efforts."

"Your efforts?" Stephen offered.

"I regret not enjoying step four but hey ho the deed is done."

"If I were you Al I'd thank them for their efforts next time you see my fellow musicians."

"Sadly, due to my agreement with the NYPD they won't be enjoying my patronage for some considerable time. So, where were we before our valiant efforts to help the 'stooping man'?"

"I'd explained my attendance at the 'Buble' concert and the subsequent ripples." Stephen reminded him.

"Ah yes, and I'm sorry, I can't bring myself to forgive you," Alberto tried to sound serious.

"Jonny Rotten hasn't forgiven me either."

"I thought you'd replaced him with 'The Boss'?"

"Still love 'The Boss', but I've fallen back in love with my old punk hero, despite the butter business."

The two watched a couple of attractive joggers run by. There was a brief silence before Stephen asked a question that'd been on his mind for twenty-seven years.

"Do you ever think about Wayne and those crazy days Al?"

"Everyday," Alberto answered without hesitation.

"He was my friend, he wasn't a bad man, neither was Hank. Marvin, well, let's not speak ill of the dead."

"And are you still Jewish?"

"One hundred percent. Yes I converted so I could marry Susan but, though I fell out of love with her, the more I learned about the Jewish faith the more I embraced it."

Stephen looked the big man in the eye. "Can you forgive me Al?"

"For 'Buble', never."

"No not the 'Buble', for doubting you."

"Doubting me?" Alberto looked puzzled.

"I thought you might have been in league with the others, you arrived with them, I doubted you and I'm sorry." Stephen put his hand on Alberto's shoulder in an act of solidarity.

"Whatever happened to the Liverpudlian?" He asked, changing the subject, which threw Stephen.

"Neville, umm well, after his flirtation with animal rights, Irish and Palestinian politics, he joined a commune in Rajasthan and gave all his ill gotten gains to a guru. Eventually a dodgy Irish republican retrieved the money and Neville was arrested by a dodgy Israeli and did eight years for arson in an Israeli prison."

"And what happened to your Israeli friend?"

"The 'silent assassin' as I used to call him, he started a private security company, spent many years training some of the world's most unsavoury regimes. Last I heard he's retired, but I often think of contacting him when I have trouble getting paid by clients."

"And what about the Canadian nympho?" The big man winked.

"Marci married a posh wanker called Toby, a union I can take some credit for. She confessed to me that she had at least five affairs in their first five years of marriage. She caught him out with his secretary, she not only divorced him but destroyed him financially and gave him a terrible beating with her Krav Maga skills. I believe she is at the bitter end of a third marriage in Toronto."

"And what about the rich Jewish princess, did she ever get over Wayne?"

Before Stephen could answer his phone buzzed, it was Cassandra, they were back at the hotel and she wanted him to return right away, there was urgency in her voice.

"I've got to run big man." Stephen stood and shrugged.

Alberto hugged Stephen, who felt tears land on his neck. "It's been a pleasure you English wanker, we'll have to take a rain check on 'The Boss" tour of New Jersey."

"Not for the first time," Stephen laughed as he broke free and headed towards the nearest exit.

He'd only gone five metres when the big man bellowed, "Next time you're in town I'll fill you in on your missing thirty-six hours when you went AWOL from my wedding!"

Stephen stopped in his tracks. "What?"

"It's a shame you missed him," Alberto teased.

"What, missed who?" Stephen protested.

"He might still be with us, you only missed each other by a couple of minutes. Things could have turned out differently. I blame the wedding present!"

"You mean Wayne? Wayne turned up after I went missing?"

"I'll send you the wedding album, now get back to your lovely family, have a great life." The 'Big A' disappeared in the opposite direction.

Stephen stood digesting Alberto's ambiguous revelation before deciding to walk back to the hotel to clear his spinning head.

He realised he hadn't answered Alberto's last question about Rachel Saltzman. He smiled to himself as he exited Central Park and headed down Madison Avenue as dusk fell on the Big Apple.

He reflected on the fascination with the Jewish princess from Hampstead Garden Suburb Wayne, Hank, even that mad buck toothed arsonist Neville had an infatuation with her. He thought about his night of passion in the smelly Bethnal Green bedsit, not just about the glorious sex, but the irony of the location.

****

Six months after the weekend in Paris, Stephen and Cassandra were married. After the registry office they were joined by a few close friends (no relatives) in a pub back room in East London, where they pogoed the night away to punk classics.

They honeymooned in Thailand, two nights in 'The Oriental' Bangkok, and then took a fishing boat to Koh Samet. The journey was treacherous and both were relieved to reach the exotic island safely. They rented a spartan beach hut, from a lady boy who called herself Lulu, and spent the first day lazing under a coconut tree. On the second day curiosity got the better of Stephen and he studied a small hand drawn map with the name Wayne had given him back in the Hyderabad hospital written on it. He told Cassandra he was going for a walk, she was happy to continue lying on the beach reading a book. He'd researched the island and knew it was around six miles in circumference, the 'X' on the map was halfway round, he figured it would take no more than an hour to walk there following the coastal route.

He walked briskly passing clusters of beach huts and eventually reached a battered jetty that signaled he was halfway. He planned to walk straight into the complex and ask for Klaus, claiming a German traveller had recommended his accommodation and he was checking it out. He recalled his promise to his new wife that he'd finished with his shenanigans, he had, this was simply curiosity. *But what if the old Nazi suspects he is snooping? What if he has stooges?* He could get himself in trouble, he could get Cassandra in trouble. He hesitated, went to turn back, then Trevor the sadhu's words came to him, 'Sometimes you let go of the handrail'.

He guessed he had under a mile to go, it was midday and the sun was at its height, he could feel the back of his neck burning with no protection from a hat. Suddenly the coastal path disappeared and there was only a craggy formation of rocks. He gingerly tried to continue but it was too treacherous, so he climbed up through thick bamboo instead. He stumbled a couple of times resulting in the sharp vegetation cutting lacerations into his legs and arms. He started to feel delirious, he couldn't see the sea below him but he guessed he was almost at his destination.

He sat down and breathed deeply to calm himself, he decided to head down again towards the water. He pushed through the heavy growth and could see a small bay twenty metres below. Relief was swiftly replaced by panic as he spotted two figures on the beach. They wore what he assumed were military uniforms and were carrying machine guns. "Shit," he whispered and backtracked. He scrambled through what seemed an endless forest of spiteful bamboo, bleeding from a multitude of lacerations. He'd come this far he had to see Klaus, he wondered if the men he saw were police or the German's stooges.

He was sure Cassandra would be starting to worry about him. The sensible thing would be to simply go across to the middle of the island and jump in the sea, continue his honeymoon. He wasn't sensible though, he'd become a zealot like Wayne. He got a second wind and carried on with gritted teeth, ignoring the pain. He reckoned he must be clear of the bay, the old Nazi's complex should be just the other side.

The forest of bamboo began to disappear but he stood looking at the spot marked 'X' on Wayne's map. It was absolutely accurate. He could see the identical small bay on the other side. it must have been a spectacular place to live, Stephen had never see a bluer sea or a whiter beach. Klaus, his young Thai wife, cook/mistress and twin toddlers must have truly thought they were in paradise. But not anymore, there was only a crater left of what was once been their paradise home. Stephen couldn't believe the devastation was caused by sabotage on the ground. From his vantage point it looked like a bomb had been dropped from the air. He could follow the line of the explosion outwards from its epicentre, where Klaus' bungalow had stood just a few weeks earlier.

He looked down by his feet and saw a discarded pair of sunglasses on the flattened vegetation. He went to pick them up and noticed one of the lenses was broken. He thought of Avi, of Yakov, Clara, Marci, the A team. This was where Wayne and Rachel were supposed to end their relationship, he was the only one who actually made it, albeit a little too late. It was a shame about the women and kids but he doubted anyone would miss the old Nazi. He fumbled in his short's pocket for his throwaway camera and took twenty-four photos of the devastation.

An hour later he stumbled into a beach bar and downed four bottles of coke, attracting strange looks from the other tourists. Eventually he staggered back to his beach hut where Cassandra burst into tears in a mixture of relief and shock. Stephen looked like he'd been to war.

On his return to London he sent a photo to Avi with '*KOH SAMET*' and the date written on the back. Two weeks later he received the same photo back with an added comment. '*You should have seen it three weeks earlier, such a beautiful home. Best wishes, Avi. p.s. Congratulations.*'

Cassandra got pregnant about two years after their honeymoon, they managed to buy a small second floor two-bedroom apartment in Barking. They just about met the mortgage payments but found themselves really stretched when Jessica arrived. It was something of a blessing when six months later Stephen received an A4 envelope, containing the deeds to the Bethnal Green bedsit with a short covering letter.

Dear Steve,

Rachel was married to Paul Goldberg at St Johns wood synagogue last Sunday. If you prefer send the deeds back to me and I'll give you the market price for it.

Hilary and I will never forget your contribution to our family's continuing happiness.

Good luck and best wishes,
Maurice Saltzman

Not long after they moved into their three-bedroom semi in suburbia. It was his last contact with the Saltzman family for ten years, until he received an enquiry to quote for the re-glazing of a large property in Chelsea. He was stunned when Rachel Saltzman opened the door.

"Hi Stevie, long time." She said, kissing him on the cheek. He noticed she was no longer the slender princess she was the last time he saw her, naked on his bed. She was at least twice the size. "Four kids," she shrugged.

They indulged in small talk before she introduced him to her husband, who must have been five foot nothing and eighteen stone. He was charmless and Stephen was relieved when he made his excuses and left for work.

"You don't like him do you Stevie?" Rachel said bringing him a coffee.

"I don't know him," Stephen said, slightly embarrassed by his obvious reaction.

"I heard you married the old receptionist."

"Cass," he confirmed.

"Kids?" She asked.

"Two."

"I bet she still has a fantastic figure, unlike me."

Stephen didn't know how to agree with her without causing offence.

"My parents like him, my kids love him, everyone's happy. Well, almost everyone. Everyone except me, which is why I eat like a pig."

Stephen didn't have a clue how to respond.

"I still think about him Stevie."

"Wayne?" He guessed.

"All the time." There was a long silence before she added, "and I think about you Stevie."

"They were interesting times," Stephen replied, rather ambiguously.

"Remember the holy man on the train in India Stevie? He talked about letting go of the hand rail."

"Trevor the Sadhu," Stephen confirmed, "yes, I thought I saw him on the underground one day last year, he often pops up in my thoughts. I suppose we were young and foolish back then Rachel."

"I wish I could let go now Stevie, but my hands are well and truly tied".

There was an awkward pause as they both thought of what might have been, a tear trickled down Rachel's plump cheek. Stephen reflected on how this 'Princess' who had everything was now so miserable and he, 'half a person', was so happy with his lot.

He carried out the work, got paid in cash and took his young family to Florida on the proceeds. He never heard from Rachel again.

****

Stephen entered the lobby of the hotel, he looked at the elevator and then the bar. *I need a drink*, he thought.

"Mr. Ross, you're alive! What's your poison?" Herbie, the bar manager, warmly welcomed him.

"Large JD on the rocks please Herbie. Yep it was some night, Irene caused quite a stir."

"Shame about that poor 'stooping man' but you and your buddy couldn't have done anymore to help him."

"I'll drink to that," Stephen said knocking back his drink in one.

"One for the road on me," Herbie offered.

"Thanks pal, but I'd better report in to the family, we've got a road trip to DC early tomorrow."

Stephen found his family in his room. Cassandra lay on the bed next to Florence, Jessica sat on the end of the bed, Luke in the arm chair. He sensed a strange atmosphere.

"Hi everyone, am I glad to see you all it's been one hell of a day. How you all doing? Washington tomorrow!"

There was a long silence, the four of them all exchanged glances.

"Dad, is there something you didn't tell us about the 'Buble' concert?" Jessica asked.

"Yeah, it was shit." Stephen laughed nervously.

"No dad, about after the concert, when you went to get the car," Jessica added.

Stephen looked around the room, he saw Luke nod towards his iPad. Stephen got the hint and realised he was banged to rights. He'd hoped he may have gotten away with it but he realised that there were so many people about someone may have captured his moment of madness. "Okay, I can tell you exactly what happened. I was not best pleased, I'd sat through two hours of torture I'd been beaten and assaulted by a bunch of paralytic Northern women. It was peeing down with rain and I had to go and fetch the car because the 'dickhead' couldn't walk. I was approaching the car when a mini bus pulled up next to me and there they were, the hen party from Blackburn making gestures at me."

"We've seen what happens from there dad, wow, you scared the shit out of us," Luke interrupted, nodding at the iPad again.

"There's a fifteenth upload, I wouldn't be surprised if you're not arrested at Heathrow if we ever get home," Cassandra added.

"I'm going to have a shower, then get some sleep. I'm looking forward to the Smithsonian Institute tomorrow," Stephen said, deciding it was best to ignore them as he disappeared into the bathroom.

Florence picked up the iPad, "I've got to see this again, it's insane."

The others gathered around.

> The clip starts exactly where Stephen's description ended. Whoever filmed it was only a few metres directly behind Stephen, the heads of the screaming women and their obscene gesturing are clearly visible. Stephen stops and stares at them, he seems to be laughing. The driver's shout is audible. "Beaten up by a woman you soft cockney wanker!"
>
> Obviously Jonny Rotten is not in the clip but he was egging Stephen on. "Cockney wanker, you guna take that, you're a fucking disgrace."
>
> Stephen then shouts at the driver, "Come on then, I reckon those drunken slags are harder the you, you cunt!"
>
> The driver jumps out, he is massive, with a tattooed and shaven headed. Cars stuck behind the bus can be heard hooting.
>
> 'One of those 'slags' is my misses you southern wanker!" The driver shouts and then throws a punch at Stephen who ducks under it and thrusts his right hand up into the attackers nose, before thrusting two fingers from his left hand into his attacker's eyes. The driver collapses screaming to the floor and Stephen's right foot connects with his already bloody nose. A passenger emerges from the other side of the vehicle, equally as big, but retreats as Stephen adopts an attack pose, placing his left foot on the driver's bloody head.

"Where the hell did he learn to do that?" Florence asked.

"It's a long story dear," her mother sighed.

Stephen sat on the edge of the bath sporting the hotel towelling dressing gown. "Top geezer, top geezer, proud of you Stevie boy," Rotten said, smiling from the corner.

"Cheers John, appreciated, but I won't be seeing you for a while."

ABOUT THE AUTHOR

Having left his North London 'sink' comprehensive at the age of fifteen with few qualifications, Simon travelled extensively before settling down to family life and 'blagging' a living. A ferocious gig and festival goer, he always felt he had a story to tell and *How to Kidnap a String Quartet* is the combination of his varied experiences of life and wild and whacky imagination. He is currently near to completing his follow up *The Good Poison Club*, a thriller set in an NHS hospital.

Made in the USA
Columbia, SC
13 September 2017